THE SHOCK OF DESIRE

The fingers of his right hand combed into the golden hair along her temple and rested at the back of her head.

As he took a small step closer, her eyes widened with awareness, but she wasn't immediately certain what she wanted to do about it. The softness of her voice contradicted the indifference of her words. "If this is a test, I think it's safe to say you're no longer supercharged." He stroked her cheek with the thumb of his free hand. The tenderness of it made her sigh, but she stopped herself from giving in to the urge to touch him in return.

"Funny you should say that," he murmured. "I was thinking there was enough electricity flowing between us to light up Atlanta." His hands slid slowly down the length of her arms, then just as slowly, he brought her hands up between them.

OUT OF TIME

Marilyn Campbell

A TOPAZ BOOK

TOPAZ
Published by the Penguin Group
Penguin Books USA Inc., 375 Hudson Street,
New York, New York 10014, U.S.A.
Penguin Books Ltd, 27 Wrights Lane,
London W8 5TZ, England
Penguin Books Australia Ltd, Ringwood,
Victoria, Australia
Penguin Books Canada Ltd, 10 Alcorn Avenue,
Toronto, Ontario, Canada M4V 3B2
Penguin Books (N.Z.) Ltd, 182–190 Wairau Road,
Auckland 10, New Zealand

Penguin Books Ltd, Registered Offices:
Harmondsworth, Middlesex, England

First published by Topaz, an imprint of Dutton Signet,
a division of Penguin Books USA Inc.

First Printing, January, 1997
10 9 8 7 6 5 4 3 2 1

 REGISTERED TRADEMARK—MARCA REGISTRADA

Printed in the United States of America

DEDICATION

To Kathryn Falk, Carol Stacy, and the entire
staff of *Romantic Times* Publishing Co., for
their constant support of the romance genre
and me personally.

I also wish to express my appreciation to all
the journalists who have been so helpful
in promoting my career, especially freelance
writer Don Vaughan, who warmly welcomed
me and my children into his circle of creative friends.

A special note of appreciation to Scott Wulf,
whose outstanding research talents have
provided me with a plethora of trivia for my
tall tales.

Thank you to Dan W. Crockett, a reader who
just happens to be a physicist and an electrical engineer, for showing me how to build
an electric chair from spare parts.

Chapter One

Atlanta Federal Prison, August 23, 1965

"Bless me, Father, for I have sinned. It has been, um . . . Christ, I don't know how the hell long it's—"

"*Ahem.*"

"Oh. Excuse me. Do I need to confess that now, too, or is it automatically covered under the circumstances?"

The elderly priest raised his eyebrows a notch. "If you take the Lord's name in vain on a regular basis, then I'd suggest you include it."

Luke Templeton grimaced. A confession had sounded like a good idea when it was offered as part of his last requests, but if he had to list every minor offense . . . His mouth curved into a grin as he wondered whether they'd delay his execution if the confession ran into overtime.

"This is not a laughing matter, son. In less than ten hours, you'll be—"

Luke held up a hand to cut him off. "I'm well aware of how *un*funny this whole thing is, Father. But I've already gone through fear, anger, fury, frustration, depression, and acceptance. Humor is all I have left. But I'll try to control myself. Okay, let's see. I've taken the Lord's name in vain. But I never meant Him any disrespect. It was just a bad habit."

"I see. Go on."

"I haven't gone to mass in about twenty years, since I was fourteen or fifteen. It wasn't anything against the church, mind you, I just got busy." He mentally ran through a list of potential offenses. "I didn't always obey my parents when I was a teenager, but they forgave me, and I'm pretty sure I've made it up to them since then. I've never stolen anything . . . unless you count the time I *borrowed* that one homicide case file from the police station in Detroit. But I was positive the detective in charge was burying something really important, and my article did end up leading to the arrest of the actual—"

He realized he'd gone off track and moved on from the commandments, which he couldn't fully remember, to the seven deadly sins. "I've, uh, overindulged . . . a little."

"In what way?"

"You need details, huh? Well, I mean I'm not an alcoholic or addict or anything, but there were a few times . . . well, maybe more than a few. It helps me relax, especially when I'm on the trail of a particularly, uh, complicated story."

"I'm afraid it's a sin to abuse the body God gave you regardless of your reasoning. I believe you also *overindulged* in the area of, *ahem*, lust."

Luke covered his grin with a cough. "If it's a sin to, *ahem*, lust outside the confines of marriage, then yes, I'm guilty of that one, but I don't think anyone would call it overindulging." He stopped and considered the number of women he'd had sex with in his life. "Well, I suppose *some* people would consider it overindulging, but every one of those women were more than willing. I never forced anyone."

The priest's neck flushed a bit. "Actually, I was referring to the seventh commandment: Thou shalt not commit adultery."

"Oh, that. Well, in my defense, Ginger O'Neill was the only married woman I ever . . . had relations with. And she didn't tell me she was married until the day she broke it off with me."

"Yes, you related that during the trial, but it still amounts to adultery."

"Okay. Then I confess to adultery, but I cared for her more than any woman I'd ever met. I might have even married her, eventually, if she hadn't changed her mind and gone back to her husband."

"I believe that brings us to the commandment that brought you to this point," the priest prodded.

For a moment, Luke didn't know which one he was referring to, then the lightbulb turned on in his head. "You mean, thou shalt not kill, don't you? Well, I'm sorry, but I can't confess to that one, Father. No matter what that jury of my so-called peers said, I did not kill Ginger."

"But the evidence—"

"Fuck the evidence!" Luke shouted and bolted up off his bunk. "Whoever killed her, framed me to take the fall." He turned his back on his confessor and gripped the bars of his cell until he regained his composure. "I may have committed a few sins in my life, but none of them were mortal, and I never lie. Well, almost never. Only if it's absolutely necessary. Oh, the hell with it." He turned and knelt down before the priest. "I swear to you, in the name of God, I did not kill her. Nor did I rape all those other women."

The priest patted Luke's shoulder and looked somewhat sympathetic, so Luke moved back to his bunk and repeated what he'd told everyone else. He knew it wasn't necessary for this man to believe him in order to give him his blessing, but Luke couldn't resist the opportunity to try one more time to convince someone of his innocence.

"I know I fit the description of the rapist, but so do half the men in Atlanta—white male, about six feet tall, medium weight and build."

The priest added the less common details. "The rapist was also reported to have dark brown hair, long enough to curl out from the back of his ski mask, and blue eyes."

"Lots of men have blue eyes and wear longer hair these days. Maybe it was one of the Beatles."

"At the risk of sounding biased, I feel obliged to mention that *you* were the one found bending over Mrs. O'Neill's body when the police arrived."

Luke ran his hands through the thick waves of his shagcut hair. "I got a phone call. It sounded like Ginger. She was crying. Said her husband had beaten her, and she wanted me to come get her." He closed his eyes at the memory. No matter how many times he repeated the story, it made him sick to his stomach. The end of his version of what had happened that night was barely audible. "The front door of her house was open. She was dead when I got there."

"You don't have to convince me, son," the Father said in a more kindly manner, then glanced heavenward. "*He's* the one who will be judging you now."

Luke sighed heavily. "In a way, I'm almost anxious to go have a talk with Him. I mean, if He's as all-knowing as I was taught He is, then He knows I'm innocent, and He also knows who set me up. If He can't save me, at least He might be able to satisfy my curiosity." The old priest gave him a reprimanding look. "You don't understand, Father. It's bad enough to have been framed for murder and multiple rapes, then railroaded through the justice system at the speed of light, but not knowing who to curse at for it all . . ."

"Vengeance is mine, sayeth the Lord."

"Yeah, I know, but I'd sell my soul to the devil to perform that vengeance myself."

The priest's gasp of shock was punctuated by a momentary dimming of the prison lights. He grasped Luke's arm and shook it. "Take it back quickly, son, before it's too late. Beg God to forgive you for that slip of the tongue."

Luke's response was prevented by the appearance of a prison guard.

"Sorry for the interruption, Father, but I wanted you to know there's no cause for alarm. They're just running a few tests on the electrical system . . . you know, to make sure it can handle the extra two thousand volts without shorting out tomorrow morning. Wouldn't want to cause our guest any unusual suffering." He gave Luke a nasty smirk, then reminded the priest, "Just give a yell when you're finished, and I'll escort you out of here."

"Dickhead," Luke muttered as the guard walked away.

"He's only doing his job, son," the priest stated with another reprimanding look.

Luke snorted, vividly recalling the energetic beatings he'd received from that particular civil servant. "Look, I don't have anything else to confess, so why don't you give me my penance, or last rites, or whatever, and then you can go."

The priest seemed somewhat agitated as he gave his final blessing, and Luke figured he hadn't managed to convince the old guy after all.

Finally, the priest gave Luke his penance. "Say twenty 'Our Fathers,' twenty 'Hail Marys,' and ten 'Apostles' Creeds,' and pray that the devil didn't hear what you said before."

Luke wrinkled his brow in thought. "Oh! You mean about selling my soul. That was just a figure of speech. Although—"

"*No!*" the priest exclaimed, rising quickly from his chair and stepping to the cell door. "Do not make matters worse by repeating such an evil offer."

Luke thought the holy man was carrying his religious superstitions a bit too far, but he nodded respectfully and changed the subject. "Father, I wonder if you could grant me a favor."

"If it is in my power," he replied solemnly.

Luke stood up. "Despite what that guard just said, everyone around here has gone out of their way to cause me as much suffering as possible. I don't trust them to make the execution swift and painless."

"I don't see how I—"

"You could be a witness. To make sure they do it the way they're supposed to. One electrode on my head, one on my calf. An initial charge of two thousand volts, then lowered to five hundred, then twice more raised to two thousand. The first jolt should knock me out, and my organs should be thoroughly fried within three minutes, no more. I know I'm asking a lot of you, but I don't know anyone else in a position to protect me from their sadism."

"That's a very strong charge," the priest said doubtfully.

"Would you like to see the bruises on my body from their humane treatment? I'd be glad to undress for you."

"No, no, that's not necessary. I admit, I have . . . heard things."

"Then you'll do it? Please?"

The priest frowned, but nodded his agreement.

Luke sighed with relief and shook the man's hand. "Thank you. I almost hate to ask for anything else, but, well, there is one other small part to the favor. As you know, they asked me if I had any last requests. The confession I got. For my last meal, I ordered a filet mignon, mashed potatoes, carrots, and a bottle of beaujolais. Nothing fancy. What I got was a bologna sandwich and a cup of warm water with red food coloring in it."

"I'll speak to the warden—"

"The meal wasn't important. The wine would have helped get me through the night, but I'll manage somehow without it. No, it was the third request that I was hoping you could help with. You see, I'm kind of attached to my hair. I'd like to be buried with as much of it as possible. Besides, I figured my mother is going to want to view the body, and it would be easier on her if I looked as normal as possible. So, I asked them to only shave off the small spot where the electrode goes on. Since you've agreed to witness the execution, I was hoping you'd also make sure they didn't shave my whole head."

"I'll see what I can do."

After the priest left, Luke tried to say the penance he'd been given, but quickly discovered that he didn't remember all the words to the prayers. He reassured himself that it didn't really matter since God knew that none of the sins he'd committed were that heinous.

With nothing else to concentrate on, he drifted back into the depression that had darkened the last six weeks. Since the night he found Ginger, raped, beaten, and strangled, there had been times he'd almost succeeded in convincing himself that it was all a bad nightmare. Any moment, he would wake up in his old apartment in Detroit and discover that he'd never moved to Atlanta a year ago. He'd still have his old job writing for the *Detroit Daily News.* He'd never met Ginger O'Neill.

But the nightmare was still running strong, and though it would come to the grand finale tomorrow morning, he wouldn't be waking up in Detroit, Atlanta, or anywhere else on this planet.

What he had told the priest came back to him. Somehow it really wouldn't be quite so bad if he could direct his anger at a specific person, be able to curse his nemesis with his dying breath. As it stood, there were a number of people who might have been responsible, the least suspicious of whom was the mysterious rapist who had broken into nine homes in the northeastern outskirts of Atlanta during the eight months prior to Ginger's murder. It had been suggested that there were more break-ins that had not been reported.

In each case, the victims were married women, home alone at the time he assaulted them, usually in the afternoon. Only twice had the rape occurred in the evening. All the women's descriptions of the man and his modus operandi were similar. He never spoke aloud. Although he threatened them with a large knife, he never actually used it on any of them. The only bruises he left on their bodies were on wrists and ankles from being tied to beds or other furniture, or around their mouths from being gagged.

From the interviews Luke had conducted with the victims for the newspaper, he had deduced that the rapist had actually been fairly gentle and perversely adoring once he had them secured and unable to object. Off the record, several women even admitted that he'd made a concerted effort to arouse them before entering their bodies. Every woman was left tied with the rapist's semen drying on her thighs. In all but one case, the victims' husbands were the ones to find them.

As far as Luke was concerned, the man who brutally assaulted Ginger O'Neill could not have been the same man who had raped those other women. Unfortunately, no one on the jury saw it his way. Whether gentle or violent, a rapist was a rapist, and Luke not only fit the general description, but he was caught at the scene of the crime. He was guilty. Case closed. Sentence to be carried out at sunrise.

Though he had told the priest it had been a figure of speech, he wouldn't be averse to making a deal with the devil himself if it could get him out of this mess.

His gloom was lifted considerably when the guard arrived with a bottle of red wine.

"From the priest," the man said with obvious annoyance and walked away.

Luke could see that the guard had helped himself to a swallow or two, but he didn't let that bother him. The delivery of the bottle itself gave him some hope. If the good Father could perform one miracle, there was a chance he'd be permitted to witness the execution as Luke had requested. Maybe he'd even be able to save his hair.

Luke plopped down on his bunk and took a long drink of wine. It was harsh stuff, and not nearly enough to render him unconscious, but it was better than nothing at all.

"Gotcha, Luke Templeton. You're mine now."

"Premature congratulations again, Jezebel?"

The dark one's handmaiden snarled up at the being of light. "Not this time, Gabriel. He offered loud and clear, *twice*, and I'm accepting. He's mine."

"And I challenge due to extenuating circumstances. Justifiable frustration caused him to use a figure of speech he did not mean literally."

She huffed and a smoky cloud escaped her form. "You heard his confession: disobedience, lying, stealing, excessive use of alcohol, breaking a civil law of his—"

"What law?"

Jezebel smiled confidently. "The one about possession of a narcotic substance. I know for a fact that he has smoked marijuana."

"A technicality. Just like all the rest. Nothing on his record warrants a direct trip to your lair. He deserves his judgment day."

"Is that so? What about his overindulgence in unemotional fornication? Everyone knows that's a particular peeve of yours."

"Just as everyone knows how that is your favorite form of temptation. I wonder how many of the women he encountered were acting under your provocation." The archangel remained silent for a moment. "It is true that the relationship portion of his record is rather murky, but the free love promotion of 1960s Earth was extremely hard for many humans to resist. Besides, I believe he was beginning to come around with Ginger O'Neill."

"*Hah!* He never told her he loved her. Nor would he ever have given up his own life to save hers. If she hadn't left him, he would have left her long before any promises were made."

"Then let that form the terms of the challenge.

And since you have staked the premature claim and named the terms, I have the right to set the stage for his test. Is that understood?"

"Damn you to hell, Gabriel!"

"Now you see how easy it is to accidentally use a figure of speech. You know very well you do not have the power to damn me to anything."

"We'll see who has the power on this one. I accept your challenge, with one stipulation."

"That is your right . . . as long as it is reasonable."

She grumbled at the limitation. "All right. Luke Templeton is mine if he doesn't tell a woman that he loves her and prove that he's willing to die for her, within two weeks, Earth time."

"Unreasonable. Six months."

"Also unreasonable. Three weeks."

"Six weeks, and absolutely no interference from you or yours during that time."

"The same goes for you. No guardian angels sitting on his shoulder, whispering helpful little suggestions in his ear."

"Agreed. No angelic whispers."

"Done."

Once Jezebel had slithered back into her lair, Gabriel allowed himself to smile. Once again, in her fit of temper, Jezebel had missed an important point. He had agreed to no angelic guidance, and he would not intervene directly during the specified time, but he had not agreed to refrain from using his power to create an extraordinary set of circumstances in which Luke would take his test.

Given a certain advantage and a distinct disadvantage, Luke Templeton just might be saved.

Father Peters had never regretted a promise more than the one he'd made to Luke Templeton last night. It wasn't that he had never seen a person die before. It was the manner of death he was having trouble with in this instance.

He firmly believed God was the only one who should have the power of life and death. Whether Templeton was innocent or guilty was not his concern—God would deal with that—but he did not believe that anyone's life should be ended by another man's hand. Since he couldn't stop the death sentence from being carried out, however, at least he could make sure that it was done as humanely as possible.

From behind the one-way glass, he watched two guards bring Templeton into the small room and strap him into the electric chair. He felt some satisfaction in noting that the convicted man's last request regarding his haircut had been granted. On the other hand, it was acutely uncomfortable to be close enough to see the beads of perspiration on Templeton's face. He wondered what he was thinking at this moment.

After the leather straps were tightened and the electrodes secured in place, the two guards left Templeton alone in the room.

The warden turned on the intercom and spoke into the microphone. "Any last words, Templeton?"

The man's eyes seem to bore through the glass. "I'm innocent."

The warden turned off the intercom and nodded to the executioner. Father Peters made the sign of the cross and began reciting The Lord's Prayer.

Rather than watch Templeton, the priest kept his eyes on the voltage meter. The arm jumped to 2,000, as Templeton had said it should, but then the worst thing that could possibly happen, did. All the lights went out.

"Shut it down!" the warden ordered.

For several seconds they were in total blackness and the priest prayed that the first surge of electricity had been enough to put the poor man out of his misery.

The return of power caused the lights to flicker for a few more seconds before the area was fully illuminated again.

"What the hell!" exclaimed the warden, and he burst through the door into the room where the electric chair sat. The two guards, the executioner, and Father Peters were right behind him.

"Dear God in heaven," the priest muttered as the others expressed their shock in less spiritual terms.

Where Luke Templeton had been securely strapped moments before, there was now nothing but a slightly scorched prison uniform and smoldering ashes.

Chapter Two

Forsyth County, Georgia, 1997

"Spontaneous human combustion."

Kelly Kirkwood said the words aloud, letting the idea settle into her mind through her ears, as though trying on a new dress to see how it fit.

Perhaps she had been approaching her problem from the wrong angle. Instead of starting with a motivation for murder as she always had in the past, what if she started with an unusual means? It was quite obvious by now that her usual method of developing a story idea was not going to work this time.

For the past five years, she had come up with plots by researching true homicide cases, then putting her own twists on them. Until recently, that process had proven extremely successful. Seven of her romantic suspense novels were already in print, the last three had become bestsellers, and her next release was being turned into a pilot for a weekly television series.

Unfortunately, two months ago, her well of creativity dried up.

One author friend had cited several cases of artistic people who froze after major success hit, but she didn't think success had affected her that severely.

When she accidentally blurted something out about her lack of productivity to her ex-husband, he accepted total blame. Noting that her problem seemed to have begun at the same time as they signed the divorce papers, he was certain she would get back to work once she accepted him back in her life.

As much as she hated to agree with him on anything, Will Kirkwood may have been close to the truth. During their mockery of a marriage, she had turned to writing to escape the reality of the mistake she'd made with him. She had poured every ounce of pent-up emotion into her work rather than taking her anger and frustration out on the cause of her tension. The emotional intensity had made her stories come alive, and now that she was legally free of him, she seemed to have totally lost that spark. But she would still prefer never to write another word than go back to living the way they were.

Of course, Will kept assuring her it would be different now. He had supposedly learned his lesson by losing her. She wasn't falling for it, but his continuous attempts to convince her that they should reconcile were driving her mad.

As though that wasn't bad enough, Will was not the only man trying to win her attentions since the divorce. Bruce Hackett, a longtime friend, whose legal skills had helped obtain her divorce, had taken it into his head that it was time to move their relationship from friends to lovers. Kelly had not wanted to hurt his feelings, so rather than flatly reject him, she had given the excuse that it was too soon for her to get involved with another man.

Instead of pushing him gently away, it had encouraged him to hover around her, being as solicitous as possible, so that the instant she felt ready to get involved, he would be the first man in line.

Kelly had come to the conclusion that, despite their real relationship, Bruce had fallen in love with her image, in the same way as many of her male fans had. They read the erotic scenes in her books, gazed at her press photo inside the back cover, and imagined that the words were written from her vast experience rather than a fertile imagination. Her publicist was partly to blame, but she had gone along with the plan.

In the photo she was wearing a leather jacket, a bustier that accented her full breasts, and her waist-length strawberry blond hair was draped seductively over one shoulder. It was a picture of wicked sensuality that she augmented by dressing the part for book-signings and television interviews. Generally, it worked to her advantage, but occasionally, as with Bruce, it backfired.

Perhaps she should make a point of having Bruce see her as she now looked—in her oversized T-shirt and baggy shorts to hide the extra fifteen pounds she was carrying, her hair pinned in an untidy knot on top of her head, no makeup to cover the freckles on her nose or darken the pale brows and lashes that framed her green eyes—a very average woman who cleaned up well.

Her agent, Jack Pendergast, being a man, unwittingly sided with Bruce and Will as to the solution to her writer's block. He seemed to think that all she needed was a wild fling with a young stud— he had compared it to a car getting a tune-up. Fortunately for Jack, he was an extraordinary agent so she was able to tolerate his less than charming personality.

The truth was, she couldn't imagine ever feeling ready to be with any man again. Perhaps that was the reason she was having a hard time coming up with a *romantic* suspense story.

The explanation she liked best, however, had come from her very understanding editor, Connie Engel. She had said it was perfectly normal to feel drained after going through something as traumatic as her divorce had been, and besides, she had been pushing herself nonstop for five years. All she needed was a quiet vacation to recharge her batteries. Get away from everything and everybody for a couple of weeks, and she'd be right back on track.

Kelly had liked the sound of that a lot, but couldn't imagine where she could go that she could really get away. Then, almost magically, came the perfect answer: a friend of a friend owned a slightly primitive cabin, nestled in the woods by Lake Sidney Lanier.

The two-room cabin was less than fifty miles from her town house in Atlanta, but it was remote enough to be in another country. It had indoor plumbing with running water from a well, a small kitchenette operating off a propane gas tank, and a generator that provided enough electricity to power her computer and printer. If it happened to get chilly one night, there was a wood-burning fireplace. Best of all, it had no telephone or mail delivery. If she wanted to make a call, send a letter, or buy groceries, the town of Charming was a mere fifteen-minute drive away.

Only her mother and Connie knew of her whereabouts, and if they wanted to reach her, they had to do so through general delivery in Charming. Since Jack's only reason for contacting her would be new business—which she didn't want at the moment—or to nag her about the new synopsis—which her nerves didn't need—she told him that she would call his office once a week, rather than tell him how to contact her.

The cabin seemed like the perfect place to regenerate, but after two weeks of solitude, she was no closer to a new story idea than she had been before. Even the very understanding Connie was beginning to get nervous about it.

Kelly had arrived at the cabin with some casual clothes, her computer equipment, folders filled with copies of articles and newspaper clippings for research, and a stack of other authors' novels for diversion and inspiration. So far, she had read every one of the books without being inspired, but she was getting pretty good at playing blackjack against her computer.

At least twice a day, she went through the research material and her miscellaneous notes. The clippings that had held some appeal were spread out on the table, where she kept hoping one of them would jump up and turn itself into a plot idea, but so far, they simply laid there.

There was one old case that had rung a bell of possibility when she'd first read about it, but as many times as she had reviewed the recorded facts, a story failed to gel in her mind.

Thirty-two years ago, a reporter named Luke Templeton was executed for the murder of a Charming woman and multiple rapes in Dawson, Forsyth, and Gwinnett counties. At first, it was the coincidence of her presently being in that locale that had caught Kelly's attention. Then other things posed questions in her mind.

Though Templeton denied his guilt to the end, his trial was immediate and brief, no appeals were permitted, and he was executed within six weeks of his arrest. Talk about speedy justice!

He had a probable motive for killing Ginger O'Neill, the opportunity, and was found at the scene, but Kelly did not read anything in the various clippings that suggested he had the psychological profile of a serial rapist.

Ironically, about a year later, several more rapes with the same MO occurred in the area, and a local man was caught breaking into a woman's home. He had an alibi for the time of Ginger's murder and most of the rapes, however, and thus it was generally agreed that Templeton's execution was still justified.

The other thing that kept pulling Kelly back to this case was the photo of Templeton being led out of the courthouse. Her copy wasn't that sharp, but she could see that the expression on his face was shock. That, added to the probable mistake that had been made about his being the rapist, made her wonder if, in fact, he was also innocent of the murder as he had claimed.

In those days, they couldn't check the DNA in the semen or lift fingerprints from a victim's throat. If Templeton was caught under the same circumstances today, would he still be executed, or would he be a free man?

She kept feeling as though there was something she could use here, but until this morning, she hadn't realized that it wasn't the crime or the killer. It was what happened at the execution that kept niggling at her creativity without quite getting it flowing.

Spontaneous human combustion.

As the switch was thrown to the electric chair, there was a power failure in the prison. When the lights came back on seconds later, Templeton had vanished. The room was thoroughly examined afterward, and it was determined, without a doubt, that he could not have escaped.

What was left behind in the chair bore enough similarities to other recorded cases of spontaneous human combustion that it was informally accepted as the explanation. Officially, his total incineration was regarded as an accident due to an unexplained surge of electrical power, probably due to lightning.

Kelly turned on her laptop computer and called up her research information directory. Entering a file of unusual facts and unexplained mysteries, she found a section on spontaneous human combustion, commonly referred to as SHC. To her surprise, it was quite extensive.

From the 1600s to present day, a considerable number of fiery deaths had been attributed to SHC for lack of better explanation. A number of authors, including Charles Dickens, Mark Twain, Herman Melville, and Emile Zola had used SHC to dispose of particularly unsavory characters.

Sometimes the clothes or other items within a four-foot radius were incinerated with the victim, but just as often nothing but the body itself was burned, occasionally all the way to ash.

The heat required to turn human bone to ash was likened to a bolt of lightning, yet it is not scientifically possible for lightning to destroy a human body inside a room or automobile without causing any other damage. Nor could a fire of the intensity of a crematorium leave the victim's clothes or bedding intact. Luke Templeton's case was the most recent one cited, and though lightning was mentioned as a contributing factor, witnesses swore there was no lightning that morning.

Kelly's gaze darted to the date of that morning and received another surprise. It was August 24th—today's date! Was this another coincidence, like the murder victim being from the nearby town, or was this a spiritual confirmation that she was on the right track?

Since she couldn't always explain where some of her ideas came from, she remained open to the possibility of spiritual assistance from time to time. The more she thought about it, the more convinced she was that this was one of those times.

If it was good enough for Mark Twain to use, it certainly was good enough for her. So, what if she started with a death that appears to be caused by spontaneous human combustion, but is actually murder? How could that be accomplished?

She reread all the information in the file twice,

but the answer wasn't there. SHC seemed to be a genuine paranormal mystery.

There was only one case cited that had undergone extensive investigation using twentieth-century scientific methods. It had occurred prior to Templeton's case, which had more or less been dismissed because of his being purposely electrocuted at the time. In 1951, in St. Petersburg, Florida, Mrs. Mary Reeser's body was reduced to ashes without much of her surroundings being damaged. The FBI and a series of fire and arson experts investigated the case, but no logical explanation was ever derived.

If she was going to use SHC as a method of murder, she would have to do a lot more research to find out how it could be imitated, and she couldn't do that from where she was presently sitting. For the first time since she'd arrived at the cabin, she wished she had a phone.

Energized by the feeling that her dry spell was finally over, Kelly had her sandals and baseball cap on and was driving to Charming minutes later.

Luke slowly opened his eyes and took in his surroundings. Only one thing was certain. This could not be hell. But was it heaven? There were no white clouds or pearly gates or winged angels waiting to look up his name in The Great Book.

Actually, he could see a few fluffy masses in the otherwise clear blue sky. But other than that, and the fact that it seemed to be a peaceful place, nothing else seemed very heavenly. On the contrary, his surroundings were quite earthly, with dirt beneath his bare feet and trees and plants all around him. He even heard a bird chirping and felt the hot sun blazing down on him through the branches overhead.

He touched his face, his chest, and his thighs. Why did he still have a physical body? And why was he naked? Shouldn't he have been issued a robe or something? And shouldn't someone have been here to greet him? At least to explain his rank and/or situation? Should he stand there until someone came for him or go exploring on his own?

Suddenly his stomach growled, reminding him that it had been a long time since—He stopped his train of thought as he realized that he shouldn't be hungry. He shouldn't be *anything*. He was dead!

But not only did his stomach feel empty, his bladder felt incredibly full. Hoping he wasn't desecrating a holy place, he relieved himself of the last of the bottle of wine he'd consumed last night. As he stood there, trying to decide a course of action, he distinctly heard what sounded like a car engine not far away. Since there seemed to be a narrow path heading in the direction of that sound, he began walking and immediately discovered another incongruity.

Being a city boy, he wasn't on familiar terms with the stuff, but he was fairly sure some of the prickly plants along the way were of the poison ivy, oak, or sumac variety. He was eyeing the plants so cautiously, he stepped on a twig and got a splinter in his big toe. The sliver pulled out easily, but he lost his balance in the process and ended up falling into the bushes he was trying so hard to avoid.

This place was beginning to seem more like hell every second.

Perhaps this was purgatory, an in-between kind of place, where his fate was yet to be decided. Would he be tested, then? Had the test already begun? He wondered if he'd already lost points for peeing on the ground.

A dozen more careful steps brought him to a wooden cabin. The screen-covered windows were open, suggesting habitation, but when he knocked, no one answered. A peek inside a window confirmed that someone appeared to be residing, or at least working here. He could see stacks of books, folders, and papers spread out on a table, and a desk and secretary's chair in one corner. Squinting, he determined that some of the papers looked like newspaper clippings. Since he used to be a reporter, maybe they held a clue as to what he was supposed to do.

He tried the door and was surprised to find it locked. Glancing inside again, he decided he definitely needed to go in there and that the locked door was probably just a little test of his perseverance. He removed the screen and climbed in the window, scraping his already bruised buttocks on the rough wood frame despite his careful movement.

The cabin consisted of a fairly large room, cramped with furniture and clutter, and a very small bathroom. In one corner of the main room was a kitchenette, and the rest appeared to be a combination living area and office. He started toward the table covered with papers, but was distracted by some clothing on a chair.

Was this for him? Examining the items, he wasn't so sure. The cotton T-shirt was large enough to fit him, but bore a strange phrase: "I have PMS and a handgun—any questions?" If that was a clue, he didn't get it. The elastic-waisted cotton shorts were a little small, but at least they would offer some protection against scratchy plants and splintery wood. Though the outfit wasn't the ethereal robe he'd anticipated, it was better than going around nude.

As he pulled on the clothes, his gaze was drawn to the view outside the front window. What he saw made as little sense as everything else. The dirt driveway might not have seemed so strange, but there were distinct tire tracks in it, as though a vehicle had recently been parked there. He recalled hearing a sound like a car engine. Whatever this place was, it had a motorized vehicle, which meant there was possibly a driver around somewhere.

Returning his attention to the papers he'd seen,

he sat down at the table. Although he was looking for a clue of some kind to explain his circumstances, he was still shocked to see a grainy photo of himself being led from the courthouse after he'd been sentenced. He quickly scanned everything on the table, then read all that pertained to him, including a piece on spontaneous human combustion.

From personal experience, he surmised that he was looking at someone's criminal research files and that his case was one of those being reviewed. Some had later chronological dates, even one nearly three decades in the future. He supposed time had no relevance where he now was. Several articles contained unfamiliar words, abbreviations, and phrases. With each case file was a sheet of handwritten notes and questions—the kind he would make if he was writing an article.

A half hour later, he was both more knowledgeable and more confused. According to these bits of information, his body had been incinerated to ashes, yet here he sat with flesh that could be injured by splinters. It also intrigued him to note that more rapes occurred after the date of his execution.

What did all of this mean? Was he supposed to write something using these notes or were these the scribbles of a higher power sitting in judgment of him and the others? And if that was the answer, why did that higher power need to do research? Wasn't he supposed to be all-knowing? Continuing along that line, why would a higher power need a car to get around?

Frustrated, he ran his hand through his hair and winced when he touched the burned spot on his scalp. That and the one on his calf verified that he had been in an electric chair the last time he was conscious. But if he had spontaneously combusted, as the article claimed, why wasn't his entire body covered with seared flesh instead of only two small areas? For that matter, why did he have a physical body at all?

Suddenly he remembered seeing a drop of blood—bright red, *oxygenated* blood—trickle out when he pulled the splinter from his toe. From everything he'd ever learned about corpses, that wasn't right either.

He rose and went over to the desk to see what else he might find. His curiosity was further roused by the sight of what appeared to be a flattened-out typewriter keyboard with a small television screen attached to it. The instant his hand neared the keys, a bluish spark shot out from his fingers. As he jerked back, the television behind the keyboard turned on. Rather than a TV show appearing on the screen, however, there were printed words that reminded him of the microfiche directory in the research department at the newspaper. He was about to try to figure out how it worked when he heard the car engine sound again. It was clearly coming closer.

Luke's heart picked up its pace as he stood in

the middle of the room, waiting for someone, or *something*, to come to him. Through the window, he watched a sleek black car stop amidst a great cloud of dust. A figure emerged and headed for the front door, but Luke had to wait for the key to turn in the lock and the door to open before he could see what it was.

Kelly entered the cabin with more energy than she'd felt in months. During the drive into town and back, a plot had begun to blossom around the SHC idea, and she couldn't wait to get started on an outline.

But there was a man standing in the path between her and her desk.

"Oh!" she squeaked in surprise, then realized that she might be in danger. Trying not to panic, she asked, "Who are you?" When he looked bewildered by her question, her gaze darted around the room, particularly noticing his attire and the powered-on computer. "What do you want? Something in my files? Why are you wearing my clothes?"

The man seemed even more confused by that. "*Your* clothes? I . . . I didn't know. I mean, I wasn't given anything to wear and I thought . . ."

As he continued to stammer some nonsense about being naked and getting splinters, Kelly inched her way past him to the desk. The instant she was within reach, she yanked open the drawer and whipped out her Walther PPK. When he recognized the automatic pistol, his bewildered expression altered to shock.

That response, and the lethal weapon, gave her the courage to act braver than she felt. "Explain what you're doing here right now, or I'll blow a hole right between your eyes. And don't think I can't. I'm an expert marksman." She clicked back the safety to emphasize her point.

"Hold on!" he exclaimed, quickly raising his arms in a show of submission. "This is obviously a big misunderstanding. The problem is, I was hoping you could explain it to me."

There was something very familiar about his face. She lowered the gun barrel a few inches. "Explain what?"

He eased his arms back down to his sides. "Everything. *Anything*. Where I am. What I'm supposed to do here."

"Are you trying to tell me you have amnesia?"

He made a face. "No. I know who I am, or rather who I was, and where I was. I just don't know what my present situation is. My guess is, I must have gotten lost somehow. But I gather you're not an angel come to guide me the rest of the way to wherever I'm supposed to be."

Kelly would have laughed at that, but he didn't seem to be joking. Perhaps he was mentally handicapped and truly needed help. "Look, why don't you tell me who you are and where you came from. Maybe I could help you get back there."

"*Back?* Can you really do that?" Enthusiasm

had him taking a step toward her, but a glance at the gun held him in place. "What would I have to do to go back?"

Kelly was no longer afraid of the poor man, but she didn't know what to do with the gun now that it was out of its hiding place. She decided to hold onto it, but put the safety back on and directed it at the floor. "Why don't you begin by telling me your name."

"Luke Templeton."

It took Kelly a moment to recall why that name sounded familiar. She looked at the table and noted that the files and clippings were now in neat little piles rather than spread out as she'd left them. "You went through my research materials. And you were trying to get into my computer files. Why?" When he didn't answer immediately, she brought the gun back up. "I asked you a question. Now, I want to know who you are and what you were looking for. Did someone send you to spy on me? Will? Jack? Bruce? Please don't tell me Bruce has gotten so twisted that he hired an investigator."

"Look, lady, I don't know any of those guys. All I know is *you* have a file on *me*, and that makes you the spy here, not me. Why don't you tell me why you have all that information, and yet you say you don't know who I am or what I'm doing here."

She knew he had to be playing some kind of game with her, but she couldn't imagine why. She walked over to the table, picked up the clipping with Templeton's photo on it and held it up. *"This* is Luke Templeton. Thirty-two years ago today, he was executed for the rape and murder of a woman not far from this cabin. Would you like to choose another name?"

"Thirty-two years ago today?" Luke repeated in a hushed voice, then slumped onto a chair by the table. "Where am I?"

Kelly was back to thinking he had a serious mental problem. "About ten miles west of Charming."

His eyes narrowed in concentration. "Charming? There was only one place I ever heard of called Charming, and it was anything but." He stared at her intently, then his brows raised in awareness. "Good God. You're not kidding. I'm still in Georgia? And the date is . . ."

"August 24, 1997."

He rubbed his forehead as though trying to get rid of a bad headache. "I don't understand any of this."

"It might help if you'd be honest with me."

He stared up at her with complete sincerity. "Please, look closely at that photo of Luke Templeton and look at me."

She did and had to acknowledge that the resemblance was uncanny.

"Now look at this." He pointed to the burned circle of flesh on top of his head, then his calf. "About an hour ago—or so I thought—I was strapped into an electric chair with electrodes attached to these two spots. The lights went out and the next thing I knew, I was standing in the woods behind this cabin, naked as the day I was born. I figured I was in purgatory."

Kelly smothered a chuckle. "I've heard Georgia called worse than that."

"You don't believe me."

"Can you blame me?"

He sighed and shook his head. "No, I guess not. *I* don't even believe the conclusion I'm coming to."

"Which is . . ."

"Somehow, instead of dying in that electric chair and moving on to an afterlife, I traveled in time."

She took a step back. "I see."

"I won't hurt you, if that's what you're thinking. I didn't kill Ginger O'Neill. Nor did I ever rape one woman let alone nine. And you know that part's true if you read all those clippings."

Kelly sat down across from him and placed the gun on her lap. "I read a book last week about a woman who was zapped into the past after looking at an old portrait. It was a good, fun read, but it was *fiction*. Real people can't travel through time."

"Then how would you explain my being here?"

"I would say you're a man who looks very much like the late Luke Templeton and burned two circles on his body to convince me he'd been electrocuted."

Luke threw his hands up in disgust. "Why the hell would I do that? I don't even know you. I certainly wouldn't burn myself to convince you of anything." His expression suddenly changed, and he angled his head at her. "Maybe *you're* the one who's lying, and this is all part of a test I'm being put through. We're out in the middle of the woods. You could tell me we were on Pluto and there's nothing around to prove you wrong. That's it, isn't it! Instead of being electrocuted, I was just knocked unconscious and brought here. They must have figured I'd make a full confession if I thought I was already dead."

He rose abruptly and pointed his finger at her. "Well, it won't work, lady. No matter how sexy you are or how big your gun is, there's nothing you can do to make me confess to something I didn't do. You may as well just take me back to the pen so they can finish what they started."

Kelly nodded approvingly. "You have a very fertile imagination. You should consider fiction writing as a career."

"I'll stick to nonfiction, thank you. That way I know what's real and what's make-believe. Do you admit this is a setup?"

She clucked her tongue. "We seem to be at an impasse. I don't believe you and you don't believe me. But what I've said can be proven. All you have to do is walk out that door and turn left.

Charming is in that direction. I'm sure you could buy a newspaper there to confirm where and when you are at the moment. Feel free to keep that stunning outfit . . . since you claim to have none of your own."

He frowned at her and looked down at his feet. "I don't suppose you'd have a pair of size eleven shoes around, and maybe some longer pants."

"Sorry." She set the gun on the table and stood up. "As interesting as this has been, I really need to get back to work now."

He walked to the door, then turned back to her. "Would you at least tell me why you have all that information about me?"

She smiled. "I'm an author, a *fiction* author. I mainly write romantic suspense. Love and murder mixed together. Your case—I mean the *Templeton* case, interested me."

He nodded, as if that made some sense to him. "Well it was very nice to meet you—" He held out his hand to her, clearly expecting an introduction.

"Kelly Kirkwood," she said with another smile and reached out to shake his offered hand. The instant their palms met, a bluish light crackled around their hands, a powerful shock ran up Kelly's arm, and she was forcibly projected away from him and against the wall several feet behind her.

Chapter Three

"Good God!" Luke exclaimed as Kelly dropped to the floor. He hovered over her, but didn't dare touch her again. "Are you all right?"

Kelly blinked her eyes until she could focus on him. Her mouth was dry and tasted of metal. "I . . . I'm . . . tingling. All over. You know, like when your foot falls asleep. What happened?"

He knelt down to her level. "Did you see that bluish spark when our hands touched? I saw the same thing when I tried to touch that keyboard. Then the TV came on. I didn't think I'd made it do that at the time, but now, well, I think I might have some kind of electrical charge left over from the electrocution."

She looked at him doubtfully, but she couldn't deny that she'd been shocked by him. "You really believe you're Luke Templeton, don't you? And that you were electrocuted, but didn't die?"

"I swear. If I could think of a way to prove it, I would."

She wished he could also. He certainly looked like Templeton, without having aged a day. And he did have those two fresh burn wounds, which could have been caused by electric chair electrodes. He seemed to be as disoriented and upset as he should be if his story was true. And he had definitely shocked her far beyond what normal static electricity felt like. But was he actually carrying an electrical charge?

An idea occurred to her and she tried to stand, without success. "Help me up." She moved to grasp his arm for support but he jerked away.

"I don't want to risk shocking you again." He pushed a chair next to her. "Here. Use this."

With some effort, she got to her feet and went over to the desk. She turned off the power to her laptop computer, but left it open. "Come here and show me what you did before." As he neared, she backed away . . . just in case.

Luke slowly brought his index finger close to the space bar. When he was an inch away, a blue spark jumped from his fingertip into the keyboard, accompanied by a slight crackling sound. A second later, the power was on again.

Not wanting to jump to a wild conclusion too quickly, she turned everything off, then went to the generator and shut that off as well. "Try it again," she ordered.

He obeyed, and the computer turned on again, but the moment he moved away, the power went with him. He walked over to the generator and turned it back on with little more than a touch.

"This is nuts," Kelly said with wide eyes.

"No kidding. Do you believe me now?"

"I don't know. I mean, time-travel's not really possible. Is it?"

Luke shrugged. "I didn't think so this morning, but if you were being honest with me about the date, I can't think of a better explanation for my being here, alive and well."

"Okay, let me think." Kelly wiggled her fingers to make sure she had all the feeling back again, then began to pace back and forth. "First, let's do what I do when I'm making up a story. We have to let go of what we believe to be reality and imagine that anything is possible. I suppose, if a tremendous electrical charge, like in an electric chair, could disrupt all the cells in a man's body sufficiently to kill him, then it might also be possible for a charge to cause the cells to be relocated. But why to this place? Why now?"

Luke shrugged again. "An opposite charge? Positive to negative, or vice versa."

"I don't think so. The generator's not that strong. What else would pull you here?" She mentally reviewed the time-travel novel she'd recently read and recalled tidbits from some of the time-travel movies she'd seen. "There has to be a connection. If I was writing this as a story, I'd make you innocent, as you claimed. You would be transported to me at this place and time because

I was researching your case and had doubts about your guilt."

Luke's eyes lit up with interest. "You had doubts?"

She waved at him. "Hush. I'm creating. Where was I? Oh, yes. The author had doubts and could help you—the falsely convicted man—to find the truth and set things right." She purposely left out the part where the two characters would fall in love. Not that he wasn't attractive to her. But how could there be a romance if the hero's kiss could accidentally electrocute the heroine? Talk about getting charged up by a man!

"How could I set things right three decades later?"

"What?" He repeated himself, and she pushed the question of a romantic subplot to the back of her mind. "Well, you'd have to go back in time to fix things, of course, probably by another electrocution or a lightning stroke or something. Hey, this could actually turn into a new kind of plot for me. I've never used any paranormal aspects in my books before, but I think my editor would go for it."

She could feel the adrenaline coursing through her system in anticipation of getting back to work. "You know, just this morning I was thinking about the coincidence of my researching your case right near where the murder happened, and how it was the exact date of your execution. It's not uncommon for that kind of thing to happen to me when I'm creating. Like I need to verify a fact and an hour later someone calls who has access to the information I need. I call it spiritual assistance. Maybe that's what you are. A story idea dropped right into my lap when I needed it most."

"Kelly?"

She stopped pacing and faced him. "Hmm?"

"This isn't fiction. And I'm not a spirit. I'm really Luke Templeton. I was *really* electrocuted this morning in 1965 and transported to you in 1997. And I *really* need some help. I wasn't lying about arriving here with nothing. I don't know how or why, but I've been given a second chance. The problem is, I don't even have a dime for a cup of coffee."

"You'd need fifty cents, at least. Inflation's part of this real world."

"Good God. Anyway, I'll be glad to get out of your hair, but if you could possibly make me a small loan, I swear I'll pay you back as soon as I get a job—"

"Whoa! It doesn't work that way. Weren't you listening to me? If we're going to accept the possibility that you traveled through time, then we have to accept all of it. You were sent to me for a reason—probably because I *can* help you set things right."

"*But*," he countered, "as of this minute, things are right . . for me. I'm alive and free. I can start a whole new life in this time period. I'm an ace reporter. I could get work in a heartbeat. I just need a stake, a small one. I can eat bread and water, sleep in the woods, and buy clothes at a thrift shop."

"Forget it," she said with a smug expression. "You couldn't get a regular newspaper job without identification, and you wouldn't get any paying freelance jobs without credentials. Besides, things haven't been set right for Ginger or whoever killed her . . . assuming that wasn't you. The murderer could still be alive, even living right in the area. What do you think would happen if he learned that Luke Templeton was back from the dead?"

"I could go to another town."

"The murderer could be there. You have no way of knowing where he is. And since you don't know who he is, he could spot you first. But your safety isn't the real issue here since, historically speaking, you're already dead. If you are who you say, then your being here is a sort of miracle. You can't just ignore that. You have to do whatever it is you were given the second chance to do, which is obviously to set things right. You have no choice."

Luke grimaced. "I think I liked you better when you were a gun-toting skeptic."

"How ironic. I like you much better as a helpless time-traveler than a burglar, rapist, mental institution escapee, or spy with a fetish for my clothing. But I'll go back to ordering you out of my presence at gunpoint, if it would make you happy."

"You win," he said, giving her a mock bow. "I am momentarily helpless, as you say, and thus at your mercy."

"Heh-heh-heh," she cackled and rubbed her hands together. "Just what I always wanted—a man at my mercy. What shall I do with you first?" She was thinking along the lines of ordering him to wash the windows, but he clearly took her comment in a sexual way. "Don't even think about it," she said bluntly. "Shaking hands with you nearly killed me. Are you hungry?"

He grinned, both at her quick subject change and the prospect of food. "Starved."

"There's plenty in the fridge and cabinets. You can help yourself. The stove runs on propane gas, so your personal electricity won't help. You'll have to light the burners to cook. If you'll give me your sizes, I'll drive back to town and pick up a few things for you to wear."

"Wouldn't it be easier if I went with you?"

She laughed. "We're in the backwoods of Georgia. You're barefoot, wearing shorts that hardly cover your butt, and a shirt that announces that you have PMS. I don't think so."

He looked down at the phrase on the shirt. "What is PMS anyway?"

She had to remind herself that if he really was who he said, he knew nothing of the years between 1965 and 1997. "Premenstrual syndrome.

An age-old female malady that some doctor finally gave a name to. Believe me, you don't want it. You've got enough problems already."

He gave her his sizes and another promise to pay her back, and she was ready to go again. At the last second, she remembered the gun and stuck it in her purse.

Luke frowned. "I thought you were starting to believe me."

"I am. But you're still a man. Therefore, I may believe what you say, but I know better than to trust you with my life."

As Luke watched Kelly drive away, he couldn't help but wonder why she'd say such a thing. The reporter in him always listened very carefully to what people said aloud, then he guessed at what they were actually thinking. When Kelly had accused him of spying, she'd mentioned three men's names. He'd bet at least one of them was responsible for her derogatory comment.

Under different circumstances, he would have automatically been tempted to pick up the gauntlet she'd unwittingly thrown at his feet. Given time, he had no doubt he could get her to trust him.

Then again, his methods of changing a woman's mind usually involved considerable physical contact, something that was completely out of the question at the moment.

He supposed that was a good thing. Even with Kelly wearing a boy's cap and unflattering clothes, and pointing a gun at him, he thought she was extremely sexy. The big T-shirt failed to hide her terrific figure, and she certainly had great legs. If it wasn't for his little electrical problem, he'd definitely have a hard time keeping his mind on what he was supposed to be doing . . . whatever that was.

He wasn't at all convinced she had that part right, but he was hardly in a position to argue with her. Personally, he thought his more scientific theory of positive and negative energy was easier to accept. On the other hand, if a miracle had occurred, it was probably because God knew he was an innocent man who deserved a few more years in this life. Just in case that was the explanation, he looked upward and said, "Thank you."

In the meantime, he needed Kelly's help to get on his feet, so he would go along with whatever she had in mind. Once he figured out how to survive in this time on his own, however, he'd take off, disappear into a crowded city to quietly live out the bonus days he'd been granted, and leave Miss Kirkwood to her world of make-believe.

"Did you hear that, Gabriel?" Jezebel shouted toward the light. "You may have tricked me with the circumstances for his test, but it won't make any difference. He'll never stick around long enough to fall in love with her. And don't you just hate the way he keeps using your lord's name in vain, even after that priest brought it to his attention? Give up the challenge now, Gabriel, and I promise not to remind you of your loss any longer than, say, a millennium."

The archangel ignored her taunt. It was too soon to give up on Luke Templeton. Kelly Kirkwood had every attribute Luke was usually attracted to, and more. Why, he hadn't even seen her glorious hair yet. Besides, Gabriel was certain that the fact that Luke couldn't touch Kelly would make her seem that much more desirable to him. It was only the first day of his test. There was still plenty of time.

Kelly parked her Camaro, but didn't get out. It hadn't occurred to her until now that Charming didn't have any department stores, and she wasn't sure if any of the stores it did have stocked a selection of shoes or clothing.

Besides that, when she was here an hour ago making a call from the public phone in front of the drugstore, two people had greeted her by name. She'd only been into town three previous times to buy groceries, do laundry, and check general delivery for mail, but she supposed that was often enough in a town this size, especially with several of her books on sale in the drugstore.

Did she want anyone here to know she was looking for clothes for a man? Her intuition told her it was a bad idea. She should go elsewhere.

As she pulled out of the parking space, she saw something she'd failed to notice before. The sign over the drugstore read O'NEILL DRUGS AND SUNDRIES.

Could that be O'Neill, as in Ginger-the murder-victim O'Neill? If so, it was a place to start asking questions about what happened here in 1965.

As she drove toward Buford, a considerably larger small town than Charming, she gave some thought as to how she should proceed with her Luke Templeton project and came up with the simplest solution possible. She would proceed as though she were actually writing a book based on Ginger O'Neill's murder. Considering her reputation, no one should be suspicious of any ulterior motive on her part, and most people were very helpful when she told them why she wanted to interview them, especially if she promised them a mention in her book.

That decided, she made herself think about her parting remark to Luke.

Did she believe that was his name? Maybe. Maybe not. It was better than calling him that man that shocked the hell out of her.

Could he truly be who he claimed? Did he actually travel through time? Were all the coincidences only that, or had a genuine miracle occurred? Maybe. Maybe not. Her overactive imagination was leaning toward the miracle, as usual.

The bottom line, however, was this question. Could she refuse to believe any of it and send him away? No. Absolutely not. The miracle theory was too enticing not to follow up, if for no other reason than to see how the story would end.

So that was it. From this moment on, she would stop doubting that Luke Templeton was the man she'd been researching. She would accept him at face value. As a precaution, though, she would continue to keep her gun close at hand. After all, he had been convicted of rape and murder, whether he denied his guilt or not.

Just outside of Buford, Kelly spotted a free-standing discount department store, which would have been satisfying in itself, but the name of it gave her an eerie shiver.

O'NEILL'S. Could there be a connection?

O'Neill's was a successful retail chain in Georgia. She'd shopped in one of the Atlanta stores not long ago. The goose bumps on her arms told her this was important for some reason.

She found everything she was looking for inside the large store, including an informant in the men's clothing department. The elderly saleslady, whose name tag identified her as Mrs. Lawson, was pleased to be of assistance.

"I've just moved to Georgia," Kelly told her with a bright smile. "But I've seen O'Neill's stores all over the state. In fact, I was passing through a little town called Charming and saw a drugstore with that name."

"Why that was Mr. O'Neill's first store. He opened it in 1962, as a wedding present to his wife."

"How romantic," Kelly said taking her cue from the soft expression on the woman's face. "It must have been very exciting to watch the business grow over the years. Do they still live around here?"

"Mr. O'Neill still lives in the same house where he grew up as a boy. In Charming. 'Course he's fixed it up a lot from what it was like back then. He comes in here once a week, just like he visits every one of his stores. The years haven't slowed him down a bit. Unfortunately, his wife never saw the success he made of it." Mrs. Lawson clucked her tongue.

"Oh? Why not?"

The woman leaned forward to share her knowledge and spoke in a lowered tone. "She was murdered when they were only married a few years. It was a tragic story. Raped and strangled in her own home. Most people hereabouts know of it, but no one speaks of it anymore."

Kelly looked appropriately sympathetic, yet intrigued. "How awful. Did they ever catch the murderer?"

"Oh, yes. Right away, in fact. And he was electrocuted right away, too."

"Well, thank heavens for that. Not that justice could ever bring back a loved one. I suppose, after such a tragedy, Mr. O'Neill must have put all his attention into expanding his business."

The woman nodded. "He never remarried. They

say his wife took his heart with her when she died."

"Boy, someone should write a book about Mr. O'Neill. You know, like the Wal-Mart guy."

"Why, that's a very good idea, miss. Someone should do that."

"Marv, go see if there's a problem down on the floor, or if Mrs. Lawson's doin' her socializin' on company time again. She's been jawin' with that customer in the baseball cap for five minutes now."

Junior Ramey took his position as manager of the Buford store very seriously. He had to. Between having a criminal record and a face that made babies cry, his options were limited. If it hadn't been for Reid O'Neill, he might have ended up in a gutter somewhere.

At five years old, he'd knocked a skillet of hot bacon grease off the stove, severely burning the right side of his face. After high school, the only one who would hire him was Mr. O'Neill. It didn't matter that the work was menial and that he had to stay out of the public eye; it was a paying job that freed him from his father's tyranny.

Mr. O'Neill even let him come back to work after serving time in the loony bin. He proved himself to Mr. O'Neill and, in return, was promoted to office work as the business expanded. With the help of an assistant manager like Marv,

Junior was now able to run a profitable store without frightening the customers away.

Marv returned with a smile on his plump face. "It's okay, Mr. Ramey. The customer is new in the area and was asking a lot of questions. She's got about three hundred dollars' worth of merchandise in her cart."

Junior returned the smile as well as his distorted face allowed. "Well, then, we must remember to commend Mrs. Lawson for her friendly, courteous service."

"Will do. You might get a kick out of this. She said they were talking about how Mr. O'Neill's life story is so interesting someone should write a book about it."

The hairs on Junior's neck twitched. "You said the woman was asking a lot of questions about the area. How did Mr. O'Neill's life story come up?"

Marv shrugged. "Damned if I know. You know how Mrs. Lawson likes to talk."

Junior stared at the old gossip through the one-way glass of his upstairs office. What had gotten her talking about Mr. O'Neill's *interesting* life? The last thing he or Mr. O'Neill needed was people dredging up the past. It was dead and buried.

Just like Ginger O'Neill, her Yankee lover, and his own misdeeds.

"We have to talk," Kelly blurted out even before she closed the cabin door.

Luke glanced up from the book he was reading.

"Give me a few minutes. I want to finish the chapter."

"What are you reading?" she asked as she walked over and deposited the shopping bags on the sofa next to him. "Oh! You found the time-travel story I mentioned."

He made a face at her. "You didn't mention that it was a *love* story."

"Don't worry," she said with a chuckle. "You won't turn into a woman by reading it. In fact, you might even gain a little insight. Women's fiction has changed drastically since your time. It all started in the early seventies, when—"

"Okay," he said, closing the book and setting it aside. "I can take a hint. What do we have to talk about?"

"Details. I need to know everything about your case. Everything you know about the people of the town. Even details that don't seem to have anything to do with you or the murder."

"Fine. Can I see what you bought first?"

She opened one bag and dumped the contents out. "This should do you for a while—jeans, T-shirts, underwear, sneakers, a toothbrush, and some other stuff. There's some ointment in there that should help your burns. I also bought a copy of today's newspaper, just in case you still had any doubts about when and where you are. You go ahead and browse, change if you want. I'm going to fix myself a sandwich. Then we can get started."

"Good God!" Luke muttered when he found the receipt. "I once bought a car for this much."

Kelly laughed. "Believe me, this stuff was cheap. If I'd gone to one of the mall department stores in Atlanta, the bill would have been at least twice that."

"But can you afford this?" He was genuinely worried about the amount of his debt to her.

"It's nothing. Really. I'm considering it an expense of my new book." He didn't look convinced. "Honestly, I'm a *very* successful author. They're even making one of my books into a movie."

"No shit! Oh, excuse me. I mean, I'm impressed. Why don't you have any of your books here?"

"I don't live here. I'm only using this place as a sort of retreat for a few weeks, which is just one of the many strange coincidences about this whole situation. Anyway, they have some of my books in town. I'll pick one up for you if you'd like."

"I would," he replied sincerely.

"But you have to promise not to fall in love with me."

"Huh?"

She waved her hand at him. "Nothing. Private joke."

He didn't ask her to explain. He hadn't even heard her. He was totally focused on the front page of the newspaper. After a few seconds, he looked at the sales receipt again. "Amazing. It really is August 24th, 1997."

"Yep. And I'll be happy to fill you in on what changes have occurred besides inflation *after* I interview *you*."

"Would you mind if I took a shower before we get to work? I fell in the bushes outside and I feel cruddy."

"You're welcome to use the bathroom, but there's no shower. Only that old metal washtub that someone fitted with plumbing. You'll be a little cramped, but it's functional."

Kelly had finished her sandwich and was waiting impatiently to get started questioning Luke, when he called out her name in a worried tone.

"Kelly? I think you need to see this."

She walked to the closed door, but the fact that he hadn't opened it himself made her hesitate. She didn't like surprises. "If you've found one of those mutant cockroaches, you have my permission to kill it."

"Please. Just open the door."

His voice sounded so strange, she thought he might be playing a practical joke on her. She lightly touched the metal doorknob, in case he was holding the other end, but she felt nothing unusual.

"Kelly? Are you—"

She opened the door and gasped. He was glowing from head to toe, as though a thousand lightbulbs had been turned on beneath his flesh. A white-gold aura extended about six inches beyond his body. It was such an incredible sight, she *almost* didn't notice that he was naked.

Standing in the metal tub with his arms stretched out, he was too frightened to care about his nudity. "Do y-you s-see what I s-see?" he asked.

She swallowed hard and kept her gaze on his face. "That depends on whether or not you see a man who could star in his own science-fiction movie. Boy, we sure could have used you the night the lights went out in Georgia."

"This is not funny!" he snapped at her, but as he watched her trying hard not to make another witty comment, his mouth curved into a grin. "Well, maybe it's a little funny."

"Do you feel all right?"

He did a mental check of his body. "I feel fine. In fact, I feel terrific, except that my heart's pounding a little hard, but that could be because I just had the hell scared out of me. I guess it has something to do with the metal tub and the water. I wasn't sure what would happen if I got out."

"Well, you obviously can't stand there for eternity." She pulled the bath towel off the rack and tossed it to him. "Start drying yourself. I'll be right back." A few seconds later she returned with her rubber flip-flops. "I have no idea whether these will make any difference. They'll be a little small, but they don't conduct electricity. Step into them, then follow me outside." She grabbed a fireplace poker on her way out.

When he joined her outside, the glow was still evident in spite of the midday sun. She was somewhat relieved to see that he had made use of the towel, but the parts of his body that weren't covered were still quite distracting. Jack's suggestion that she needed to have a fling came back to her, and she realized he may have been right. If a man charged with enough electricity to glow in the dark could turn her on, she had clearly gone too long between tune-ups!

Luke noticed the way she was stroking the poker in her hand. "Unless you have a death wish, you'd better not touch me with that thing."

His warning broke into her lascivious thoughts. "Oh! I know that. What I was thinking was, maybe this could help drain the charge off you. You know, like how the guide wire on a house directs lightning into the ground." She placed the poker on the ground and moved away. "It's worth a try."

Not having any better idea, Luke picked up the poker by one end and stuck the other end into the dirt. Instantly, Luke's body stiffened and a visible wave of electricity shot down the iron staff. A few seconds later, Luke collapsed to his knees.

Kelly rushed forward and touched him before she thought of the consequences. "Are you— *Ouch!*" she cried and jerked her hand back.

"Are you okay?" they asked simultaneously, then laughed despite the seriousness of her mistake.

"I'm fine," she said quickly. "It was only a spark. I guess that means my lightning rod idea worked."

He took a deep breath, then used the poker to help himself stand. "I feel like . . . more was drained out of me than . . . an excess charge of power. I feel . . . weak."

She thought he looked terribly pale. "Drop the poker, Luke. Maybe that was a bad idea after all. Maybe the electrical charge is what's keeping you going."

He gave her a lopsided smile. "Does your imagination ever turn off?"

She shrugged. "I don't think so. That's probably why I write fiction—to get rid of the overflow. You were a reporter. Didn't you always have questions or theories, or something like that going on inside your head?"

"Yeah. I did." He took another deep breath and some of his natural color returned.

"The charge is building back up on its own, isn't it?"

He nodded slowly. "I think so. I feel better."

"Good. Then we can finally get to work."

Although Kelly had seen every masculine inch of his lean body, Luke went back inside the bathroom to get dressed. She couldn't decide if she was glad about that or not. When he came back out, she noted that he had tried to comb back his damp hair, but it was already forming waves around his face again.

"Don't you look spiffy," she said, admiring the

nice fit of the clothes she'd chosen. He was really quite a handsome man.

"You have red hair," he said, as though she didn't already know that.

Apparently his personal crisis had prevented him from noticing it earlier. While he was bathing, she had taken off the cap and brushed her hair out only because the bobby pins were irritating her scalp. She hadn't been thinking of making herself more attractive for him, but his reaction was very flattering. "When I spend time in the sun, it turns more blond than red, but I haven't been out much this summer."

He walked around behind her, clearly entranced. "It's so long." Momentarily forgetting himself, he extended his fingers to touch the red-gold strands. There was a snap of static electricity and a whole handful of her hair lifted into his hand. He quickly jumped away. "Did I hurt you?"

She shook her head. "Not at all. It just felt very weird." When he kept staring at her hair, she spoke to him more sternly. "Sit down. I have a whole list of questions."

He straddled the chair on the other side of the table, but he still seemed distracted by her appearance. Men and their one-track minds! Considering the route her mind had taken in the last hour, she decided it was best to get him on another track as quickly as possible.

"Tell me about your relationship with Ginger O'Neill."

Chapter Four

"You're different from most women."

Kelly clucked her tongue. "My hair is this color because I inherited it from my father. It's long because it goes with my public image. It has nothing to do with—"

"I wasn't talking about your hair. I was talking about your reactions. You see a strange man in your home, you calmly pull a gun on him. That man says he's traveled through time, and you accept that, albeit after some reasonable disbelief. He turns on like a lightbulb and you think of a way to normalize him. Most women I know would have flipped out, screamed their heads off, or started crying."

She laughed. "Then you're right. I'm not like most women you know. But most of the women I know today don't have the luxury of acting like twits in emergencies. They've learned to think on their feet, respond intuitively, and use the brains God gave them."

He scratched his lower back on one side, then the other. "Well, amen to that."

She thought he looked and sounded like he really meant that. Lucky for him. "Now quit stalling. Tell me about Ginger O'Neill."

Kelly could almost see him arranging his thoughts before speaking aloud. She'd have to remember this man interviewed people for a living. With her pen poised over a pad of lined paper, she waited for him to open up to her.

"I didn't know she was married."

She arched one eyebrow questioningly, and he hurried to explain.

"She wasn't wearing a ring when I met her, and she never told me she had a husband until the day she broke it off with me." He took a deep breath. "Let me start at the beginning. It'll make more sense that way. I moved to Atlanta from Detroit in October of sixty-four. I was doing well with the *Daily News*, but I couldn't stand the winters, so I applied for staff positions in milder climates. I got a few offers, but the *Journal*'s location appealed the most. Besides the weather, Atlanta was in the eye of a political hurricane."

"What do you mean?"

He looked surprised. "The march on Washington in sixty-three. The Civil Rights Act. Racial equality. Don't tell me it was all for nothing."

"Oh no. Tremendous progress was made. In fact in some areas, like employment and housing, minorities—and that includes women now—are given advantages over white male Americans. Unfortunately, you can't legislate people's attitudes.

"I'm a transplanted Georgian also. I moved to Atlanta from Scranton, Pennsylvania, when my husband—my *ex*-husband that is—was transferred. I had encountered prejudice up north, but here it seemed more, I don't know, out in the open. I have to admit, though, I'm not that knowledgeable about the early sixties. I was only born in 1966."

"Hmm. What about the space program? That was one of the other major issues in the national news the last I was around. Did we ever put a man on the moon?"

"Yes, in 1969. But a lot of other issues like the Vietnamese War and environmental pollution pushed space travel out of a priority position."

"The Vietnamese *War*? Damn. We had no business getting involved over there in the first place. How did it turn out? And what about Russia? Since we're sitting here, I will assume there was never a nuclear war as everyone feared."

"No, but—Hey, wait a minute. Who's being interviewed here anyway?"

He grinned at her. "Sorry. I didn't do that on purpose. It's just that I suddenly realized how much I have to catch up on."

"And I have something here to help you do that." She pointed at her laptop computer. "One of the wonders of my time, the home computer. If I'm not mistaken, in the sixties, a computer system was about the size of this cabin, made a lot of noise, and took forever to spit out information. Among other things, that little box contains a fair-sized research library that you can access in seconds. I promise to show you how to use it . . . *later*."

She noticed the way he kept repositioning himself on the chair and making a face as though he couldn't quite get comfortable. "Are you all right?"

"Yeah, but I don't think I got all the soap off when I rinsed. Go ahead."

"No, *you* go ahead. I want to hear your story now."

He was clearly more interested in the questions bouncing around his head, but he agreed to answer hers first. "Okay. So, I moved to Atlanta and got into hot water by the new year. I covered some local stories that obviously had racism at their core. All I did was point out the new civil rights laws that were being ignored and write an editorial or two. You would have thought *I* was the one breaking the law. At first, there were subtle hints for me to back off, notes, anonymous threatening phone calls, that sort of thing. Nothing I hadn't dealt with before. But after I wrote a piece offering proof that several confirmed Ku Klux Klan members were behind one of the cases of violence, they got serious.

"One night, on the way between my car and my apartment, I was bashed on the head, blindfolded, bound, and taken for a long ride in the back of a pickup truck. When the blindfold came off, I was in a clearing in the woods, surrounded by people wearing white sheets and pointed hoods, and there was an enormous wooden cross burning in front of me. One man did all the talking. He warned me to 'stop writing all that Yankee shit or the next cross they burned would have me tied to it.' "

"Sounds like the Klan to me," Kelly stated in a matter-of-fact tone.

He nodded. "They played kickball with me for a while—you can guess who got to play the part of the ball—then they left me to find my way back to Atlanta on my own, which took the rest of the night. As a matter of fact, I wasn't all that far from here."

"Did you report the incident to the police?"

"The emergency room doctor, who stitched up the cut on my head and taped my ribs, strongly suggested that I mind my own business. When I told my editor about it, his solution was to give me an assignment that had absolutely no racial aspects to it. There had been several rapes of white housewives, allegedly committed by a white man, around Lake Sidney Lanier. Besides keeping me out of trouble with the Klan, it was also right up my alley. I cut my teeth on crime reporting, even helped the Detroit police solve a case or two."

She noted the pride in his voice. "But instead

of helping to find the rapist, you were eventually accused of being him."

"Right. And my traveling in and out of the area on that assignment was part of the prosecutor's case against me. But we're jumping ahead. First came the assignment. Then I met Ginger. It was the second time I was up here, trying to get interviews with the victims, without much success. I was driving through Charming and stopped at the drugstore for a soda. Ginger was working there. At first I thought she was just a high-school kid, but once we started talking, I found out she was twenty-one. It was a good thing, too, because the sparks started flying the minute I—" He cut himself off with a somewhat sheepish look.

"Don't censor your story on my account. I assure you, there's not much you could say that would shock me. In fact, the kind of things I write might shock you. Just tell me what happened, without trying to decide what I should and shouldn't hear."

He looked skeptical, but got back to his story. "Anyway, we hit it off immediately, and she ended up calling two of the victims and convincing them to talk to me. But when I invited her to dinner that night, she turned me down, saying that it was not possible for her to be seen with me socially. I thought she meant because of my reputation for liberal journalism. Instead, she took my card and promised to call me the next time she was in Atlanta.

"A couple of weeks later, I heard from her. She told me she'd had problems at home and had moved in with a girlfriend in Atlanta. At no time did she mention that the problems involved a husband."

"Would it have mattered?" Kelly asked.

"Yes, dammit. It would have mattered. Not only had I never messed around with a married woman, in this case, it would have kept me out of jail."

"Maybe. Maybe not. Could she have been part of your frame-up?"

His eyes opened wide in surprise. "What? How could you think that? She ended up dead."

Kelly shrugged. "Maybe she was set up also. I realize I haven't heard it all yet, but I'm already thinking the Klan may have been behind your conviction. If you riled them that much, they may have gone to extremes to shut you up."

"Not that extreme. She once told me her father and brother were members of the local chapter. They wouldn't kill one of their own to set me up, especially not in such a brutal manner."

"Okay, we'll put that theory down on the bottom of the list. Go on."

"To make a long story short, things got very serious between us. For the first time in my life, I was thinking about settling down with one woman. Then, out of the blue, on the Fourth of July, it was over. She came to me, with her eyes all bloodshot, like she'd been crying for a long time."

Kelly remained quiet as he sifted through his memories. The events he spoke of may have occurred over thirty years ago for her, but for him, the hurt was still fresh.

"All that time, I thought the drugstore was her father's, but it was her husband's. She had gotten married right after high school to a man who was a friend of her parents'. Reid O'Neill was nineteen years her senior, but Ginger said that everyone considered him the most eligible bachelor in the county. Enough people told her how lucky she was to have him interested in her that she believed it. However, as she put it, all those people didn't have to live with the old fart. Mind you, I was fourteen years older than her myself, but she insisted that I acted like a teenager compared to him."

He stopped to scratch an itch on his leg, fidgeted a little more, then continued. "She told me that she had thought about leaving him for some time, but meeting me was what pushed her into doing it. She didn't tell me she was married because she was afraid I'd have nothing to do with her if I knew. Apparently, her husband and parents accepted the fact that she'd gotten married too young and were willing to give her a few months on her own in the big city to come to her senses.

"Now her time was up, and they'd given her some kind of ultimatum; she never told me exactly what it was. She would only say that she was going back to her husband and that under no circumstances was I to try to see her again."

Kelly stopped him for a moment to make a few notes on her pad. "You know, if this were a fictional romance, the ultimatum would have been some sort of threat against you. You said Ginger's father and Reid O'Neill were friends, and if Ginger's father was a Klan member, maybe O'Neill was also. I think it would be safe to assume that their views about interfering Yankee reporters would be similar. It might have been okay to let Ginger spread her wings until they found out who she was spreading them with."

"I don't know," Luke said, frowning. "You're making a lot of assumptions without any facts on which to base them. She told me flat out that her time with me was just a fling, and that the man she wanted to spend the rest of her life with was her husband, even with his faults."

"Which is what she would have to say to keep you safely away from her. Didn't you say she'd been crying? Why would she be crying if she was going back to the man she truly loved?"

"Women cry for all sorts of reasons. Maybe they were tears of joy."

"Yeah. Or maybe it was PMS," she added sarcastically.

He thought about that for a moment, then grinned. "Oh, I get it. Well, it really doesn't matter now. She moved back to Charming and someone killed her a few days later."

"The newspaper account put you at the scene of the crime."

"Hmmph. I was there all right. I got a phone call from Ginger, at least I assumed it was her. It was a woman's voice, and she was sobbing. She said her husband had beaten her, and she needed me to come get her. I knew something was wrong when I found the front door slightly open and no one answered when I called out, but I was only thinking of Ginger being hurt and needing help. It never occurred to me that I was walking into a trap. No sooner did I find her in her bedroom, than half the police in Forsyth County burst in and found me leaning over her trying to check for a pulse. The timing was impeccable."

"Where was her husband while she was being raped and strangled?"

"Very conveniently attending a *lodge* meeting with most of the other men in the area. It provided all of them with the same airtight alibi."

"Was it a Klan meeting?"

Luke shrugged. "No one called it that during the trial, but that's my guess."

"So, we have a cuckolded husband who probably wanted to see you and Ginger dead, or at least punished. Then we have a countless number of suspects who just wanted to see you eliminated and may have been annoyed with Ginger for mucking it up with a Yankee."

"And don't forget the real rapist who I might

have unknowingly been closing in on. By setting me up he got off the hot seat himself."

"But only for a while," Kelly reminded him. "And when he was caught, he still denied killing Ginger."

Luke pulled the stack of files closer to him and sorted through the papers until he found the article he was looking for. " 'Buford resident, Beauregard Ramey, better known as Junior, was arrested last night for breaking and entering and attempted rape. It has been suggested that he may have been the actual Lake Sidney Lanier rapist rather than Luke Templeton . . .' and so forth. That guy's name sounds familiar, but I don't know why. Do you have anything else on him?"

"I don't think so. I was only pulling articles that had your name in them."

"Damn. I wish I had my notes."

"I doubt if they're still around, but since I got these from the *Atlanta Journal*'s old files, I'm sure they'd have more information on Ramey's arrest and trial."

Luke snapped his fingers. "They'd also have my columns. Maybe his name sounds familiar because I wrote something about him. Do we have time to go today?"

Smiling, she said, "You look like a bloodhound that just caught the scent of a rabbit. Glad to see your reporter's instincts weren't destroyed during the electrocution. However, it's too late to do anything about it today. We can go in the morning if you'd like, but there are sources of information right nearby, too."

She related her conversation with Mrs. Lawson. "I figured there are probably a lot of people still in the area who remember that time. I should be able to ask all the questions I want if they think it's for a fictional book."

"What happened to your argument to me that the killer might still be living in the area? If he is, he's not going to want you snooping around, resurrecting old news, no matter what reason you give."

"So-o-o . . . I'll carry my gun," she replied with false bravado.

He made a face at her. "Do you really know how to use that thing?"

"I took lessons."

"Lessons that probably didn't prepare you for actually pulling the trigger on another human. Why did you buy a gun as powerful as a Walther PPK anyway?"

She shrugged. "I bought it after a fan took it into his head that I was writing my love scenes directly to him. I chose that make because I'm a James Bond fan. You probably don't know who—"

"Of course I know who that is. I read Ian Fleming long before they made *Dr. No*."

"I didn't realize *Dr. No* was that old. You might enjoy seeing the 007 movies that followed. I have most of them on video at my town house in Atlanta. When we go down, we could play one or two." After she said it, she realized he didn't know what she was talking about. Back in his day, colored television was still a fairly new invention. She couldn't wait to see his reaction to her VCR. And MTV. And a microwave oven!

"*Kelly.* You went away again. Do you do that often?"

She smiled. "I'm afraid so. It's the downside to an active imagination."

"Hmmph. Anyway, back to your questioning people. I can't let you do that."

Her eyebrows shot up. "You can't *let* me? Listen up, macho-man. One of the big changes that have occurred in this country is that a woman no longer has to get a man's permission to do anything."

He held up his hands as if to ward off her attack. "Okay. No problem. I'll just go with you."

She could see several advantages to having him accompany her, the primary of which would be his thinking of questions she might not. The least of which would be that she wasn't nearly as confident as she claimed, but there were risks involved in his going out in public. "It's been a long time, but someone might still remember what you looked like."

"Even if someone thought I looked familiar, wouldn't simple logic eliminate any question of my being the same man?"

She paused, then shook her head. "You could be the son of the man who was executed, come back to get revenge. We can't take any chances. If you want to come with me, you'll need a disguise."

He reached for her baseball cap and put it on with the brim low over his forehead.

"Maybe if you hunch over a bit, make yourself smaller. And since your hair length and eye color were specifically mentioned in connection with the rapist's description, you might want to trim the back of your hair and keep anyone from seeing your eyes. They're pretty distinctive."

He wiggled his eyebrows at her. "You think so?"

Rather than give him more of a compliment, she continued. "It might work if I introduce you as my secretary and you keep your head down by focusing on writing notes while I'm interviewing someone. And you'll have to remember not to jump into any conversations. I'd have to appear to be in charge at all times. If you think of a question, you can whisper it in my ear."

"That should be interesting," he replied with a smirk. "Especially if I accidentally brush my lips against your ear and you go flying across the room like you did before."

She frowned. Instead of being concerned about getting shocked, her imagination was responding to the thought of his lips brushing her ear.

"It's nice to see that women can still blush," he said, giving her a look that implied that he knew exactly which part of his statement had pinkened her cheeks.

She silently damned her fair complexion. "Never mind. We'll figure it out as we go. Now, here's something that I thought about after my chat with Mrs. Lawson. After Ginger's death, her husband immediately started expanding his business in a big way. I'm guessing there might have been a huge death benefit on Ginger's life insurance."

"It's a guess worth checking into. We should also try to find out what else he inherited from her. I seem to remember her mentioning a trust fund that she received when she turned twenty-one. At least that's how she explained why she didn't need to work while she was in Atlanta."

Kelly was very pleased that he now seemed as intrigued by the project as she was, though he was sporadically distracted by the need to scratch. She suggested he try rinsing off again, in case it was leftover soap film as he'd guessed, but he didn't want to risk another overcharge so soon. At any rate, theories, suppositions, and forming a plan of action, interspersed with his questions about the political and social changes of the last three decades, kept his mind sufficiently occupied for several hours.

But as the light in the cabin grew dim, the focus of their attention changed.

Chapter Five

He stood outside the kitchen window, watching her do the dinner dishes, her pink ruffled apron tied around her waist, the seams in her stockings not quite straight up the backs of her shapely calves. The perfect little housewife.

But where was her husband? Why wasn't he there, untying the little bow at her back, wrapping his arms around her waist, kissing her neck, seducing her away from her chores and into the bedroom? She was probably wondering the same thing, feeling sad because she didn't have a man who understood her needs.

He understood. He vividly recalled the conversation between his mother and aunt one night when they didn't know he was listening—the very private conversation that explained why Mama always looked so unhappy.

If this woman were his wife, he would never leave her unsatisfied.

He took a deep breath and pulled the ski mask over his head. If she didn't see his face, she could pretend that he was her husband come home early to surprise her. He walked around to the other side of the house, where he knew of an unlocked window, and quietly entered the neat bedroom. As much as he wished it was unnecessary, he slid the knife out of the sheath that was strapped to his leg.

His heart picked up its pace as he silently tread toward the kitchen. The instant he stepped through the doorway she saw him, but a wave of the wicked-looking knife warned her not to scream. In a flash, he moved behind her, covering her mouth with his free hand as he used his body to nudge her toward the bedroom.

The moment he freed her mouth, she begged, "Please don't kill me. I'll do whatever you say, only please don't hurt me."

Wordlessly, he directed her to keep quiet as he untied her little apron and tossed it on a chair. Then piece by piece, he slowly undressed her until she stood before him wearing only her garter belt and hose . . . and a terrified expression on her face. He tenderly stroked her cheek to assure her that she had nothing to fear as long as she cooperated with him.

Following his unspoken order, she laid down on the bed and gave no resistance as he took four silk neckties from his pockets and used them to tie her ankles and wrists to the bedposts. Once he was certain she could not run off, he set down the knife and caressed her cheek again. Soon she would understand that he was doing this for her.

For the next half hour, he concentrated on arousing every inch of her body with his hands and mouth, until she was moaning and writhing in near delirium. She sounded as though she were upset or in pain, but he knew the truth. He was giving her the kind of pleasure she wished her ignorant husband would provide. He was showing her that she should have married him instead. It felt good to know that realization would haunt her long after he left her tonight.

But he was not yet finished. There was still the message to be left behind for her husband. That man had to be made aware that his lawfully wedded wife had enjoyed another man's lovemaking.

As he undid his belt buckle, he noted how the woman kept shifting her eyes and cocking her head to direct his attention to the nightstand. He glanced at the plastic-wrapped condom and remembered how it had interfered the last time. His gaze returned to the woman's damp, squirming body, and he hurriedly shoved his pants past his hips to show her that he was more than able to finish the job he'd started on her. She smiled and shyly lowered her eyes.

As he moved to enter her, however, she shifted her hips and loudly cleared her throat. He understood what she wanted him to do, but he ignored her and continued forward.

"Damn you!" she cried out and twisted away from him in earnest. "You know the drill. No diving without a wet suit. I'll play along with almost any game you have in mind, but I ain't risking my life for a couple of hundred bucks!"

Junior slapped her face as his fantasy disintegrated. Within seconds, his erection was gone as well.

"That'll cost you," she said with a sneer. No trace remained of the sweet little housewife. "The boss don't like it when a john gets rough with one of his girls, unless it was paid for in advance."

He felt his dinner backing up into his throat. With effort, he got both the nausea and his anger under control sufficiently to get off the bed and straighten his clothes.

"Hey, what are you doing? I didn't say you had to stop."

He began untying the neckties.

"All I wanted was for you to wear a rubber. It's for your protection, too." Although he had removed the last tie, she remained sprawled on the bed. Stroking her own body, she switched to a kittenish voice. "Come on, honey, don't be like this. You got me all hot for you."

He took a twenty-dollar bill out of his wallet and dropped it on her stomach. "That's for the slap. Now get out of my house."

Her eyes were wary as she rose. "Don't think you can get away with complaining about me—"

"I'm not going to complain and neither are

you." He pulled off the ski mask and let her see the disfigured side of his face. As expected, the grotesque sight got her moving.

After she left, he forced himself to acknowledge the mistake he'd made. It was partly her fault though. She was so damned convincing, it was as if she had really taken him back into the past, to the time when he had total control of the situation.

He would have been able to come with this one. He knew it. Then she ruined it. By speaking lines that weren't part of the script. By wanting him to wear a damn rubber. He hadn't worn a rubber back then. He wanted it to be exactly the same as before. He *needed* it to be the same. And yet, he also remembered how acting on that need had nearly destroyed him.

Only his father's power and money had saved him from destruction. It had also hired a discreet shrink who had helped him to understand that even if the women enjoyed what he did for them, his behavior was not socially acceptable. His good intentions did not exclude him from the law. He had to accept the fact that he might never have a wife of his own.

Unfortunately, understanding wasn't always enough, and when the emptiness became unbearable he found that pretending sometimes took the edge off. By using an escort service, he was able to order his particular fantasy with very little legal risk, especially if the woman came to his home.

Living in a farmhouse surrounded by several acres of woods ensured his privacy.

Most of the time, the girl wasn't much of an actress, or he simply remained too aware of reality to completely let go. For a few minutes tonight, however, fulfillment had been within his grasp. Then the damn whore opened her mouth, and he was empty once again.

He knew it was wrong, even dangerous, to think about it, but he would give almost anything to be able to experience the real thing one more time.

Chapter Six

Luke yawned for the third time in as many minutes. "I'm sorry, Kelly. I'm beat."

She pretended to look surprised. "I can't imagine why. All you did today was get electrocuted and travel thirty-two years into the future." A yawn of her own proved that he wasn't the only one feeling the effects of a long, stressful day. She had run out of new thoughts an hour ago, but had kept the conversation going by rehashing things they'd already covered.

It was probably illogical, but she was nervous about spending the night in a remote cabin with a man who was not only a stranger, but a convicted murderer, who just happened to have the power to seriously injure her with the merest physical contact.

"Does that sound okay with you?" When he realized she hadn't been listening to him, he shook his head. "It would help if you'd give me some kind of signal when you're about to drift off."

She blushed. "I'm sorry. I really don't mean to be rude. My only excuse is that I haven't spent much time around other people the last few years. I guess my listening skills have gotten rusty. I'll try to control my daydreaming while you're here."

"And possibly hinder your creative flow? Uh-uh. I don't want that on my head. I think the signal system would be easier. I'll just have to watch you more closely and figure out what the signal is. In the meantime, what I suggested was for you to take the sofa bed, and I could sleep on the couch."

"That sounds fine," she said, relieved that he had already solved one of the causes of her nervousness. Keeping the gun under her pillow would take care of another. Besides, his state of exhaustion should ensure an uneventful night.

As they prepared their sleeping areas, her agent's suggestion echoed in her mind again. Well, she was about to spend the night with a handsome stud as he'd recommended. They just weren't going to be engaging in any of the activities Jack had had in mind.

Too bad.

She ordered that thought back into the secret desires compartment of her mind. Luke Templeton was definitely not the man of her dreams. He wasn't even a man of her time period.

Luke was certain he'd be asleep the moment he closed his eyes. Though the couch was a bit short, it was more comfortable than the jail cell cot had been. The chirping crickets and rustling leaves were a lullaby compared to the night sounds within the prison walls. He was physically, mentally, and emotionally exhausted. Sleep should have come instantly.

Instead, he felt restless, almost agitated. Was the electrical charge causing that sensation, or was it something else?

He heard Kelly rearranging her pillows and part of the answer came to him. She believed he was here to find the truth. Their conversation tonight had roused his reporter's instincts, but the nonreporter in him just wanted to take advantage of the unexpected gift of additional time to live and breathe.

The question was, was it a gift, free and clear, or was it as Kelly insisted—a temporary stay of execution that could only be made permanent if he righted the wrong that had been done? Did this incredible gift have strings attached, or not? It was probably that question that was preventing him from falling asleep.

Kelly let out a soft sigh as she settled into the position she must have been trying for, and another answer whispered through Luke's mind. The extraordinary events of the day should have completely blocked out any thoughts of sex, or even flirtation. Yet, those thoughts had flashed in and out at the oddest moments.

Habit. That's all it was, he decided. Being electrocuted hadn't short-circuited his hormones. Kelly was a very attractive woman, with a very, very sexy body, and the most gorgeous hair he'd ever seen.

Until the moment he saw Kelly without her cap on, he had thought Ginger held that honor, but Ginger's hair wasn't nearly as long and had less gold highlights. Now that he thought about it, he realized the two women had similar figures as well, only Kelly was a few inches taller, which made her full figure seem better proportioned.

Beyond physical appearance, however, the two women were drastically different. Ginger was rather timid and mainly used her brain to decide which accessories to wear with what dress. She was the type of woman who probably would never have left her husband if another man hadn't shown up on her doorstep to take his place.

Kelly, on the other hand, was thoroughly independent and successful in her own right. And imaginative. Brave. Confident. Cool. The list of complimentary adjectives seemed endless, and she was lying there, all soft and cuddly, only a few feet away. How could he help but have thoughts of sex?

He immediately corrected himself. Sex wasn't the only thing she made him think of, though it was the front-runner. She also made him think of friendship, the kind he had only known with other men, but for some reason, he felt certain that he and Kelly could be pals.

Was she really the most intriguing woman he'd ever encountered, or was it the extended celibacy imposed on him by prison that made her seem that way?

And what could he do about it anyway? He couldn't touch her even if she was as attracted to him as he was to her, and he definitely couldn't make plans for the future when he had no idea whether his future was here and now, back in 1965, or in a place other than earth.

Since he couldn't answer any of those questions tonight, he wanted to go to sleep, but his agitation had increased by the minute. If he didn't know better, he'd swear there were ants crawling all over his skin.

Kelly turned onto her other side, though she knew her sleeplessness wasn't due to discomfort. It was Luke. Why didn't he stop squirming around and just go to sleep?

"Damn!"

Kelly rolled back over and saw him bolting to his feet. There was just enough light in the cabin for her to note that he was naked . . . *again*. And again, she pretended not to notice. "Come on now. The couch can't be that uncomfortable."

He was practically dancing in place, contorting his body and scratching like a dog with a bad case of fleas. "I'm itching all over. I think you've got ants in here."

"Ants? I don't see—" Rather than continue, she got up and lit the kerosene lamp on the table. Keeping her back to him, she asked, "Would you please put something on? I understand that nudity was quite the thing back in the sixties, but I'm not, I mean, I'd appreciate it if you'd—"

"Good God, Kelly! I wasn't showing off. Something's eating me alive."

She peeked at him over her shoulder and noted that he had slipped his briefs back on. It didn't make much difference as far as she was concerned, but to ask for more under the circumstances might seem eccentric. She bent over and inspected the sheet he'd been laying on. "I don't see anything."

'What the hell?" Luke was doing contortions again, trying to look at the backs of his arms. "Look at this. Are these bites, or what?" He turned around so that the light was on his back.

For a few seconds, Kelly was distracted by the strong, masculine lines displayed so nicely before her, then she saw what was bothering him. "Oh my. Those aren't bites. It looks like poison ivy. Didn't you say something about falling in the bushes?" She could see for herself that his story about arriving naked must have been true. The rash was all over the back of his body. He twisted one arm behind him to scratch. "No! Don't scratch. You'll only make it worse."

Turning to face her, his jaw was clenched with the effort it took not to scratch. "I find it hard to believe that it could get worse than this."

"I know. I had it once when I was a kid. Fortunately, it doesn't last long, unless you're highly allergic. It will probably help that you took a bath not long after you came in contact with the plants. Also, lucky for you, I bought myself a big bottle of calamine lotion last week because of mosquito bites. It's in the bathroom cupboard." She snapped her fingers as she remembered what else might help. She went to the refrigerator and got out an open box of baking soda. "First, take a baking soda bath. Wash your skin well, but don't scrape. The idea is to get off any of the poison you missed with your earlier bath. Then when you're dry, cover yourself with the lotion. I'd offer to help, but there's that other little problem of yours that I'd rather not deal with." He didn't appreciate her attempt at humor.

While he was in the bathroom, she gingerly removed the sheets, and gathered all the clothes he'd worn. Everything that had been next to his skin would have to be washed in hot water, which meant a trip to the laundromat in Buford tomorrow. To be on the safe side, she scrubbed her hands with soap and water before putting clean sheets on the couch.

The only other thing she could think of doing for him was to brew a pot of chamomile tea and keep him company until he was relaxed enough to fall asleep.

When he came out of the bathroom, he was glowing again, but Kelly was positive that the aura wasn't nearly as bright as before. Without discussing it, he took the fireplace poker outside, and when he returned seconds later, the glow was gone completely. She poured them each a cup of tea while he returned to the bathroom to apply the calamine.

As inappropriate as it was, she couldn't help but think of what he was doing behind that closed door. In her mind, she saw him filling his palm with lotion, then transferring it to the parts of his body that were irritated by the rash—private parts that made her much too aware of how long it had been since she'd run her hands over an attractive man's hard body.

It was probably a very good thing that she was unable to touch him. Otherwise, she wouldn't have been able to resist *helping* him apply the lotion all over every delicious inch of his—

"How do you feel?" she asked as he reappeared, his skin smeared with pink lotion. He was wearing only a towel, but knowing where the worst of the rash probably was, she couldn't blame him for being underdressed.

"Considering how bad I felt less than an hour ago, pretty good."

She handed him the cup of tea. "Drink this. It should help you feel even better. Tell me, did you notice anything different about the electrical charge when you got out of the tub?"

"Not really, but the drain-off outside was faster and didn't weaken me as much."

"Hmm. I wonder if that means the charge is diminishing. Maybe by tomorrow you'll be back to normal."

He snorted. "After everything that's happened to me today, I don't even want to think about what might be in store for me tomorrow."

Kelly felt the atmosphere in the cabin calming down as they sipped their tea in silence. The soft glow from the lamp complemented the relaxed mood and soon they were both growing drowsy again. She took the empty cups to the sink and extinguished the lamp, certain that they would be sleeping peacefully in minutes. The moment she was comfortably settled, however, Luke broke the spell.

"How long have you been divorced?"

"Go to sleep. It's late."

"I answered all your questions."

She let out a loud sigh. "I left my husband almost a year ago. The divorce was final in June."

"Was it bad?"

She paused a moment before answering. "The divorce was relatively easy. It was the marriage that was bad."

"How long were you married?"

"I bet you were one of those children who demanded a bedtime story before you would go to sleep."

He chuckled. "I do seem to remember using that excuse on occasion. Come on, Kelly, tell me the story of your marriage."

"All right. But then you have to promise to go to sleep like a good little boy."

"Yes, ma'am."

"Once upon a time, there was a young, starry-eyed maiden who journeyed to the strange land of college and met a dashing knight who swept her off her feet. Naturally, she was flattered since he could have had his choice of maidens. But this maiden had certain attributes that made the knight want her more than the others. Most of all, he wanted to possess her treasure. No matter what he said or did, however, she was determined not to give the treasure to any man but her future husband. Being a handsome man of excellent prospects, many other girls were happy to share their treasures with the knight, but he was never satisfied with them.

"By the time coronation day arrived at collegeland, the knight became so obsessed with the maiden's treasure, he asked for her hand in marriage. At first, the new bride thought she'd been taken into paradise. Her husband could not have been kinder or more loving to her. But all too soon his career began demanding more and more of his attention. The king that he worked for promoted him to duke status, and the thingamajigs they made and sold became more interesting to him than his wife. Or at least she thought that's why he was spending less and less time at home.

"Her intuition was telling her that he might be enjoying other women's treasures again, especially since he had lost interest in any sort of treasure hunting at home, but the lady of the manor rationalized her concerns away. After all, he treated her politely, she had enough gold to buy anything she wanted, and she had the freedom to pursue any interest that occurred to her. So she threw herself into a career of her own and, for too many years, she pretended not to care about the lack of attention from the duke.

"Until the day she walked into his office unannounced and caught him and his secretary in a very compromising position . . . on top of his desk. In the months after that day, the lady learned that her intuition had been right all along—that for most of the nine years of their marriage, her husband had been jousting with every woman that crossed his path . . . except her. Apparently it was only the chase and the initial conquest that he found exciting."

Luke coughed. "I, uh, I think I know some men like that. I'm sorry he was such a bastard to you. You sure didn't deserve to be treated like that."

"Maybe not, but it wasn't all his fault. I chose to ignore the problem because it was easier that way. That was stupid, so maybe I did get what I deserved."

"You weren't stupid; he was. You were naive and optimistic, hardly a punishable sin. Maybe the next guy will be smart enough to realize how lucky he is to be with you."

She chuckled. "Let's just say my experience taught me to stick to writing about romance and to forget about the real thing."

He was quiet for several heartbeats, then he let out a huff.

"What was that for?" she asked defensively.

"You don't want to know."

"Yes, I do. Don't you think a woman can make it without a man in her life?"

He huffed again. "I wasn't thinking that at all. I just had a rather startling, and not very attractive, revelation about myself. It put me pretty much in the same category as your ex."

"That's a pretty lousy thing to say about yourself. Tell me what you were thinking, and I'll be the judge."

"If I tell you, you'll get mad."

"No, I won't. I swear. I need to understand more about how men's minds work. For my books."

"Okay. You just told me a painful story and implied that you've given up on men. My instinctive reaction was that it was a great excuse to take you into my arms to offer you comfort. I could actually see myself holding you and lightly stroking your back until I felt you leaning into me. I'm sorry, Kelly. If I could give you a real hug, without electrocuting you or making a pass at you, I would."

Now it was Kelly's turn to be pensive, and when she spoke, her voice came out in a husky whisper. "And then what?"

"Pardon?"

"I lean into you, and then what?" When he didn't answer, she added a credible explanation. "You made me think of a possible scene in a story. I'd like to know how you would proceed."

"Oh. Well, um, and then, I, uh, I'd shift my body as I increased the pressure of my hands on your back. Then I'd hold you completely still, making sure you could feel my heart beating and my breath against your hair."

She took an audible breath. "And then?"

"Then you'd sigh and tilt your head back. Our eyes would meet long enough to say, *yes*, then your lips would part, openly inviting me to taste."

"And would you?"

He laughed. "Of course. Any conscience I had fled the moment you leaned into me."

"So, what you're saying is, if you weren't electrified, we'd be having sex about now."

The tone of her voice should have warned him to answer carefully, but he charged ahead anyway. "*Now* might be a bit premature. I'd say more like fifteen minutes from—" a pillow hit him in the face, cutting off his sentence. Without hesitation, he hurled it right back at her. "Just like a woman," he said with a laugh, "demanding the truth, then getting mad when she hears it."

That got him a double retaliation, and suddenly they were immersed in an old-fashioned pillow fight, complete with nonsensical name-calling and fits of laughter.

The silliness came to an abrupt end when her hand contacted his arm and she received a shock that made her yelp.

"Oh, my God, are you okay?" he asked, totally serious.

She wiggled her fingers. "Fine. I think I was right about the charge diminishing. That was stronger than a static electric spark, but it was nowhere near what you did to me when we tried to shake hands before." As they moved back to their separate beds, Kelly sensed his uneasiness. "You're not guilty, Luke. I baited you."

"I know," he said with a smile in his voice. "I saw it coming."

"Your seduction scene was actually quite good. If you can't get a newspaper job, you might consider writing romance novels." His easy laugh gave her a nice feeling. "Thanks for the pillow fight. It was more fun than I've had in a long while."

"Maybe that's why I'm here—to remind you how to laugh."

Kelly took a slow breath and turned onto her side. Until that moment she had not considered that possibility. She had assumed he was sent to her so that she could help him. Could it be mutual? Could he also be here to help her with something bigger than a plot idea?

A cool draft of air made her shiver, seeming to confirm that thought. She let her imagination dance through some possible ways he could help her. Though a romantic interlude would not be unwelcome, her imagination didn't linger there. Rather, it suggested something more sinister was about to happen.

The big question was, would Luke be her hero, or would he turn out to be another villain?

"Are you sure you've got it? I mean, I can't stress enough how important it is not to press the wrong—"

"I understood the first three times you explained it," Luke said testily. "I didn't travel here from the Stone Age."

"Okay. Sorry. I just—" His warning glare cut her off, and she headed for the door. "I'll be back as soon as I can." He waved a hand at her, but his attention was on the computer monitor.

After staying up half the night, it was late morning by the time they had finally gotten moving. Between the hour and how uncomfortable Luke was, they decided to put off the Atlanta research trip another day. Kelly had a number of phone calls to make, laundry to do, and she needed to buy more calamine for Luke.

Rather than tag along, he asked her to show

him how to use her computer so that he could catch up on the past three decades of history. Kelly was concerned that he might damage the circuitry with his electrical charge, but he solved that by using a wooden pencil with a rubber eraser to press the keys.

For the sake of efficiency, she drove to the laundromat in Buford first and made her calls from the pay phone there while the washers were running.

The first call was to her professor friend at Penn State to let him know that there was no longer a rush on her question about spontaneous human combustion. She would still like to know how it could be intentionally caused, but she had decided on a different plot for her current book.

She then called Connie and Jack to let them know her brain had been reactivated and gave them each a brief summary of the story line. As she had hoped, Connie loved the idea of adding a paranormal twist.

"Will called me again," Connie said after their business was concluded.

"Aw, geez. Jack said he called him, too. I'm sorry."

"It's okay. At least he's always very polite. I told him the same thing as the other times: 'I don't know where she is. I have to wait for her to call me.' I've got to tell you, Kelly, he really sounds pitiful. Are you absolutely sure—"

"Hush your mouth! Don't you dare say it. You know as well as I do, that it's just an act. If I went back to him, he'd be bored with me again in a week. I believe *you* were the one who first explained that to me."

"You're right, of course. But he really is good, isn't he?"

"He's one of the best, Connie, a genuine master at manipulating women's emotions."

Her final call was to her mother, and it went along the usual lines. They compared the weather in Pennsylvania and Georgia, and touched on the latest neighborhood gossip. Her mother complained about how much television her father watched, then asked her if she'd done anything interesting in the last week. That was Mom's subtle way of asking if she had had a date with a man. This time, Kelly surprised her.

"As a matter of fact, I met the most fascinating man yesterday. He just showed up at my cabin, without a stitch of clothing. He claimed that he'd been electrically transported to me from 1965."

"You know, Kelly, it's not healthy for you to spend so much time making up romantic nonsense. I swear, Prince Charming could walk right up to you and all you'd do is write a story about him. Which reminds me, Will called again yesterday. He truly sounds sorry."

"I'm sure he does. Sincere is one of his best acts."

"I think you should at least listen to what he has to say."

Kelly knew better than to waste her breath. Her

mother had always been a sucker for Will's charm. "I'll think about it," she responded halfheartedly.

"And think about this, too. I never told you, but once, when you were a teenager, I found out that your father had been with another woman."

"*What?*"

"I'm only telling you this now so you'll realize that it happens to the best of them. They start feeling like time's passing them by, and the grass looks greener on the other side of the fence. Men can't fight temptation as well as women do. It's our job to understand and forgive them."

"Our *job?*" Kelly bit her thumb not to continue with what she was thinking. She and her mother were never going to see eye to eye on what a woman's *job* was supposed to be. She still considered Kelly's writing to be a "nice hobby." "I've got to run, Mom. Thanks for sharing." *Like I really needed to know that my father is just like other men.*

It occurred to her that she should be having some sort of strong reaction to what her mother had revealed, but it wasn't there. In truth, she didn't even feel shocked. Her parents had always had a tug-of-war relationship as far as she could tell. Her mother was always tugging and her father was always pulling away. Their constant bickering was one of the reasons she had kept quiet with Will as long as she had. She simply hadn't wanted to end up arguing all the time like her parents.

While the clothes were in the dryer, she went

into the adjacent convenience store and bought some more calamine lotion and baking soda, but they didn't have any of her books. Thus, instead of going straight home, she stopped in the original O'Neill's drugstore in Charming.

A late middle-aged man greeted her from behind the counter. "It's good to see you, Mizz Kirkwood."

She glanced at the name tag on his white lab coat. "Hello, Mr. Scanlon. Any mail for me?"

"Nope. But there was a man askin' about you a little while ago."

She set two of her books down beside the cash register. "A man? Did he leave his name?"

"Nope. Looked like a salesman, wearin' a suit and tie in this heat. Had a salesman's smile, too. Don't y'all get these books for free?" he asked as he rang up her purchase.

"I get a few, but I promised someone . . ." She didn't really think an explanation was necessary. "About this man. What did he look like?"

He rubbed his chin. "Taller than me. Light brown hair, slicked back real neat—"

"What did you tell him?" she asked abruptly.

"Not much. Only that I'd be happy to pass on a message if you happened to come in. I figured if you wanted folks to know where you were, you'd have told them yourself."

Kelly exhaled with relief. "Thank you. I appreciate that." She knew without a doubt that the "salesman" had been Will, and it took little analysis to figure out that her mother had probably been his informant, at least as far as directing him to Charming. Kelly was annoyed, but not all that surprised after their last phone call. Hopefully, anyone else Will approached about her exact whereabouts would be as considerate as Mr. Scanlon.

Before she left, she decided to find out how far his tight-lipped policy went. "I heard that this store was Reid O'Neill's first."

"Yessirree. And we're all mighty proud of that fact here in Charmin'."

"As you should be. What he's accomplished is very impressive. I heard he still lives nearby."

The man bobbed his head several times. "Y'all cain't miss his house. It's the biggest one on Orchard Lane. Every Fourth o' July he invites the whole town over there for fireworks. Y'all shoulda come up a little earlier this summer. Everyone said it was the best yet."

Kelly was sorry she missed such a golden opportunity. She probably could have interviewed everyone who remembered anything in one day.

On her way out of town, she couldn't resist making a short detour down Orchard Lane. Luke had made her promise not to do any investigating on her own, but she had had her fingers crossed behind her back. After all, if an opportunity to learn something important fell at her feet, she could hardly ignore it.

The man in the drugstore was right. One couldn't possibly miss Reid O'Neill's house. It was a smaller

version of Tara, surrounded by at least three acres
of landscaped lawn, where most of the other homes
along the lane looked like a tract development.

She remembered Mrs. Lawson's comment about
O'Neill fixing the house up a lot and wondered if
he had managed to do so with money he came
into upon his wife's death.

She stopped her car in front of the estate and
let her gaze move slowly over the entire property.
It was a beautiful view, a picture-perfect setting
for a historical romance. Few people would see it
as she did—a backdrop for a brutal murder.

Had Ginger O'Neill screamed that night? That
was what it said in the newspaper. Someone had
heard her screaming and anonymously called the
police, who conveniently arrived in the precise
amount of time it supposedly took Luke Templeton
to beat, rape, and strangle her. Looking at the distance
to the nearest house, Kelly decided that Ginger must
have had a powerful set of lungs. And considering
the size of town Charming was in 1965, either the
police were very slow, or Luke was incredibly fast.

Also, since it was a very small town, why didn't
the person who called about the scream try to help
or at least check it out firsthand?

As she sat there, trying to re-create the scene in
her mind, an old station wagon pulled into the
O'Neill driveway and stopped. A thin, caramel-
skinned woman with gray hair got out and walked
to Kelly's car. The neat, white uniform and work
shoes suggested several possible lines of work.

"May I help you?" she asked Kelly in a rather territorial tone of voice.

Kelly decided this qualified as an opportunity being dropped at her feet and got out of the car with a friendly smile. "Hi. I'm Kelly Kirkwood. I'm staying in a cabin near here while I'm working on a new book. I'm an author."

"Yes, I heard," the woman replied with no return smile.

On a hunch, Kelly asked, "Do you live here?"

"Yes. I'm Mr. O'Neill's housekeeper."

"Oh, that's great. You see, I've been hearing about what an enterprising man Reid O'Neill is, and it got me thinking that he might be a good subject for a biography, you know, like the Wal-Mart man."

The woman's black eyes narrowed. "I heard you wrote mysteries and love stories."

"I do, usually. But I've been wanting to do something different. I would need to speak to Mr. O'Neill before I decide. Is he at home?"

"No. He don't come home till five o'clock. Not five minutes before. Not five minutes after. If you'll give me your card, I'll pass it on to him."

Since her card wouldn't help someone to reach her at the moment, Kelly took out her notepad and pen, and wrote her name on it. "There's no phone in the cabin where I'm staying, but they'll take a message for me at general delivery in the drugstore." She added that information below her name. "I'd be happy to make myself available anytime that Mr. O'Neill would be able to meet with me." She wrote the phrase *appointment to discuss possible biography* on the paper and handed it to the housekeeper. "Thank you. I really appreciate this, Miss . . ."

She put the paper in her uniform skirt pocket. "Folks just call me Hannah."

Kelly wondered if Hannah always looked so stern. "Have you worked for Mr. O'Neill a long time?"

"Thirty-two years last month."

Kelly's mental red flag flew up its pole. The fact that Hannah's employment began in the same month as Ginger's murder occurred could have been just another coincidence, but it was one worth keeping in mind. "Wow. That is a long time. Perhaps I could ask you some questions about your employer . . . for the book. I'm sure you must have some fascinating anecdotes about him and the people of Charming."

Hannah's deadpan expression altered for the first time. A distinct hint of fear flickered in her eyes, and she lost her stilted speech. "I don' know nothin' 'bout nothin'. I have to git the groceries put away now. I'll give your note to Mr. O'Neill." Seconds later, she was back in her station wagon, continuing up the brick-paved driveway to the house.

"We got a winner," Kelly muttered as she got back into the Camaro. If Hannah wasn't a woman with secrets, she should give up writing suspense!

Chapter Seven

Though Luke heard Kelly's car pull up, he was too entranced by the information on the computer monitor to get up to greet her. Only when there was a knock on the screen door did he realize it wasn't her. Reluctantly, he left the computer and went to the door.

"Who the hell are you?" a slick-looking man demanded as he scanned Luke's bare chest.

"You first," Luke countered.

"The name's Kirkwood, and my wife is supposed to be here. *Alone.*"

Luke focused on the word "wife." Had Kelly lied to him about being divorced? Perhaps she had more in common with Ginger than physical attributes after all. "If you're referring to Kelly, I understood she was divorced."

Kirkwood waved a hand that sported several ounces of gold in the form of a pinky ring and watch. "A misunderstanding that will be corrected in a few days. In fact, that's why I'm here—to let her know that I've already made the arrangements for our remarriage."

Before Luke could voice a response to that rather surprising statement, Kirkwood opened the screen door and extended his hand for a shake. Luke had to quickly step back to avoid making contact with him. He had already decided he didn't like this guy, but he didn't think he should electrocute him until he found out which one of the Kirkwoods was telling the truth.

Kelly's ex-husband withdrew his hand and stepped inside the cabin, causing Luke to retreat further. He obviously got the impression that Luke was afraid of him and his mouth twisted into a sneer. "I believe it's your turn now. What the hell are you doing here with my wife?"

Kelly drove back to the cabin in a bubble of enthusiasm. She couldn't wait to delve further into the mystery of who killed Ginger O'Neill and why. She was also anxious to ask Luke if he knew Hannah.

Her bubble quickly burst, however, as she neared the cabin and saw a silver Mercedes sedan parked in front.

Will had found her.

Her first thought was to drive off and stay away until boredom sent him back to Atlanta. Knowing what a sacrifice it must have been for him to abandon his office on a Monday, she figured he wouldn't hang around more than a couple hours.

Her second thought wiped out the first. Will wouldn't be bored. He had Luke to visit with! Her mind racing, she quickly got out of the car. How had Luke explained his presence? It didn't matter. Regardless of what he said, Will would jump to only one conclusion—that Luke and she were lovers. In all their years of marriage, she'd never given him a single cause to be jealous of her, and now that they were divorced, her relationships were none of his business. Yet, she had no doubt how he would react if he thought she was having an affair with another man.

Her assumption seemed accurate as she entered the cabin and saw the tense body language of the two men. The air was disgustingly thick with testosterone.

Will's gray eyes sparkled with love as he walked toward her with arms outstretched. "Kelly, honey, you look radiant." She swiftly side-stepped to avoid the embrace he was determined to give her. "What are you doing here, Will?"

He added a touch of hurt feelings to his adoring expression. "I was worried about you, honey. You seemed so down the last time I saw you. I wanted to make sure you didn't, you know, do anything *drastic.*"

"Drastic? Like what, suicide? Or do you mean drastic like forgetting that you exist? Well, either way, you're too late, Will. As you can see, I'm alive and have a new man in my life. And unlike you, he does a hell of a lot more than just *sleep* in the same bed with me!"

She was rewarded for her uncharacteristic criticism by seeing Will's neck turn a deep shade of scarlet. As the color rose into his fair cheeks, she finished him off. "For the last time, I am not interested in a reconciliation, and if you continue to harass me or anyone I know, I will have Bruce file an injunction against you."

"Oh sure, throw ol' Brucie at me again. How long were the two of you screwing each other before you decided to screw me?"

Kelly raised her hand, but rather than strike him, she pointed at the open door. "Get out."

"Ah, Kell—"

"*Out!*"

"You're making a big mistake," he said as he backed toward the door. "This guy's not in your class. He wouldn't even shake my hand."

"That just proves that he's not a phony like you."

"But a longshoreman, Kell? And since when did you start picking up hitchhikers? You could be in mortal danger alone out here with somebody like him."

She glanced at Luke, but he kept his narrow-eyed gaze pinned on Will. "That reminds me," she said, giving Will a glare of her own. "I assume you badgered my mother until she told you I was picking up mail in Charming, but how did you find this cabin?"

His mouth curved in a cocky grin. "It was rather ingenious actually. For some reason, the people in town are being overly protective of your privacy, but I found a kid who'd seen the pretty redhead and heard his mother talking about where the famous author was staying. For five dollars, he gave me very good directions. Shows you what dumb hicks these people are. He could have held out for twenty."

Kelly clenched her teeth. It was so typical of Will to be proud of having taken advantage of someone's naïveté. "In case I haven't made myself absolutely clear, I want you to listen very carefully to my next words. I am extremely happy, in fact, I'm *ecstatic*, that you are no longer my husband. I would volunteer as a crash dummy before I would consider getting back together with you. Do I need to continue?"

Will spun on his heel and strode out. To make sure he didn't do anything childish like scratch her car with his keys, Kelly watched him from the doorway until he drove away.

"A *longshoreman*?" she asked incredulously as she turned back to Luke. "What in heavens name made you say that?"

He chuckled. "I was trying to make him believe I was too mean to tangle with and that was the first job that came to mind. Not that I couldn't take him in a normal situation; I just didn't want him to find out about my electrical charge."

"Oh, of course," she replied, not quite suppressing a laugh. "That would explain the no-handshake comment. But you didn't need to worry about tangling with Will. He's never been much of a straight-forward fighter. Guerrilla warfare is more his style. Actually, he would have been much more intimidated if you'd said you were a brain surgeon or some other highly paid professional. Still, your being a longshoreman isn't nearly as bad as your being a hitchhiker that I picked up."

Luke made a face. "I am sorry about that. I knew how bad it sounded as soon as it was out of my mouth, but I'd sort of boxed myself in with my employment. He wanted to know how we met, and I didn't think you'd been hanging around any loading docks recently. It was just a good thing that your explanation didn't contradict mine. How did you figure that I'd implied we were sleeping together?"

"I used my psychic powers." She went to the refrigerator for a soda and, when she looked back at him, he was eyeing her warily. "I'm kidding. I just have a well-developed sense of intuition when it comes to men."

"He told me you were getting remarried."

Her eyes rolled heavenward. "Gawd, you didn't believe him, did you?" His momentary hesitation disappointed her. "Geez, Luke, after everything I told you—"

"You said it yourself. He's very good at lying, and I . . . well, it was only a momentary doubt. Then I used my instincts to hear what he wasn't saying and decided he was a horse's ass who needed to be brought down a peg or two."

"So you implied that I picked you up off the street and we've barely been out of bed since." The look she gave him was part reprimanding, part appreciative.

"I'm sorry if I caused more problems for you."

"Don't be sorry," she said, as she sat down across the table from him. "I should thank you for providing me with a reason that he'd understand. You know, that was the very first time that I told him exactly what I was thinking. It felt good. If he bothers me again, I might even throw in some foul language."

Luke studied her face for a moment. "Now I understand. Last night, when you were talking about him, I thought you sounded awfully bitter for someone who'd been freed from a bad marriage. It occurred to me that you weren't really happy about being divorced."

"If I sounded bitter, it was only because I resent all the lost years."

His expression remained thoughtful. "I gather you never got mad and yelled at him, let alone giving him something he really deserved, like a punch in the nose. It's all been festering inside of you. I'm surprised you could write like that."

She gave a dry laugh. "I haven't written a single page worth reading in months."

"Then it's definitely about time you told him off. Of course, the next step's even harder."

"What's that?"

"Forgiving him and yourself and getting on with your life."

"Did you say you were a reporter or a psychologist?"

He grinned. "I once did an in-depth piece on recovering from divorce; interviewed several doctors, therapists, and veteran bartenders. That research provided me with a whole new subject on which I could be conversant at cocktail parties."

"So, tell me, did you 'forgive and get on' with regard to Ginger O'Neill?"

He thought about that for a moment. "The circumstances aren't comparable. I was so angry about being framed for her murder that being lied to and dumped wasn't all that important. I guess I forgave her though."

"And what about all the good people of Charming? Have you also forgiven them?"

He made a face at her and got up to get a soda for himself.

When it was clear that he wasn't going to answer, she gave him a verbal nudge. "Can you honestly say that you don't have a ton of resentment festering inside you?"

"What are you getting at?" he asked.

The way he was studying his soda can rather than meeting her gaze suggested he already knew where she was headed. "I'm wondering if you've accepted the fact that you have unfinished business to attend to here. Despite all the discussion we had last night, I still get the impression that you'd just as soon forget the past and start a new life."

"Well . . ."

"A guilty man would think like that, but an innocent man should want to clear his name."

He shrugged. "That might have been the case if I had had children. As it was, the only people who mattered were my parents. They believed I was innocent then, and it's highly unlikely that they're still alive now."

"Okay, then you should search for the truth for Ginger's sake. Or to see the right man punished. What if that man murdered other women since 1965? You could prevent that from happening."

"By going back in time and changing history?" he asked, raising one eyebrow.

"Yes. Don't ask me how, but I'm sure there's a way, and we'll figure it out when the time comes."

"Hmmph. Why don't we see how things go in this time first?"

"Fine. Just promise not to take off until we've looked under every rock."

"I can agree to that, especially considering the fact that I'm completely dependent on you at the moment. Which reminds me, I used the last of the baking soda and calamine."

"I bought more. It's out in the car. How do you feel?" she asked with a grimace as she walked behind him to look at his back. "Oh, this isn't bad at all. You're lucky."

"I itch, but it definitely eased up since last night. Your computer kept my mind occupied so well, I barely thought about it. Then your dear ex showed up and made my skin crawl again."

"I can empathize with that. I'm glad you enjoyed the computer though. I'm curious. What's the most fascinating thing you've discovered so far?"

He rubbed his chin thoughtfully. "I've only had a chance to skim the highlights, based on the notes I made from our discussion last night. The biggest change seems to be the giant leap forward in technology and global communication. It's overwhelming to someone who was typing out his articles on an Underwood manual typewriter. I am disappointed in the space program, though. By now, I had expected America to have a colony on the moon. It would be easier for me to answer what I considered the saddest thing, or rather things."

"Oh? What would that be?"

"The assassinations of Martin Luther King and Robert Kennedy. After I learned that, I did a quick overview of the civil rights movement and found something that supported what you said last night about not being able to legislate against prejudice. I remember when Lester Maddox closed his restaurant rather than obey the court order to serve Negroes. There were plenty of Georgians who considered him a hero for that action back then, but I was still surprised that he wound up in the governor's office in sixty-seven. After reading that, I was even more surprised to read that only six years later, a Negro was elected mayor of Atlanta. Talk about a giant step!

"Then there's the Vietnam and Persian Gulf wars. I'm anxious to do some research on them."

"After you do, I'd be interested in hearing your thoughts on how the two compare."

"Are you a student of politics?" he asked with a slightly surprised look.

"No, I study people, and your opinion on such controversial subjects would help me understand you better."

He angled his head at her. "Why do you want to understand me better?"

She smiled slyly. "Didn't I mention it? You're the hero of my next book."

He wasn't sure if that pleased him or not. "I think Ginger would disagree with your referring to me as a hero. Instead of rescuing her, I may have gotten her killed."

Kelly pursed her lips. "And therein lies another reason to set things right."

He acknowledged that he'd walked into that

one. "Anyway, how did I end up being a fictional hero?"

"Actually, the more correct term might be male protagonist. Heroines in today's stories don't require rescuing like they used to. Now they must be actively involved in the adventure or mystery solution. Sometimes they even get to rescue the men. As to your question, I've definitely decided to write your story . . . with certain embellishments or exaggerations as needed, of course. After all, no real man could compare with the traditional hero of a romance novel."

His chin lifted indignantly. "I'll have you know, I can be very romantic."

"I'm sure you can," she said, smiling. "But a hero is more than a man who brings women flowers or knows the right words to say in the moonlight."

He leaned forward and propped his chin on his fist. "I'm all ears. Go on."

After a multitude of interviews, she was more than prepared to expound on this subject. "A hero anticipates his lady's needs and finds little ways to make her hectic life easier without her having to ask for help. He would never make fun of her when she cries during a movie, nor would he pout if she's too tired to do more than cuddle one evening.

"And speaking of sex, today's hero always makes sure his partner is completely satisfied, maybe even more than once, before he sees to his own pleasure. He also understands that there are times when she'll appreciate his cooking, or doing a household chore, or baby-sitting more than an hour of lovemaking."

"Okay, okay. I got the point, and I still think I'm a pretty romantic fellow. But what about the heroine, aren't there some things that she's expected to do to make his life happier also?"

She smiled. "Most men are perfectly happy if their mate just enjoys having sex with them . . . *often*. But it's also a plus if she doesn't nag when he forgets things, like where his keys are, nor does she mind if he watches sports for hours on television or plays tennis every Sunday morning with his buds."

"It sounds like the heroines have it a lot easier than the heroes," he said with a frown.

"Hey, that's only in the fictional world. Things are tougher than ever for women in the real world. Don't worry, your fictional counterpart will have a great time no matter how much effort he has to put into winning his lady's love."

"I'll hold you to that promise. So, do I get to choose what the lady is like?"

She shrugged and reached for the pad and pen. "Sure. What would you like her to look like?"

He leaned back in his chair and folded his hands over his stomach. "Strawberry blond hair, the longer the better, green eyes that sparkle when her imagination is in overdrive, and she definitely has to have some meat on her bones. No Twiggy figures for me."

She clucked her tongue at him. "Are you being

a smart-ass or is this your way of proving how romantic you can be?"

Placing his palm over his heart, he swore, "I'm being perfectly serious. If I'm the hero, you should be the heroine."

"The heroine *is* going to be an author, and some of her personality will be mine—there's always a little of me in all my characters—but she can look anyway you'd like. Describe your fantasy woman."

He leaned forward again and held her gaze with his. "I just did."

She felt her heart take an extra beat, and she lowered her lashes. "Please don't tease, Luke. I'm not very good at flirting." His hand moved toward hers, then cautiously hovered a few inches away. The fine hairs on her arm lifted in response to his electricity, giving her a slight shiver.

"I wasn't teasing. I think you're incredibly beautiful, and so would any other man with half a brain."

She took a deep breath and met his eyes. "I see. We're back to playing amateur psychologist. You figure because my husband didn't want me while we were married, I'm suffering from low self-esteem. Well, you're wrong on this one, pseudodoc. I know very well that a lot of men look at me, and their libidos kick into high gear, but that doesn't make me feel proud. I don't *work* at my appearance." She suddenly realized how defensive she sounded and figured he was analyzing that, too. "Let's change the subject, okay?"

"Will you write the heroine to look like you?"

She shook her head. "It's a bad idea."

"You said I could choose. Why would it be bad if she looked like you?"

She searched for an innocuous explanation, but decided honesty would be more efficient with him. "Transference. Our situation is peculiar enough without the possibility of getting the fictional characters mixed up with the real people.

"I don't understand," he said, furrowing his brow. "Give me a for instance."

She was thinking of the romantic involvement, specifically the love scenes, but since she was trying to get out of the hot water, not deeper into it, she hedged. "The . . . emotional issues could . . . create complications."

His expression softened and his gaze drifted to her mouth. "And we certainly can't afford to get . . . *complicated*, can we?"

She could almost feel his lips pressing against hers as he finished that sentence, punctuating the fact that the complications had already begun despite her protest or their inability to touch.

He looked as though he had something more to say, but abruptly returned to the discussion of what he'd learned that afternoon. "If I remember correctly, your original question was what did I find most fascinating so far. Let's see, I mentioned the technology, communication, the space program, and the wars. The environmental problems appear to be truly frightening, at least on the surface. I definitely want to read more about that.

"But the most fascinating of all of it? I'd have to say it was when I looked up the presidents and saw that Ronald Reagan—*an actor who had been upstaged by a chimp*—was elected as the leader of the greatest country in the world. What were people thinking?"

She shrugged. "You already picked up on part of it. Communication is not only global and instantaneous today, it's also very visual. For a person to be elected he has to be appealing to the public eyes and ears."

"As with Kennedy."

"Exactly. One hopes that any shortcomings in the mental department are balanced out by the cabinet and White House staff. Did you get into the medical area?"

"Not yet. Anything special I should look for?"

"Organ transplants, genetic research, and AIDS would give you a good start."

He scribbled down her first two suggestions. "What was the third thing?"

"A-I-D-S, acquired immune deficiency syndrome, caused by a virus known as HIV. If you thought the environmental problems were frightening, wait until you learn about this monster. By the time you've finished catching up on the last three decades, you may be desperate to find a way to get back to the sixties."

He grinned. "I'm beginning to notice a definite pattern in your dialogue—all roads lead to my returning to 1965."

"When I'm sure you're convinced that you have a mission to accomplish, I'll quit bringing it up. Now, speaking of that mission, I stopped by the O'Neill plantation this afternoon."

His relaxed posture stiffened immediately. "I thought we agreed to do this together."

"We did, and we will. I only meant to drive by to see the house, but then his housekeeper came home. She said she's worked for O'Neill for exactly thirty-two years last month, which would make it right around Ginger's death. She appeared to be in her sixties, and her light brown complexion made me think she could be of mixed ethnic backgrounds. Her first name is Hannah. Does that ring any bells?"

Luke shook his head. "The description could be any number of women, but I don't remember any Hannah."

She related the brief conversation they'd had. "Hopefully, O'Neill will be intrigued enough to give me an appointment and a green light on the bio idea so that we'll have a clear path to everyone else."

"And if he doesn't?"

She shrugged. "If he doesn't give me his blessing, we'll just have to move on to plan B."

"Do we actually have a plan B?" he asked with a grin.

"Of course," she replied indignantly. "And I figure we'll know what it is right after we finish going through the newspaper's old files tomorrow."

* * *

"I think you have to meet with her, Reid, and the sooner the better. Put a stop to whatever she has in mind right off, before she starts stirrin' folks up with questions about your past."

Reid O'Neill stopped pacing in front of the library window and took a sip of his bourbon. Though Beauregard Ramey had stepped down as the Imperial Wizard over a decade ago, he still had the power to manipulate the lives of those around him, whether they were part of the Klan or not. For that reason alone, Reid had felt compelled to tell his old friend about the lady author's message. Their shared secrets made it mandatory.

Usually he agreed with Beau's advice, but in this case, his ego needed more convincing. "A biography could be very good for my business. If it was handled carefully—"

"It could still go sour," Beau interrupted. "We can't control the media like we did in the old days. It's best to let sleeping dogs lie."

Reid knew he was right. There was too much at stake to take a chance. "But what if I ask her not to write about me and she goes ahead with it anyway, without my authorization?"

Beau swirled the brandy in his crystal snifter and slowly inhaled its heady aroma. "If the lady can't mind her own business, I guess we'll just have to teach her some manners. I'm sure Junior and some of the other boys would be delighted to help convince her to go back to Atlanta where she belongs."

Chapter Eight

"I found it!" Luke exclaimed, tapping his finger against the microfiche screen. "Here's the article I wrote just before the Klan threw me that private party."

Kelly moved from her station to his and scanned the newspaper article he referred to.

On the drive into Atlanta that morning, they had decided to split their research. He would review everything he'd written for the *Atlanta Journal*, and she would pull any articles regarding the O'Neills, the Lake Sidney Lanier rapist, and Beauregard Ramey, Jr. In this instance, their separate tracks had crossed paths.

"I thought his name sounded familiar," Luke said. "Junior Ramey was one of the young men whose names were given to me in connection with the beating of a Negro who tried to buy—"

"Black," Kelly interjected.

"Huh?"

"The politically correct term is black, or African American, but black has less syllables."

He filed that with all the other new terms he'd been learning. "Anyway, now I remember what else I'd been told but couldn't confirm in time to turn in the article. Junior Ramey was supposed to have been the son of the Imperial Wizard, the Klan's local head honcho."

"Wow. This is getting more complicated all the time."

"Or more logical," Luke added. "If Junior Ramey was the real Lake Sidney Lanier rapist and I was getting close to exposing him, Big Daddy would have had the motivation and the clout to orchestrate everything that happened to me."

Kelly nodded. "And everyone in the area would have jumped to do his bidding. But here's where it gets a bit more complicated again. I just read the one and only follow-up article about Junior Ramey's arrest. They whitewashed the whole thing. He confessed to breaking and entering, but the attempted rape charge was dropped. After a psychiatric examination, Ramey's actions were reduced to a copycat stunt to gain attention.

"Apparently, Junior suffered a horrible facial disfigurement as a child, which made him an outcast. It was determined that he wouldn't have actually gone through with the rape even if he hadn't been interrupted by the husband."

Luke shook his head with disgust. "So, Daddy got him off again. He and the others got away with that other assault also. They claimed it was a simple case of mistaken identity, that the Negro—I mean, black man—looked just like a man who had gotten fresh with someone's sister. They apologized and no charges were filed."

"Well, charges were filed this time, but only for the *b* and *e*. Ramey's sentence was six months in a private hospital for psychiatric treatment."

"What about the other rape that occurred after my execution?"

Kelly shrugged. "I don't know. I can't find anything but a reference to it, but I'll keep looking. Based on what we've found so far though, I'll bet it got swept under the carpet. It says in the article that Ramey's intended victim and her husband were paid a settlement for their trouble. Maybe Daddy paid off the other one also."

Luke rubbed his chin. "Then the next logical step would be to verify whether the Rameys were loaded."

Kelly returned to her chair and forwarded the film to the next article. "You know what we really need now?"

"A time machine?" he asked with a grin.

"Besides that," she said with a return smile. "I was thinking more along the lines of an informant. Someone who knew all the players then, and wouldn't be afraid to talk now."

"Are you still thinking of that housekeeper?"

She shook her head. "No. She was definitely

afraid of something. I was thinking of Mary Beth Nevers."

Luke's brows lifted sharply. "Ginger's roommate? How did you know her name?"

"Someone interviewed her after Ginger's death. I must have missed it the first time through. She seemed to like you and didn't believe you killed Ginger."

He sighed. "I know. She was supposed to have been called as a character witness at my trial. Unfortunately, it interfered with her honeymoon plans, so she gave a deposition instead."

"Was it read?"

He laughed. "Oh yeah, they read it all right. Either she had a big change of heart about me, or someone reworded her testimony. It didn't come straight out and accuse me, but it was negative enough to add to the guilty picture they'd created."

Kelly had no doubt that someone had altered the deposition. Any woman who spent time around Luke would know he wasn't a rapist or a murderer. A ladykiller, maybe, but only in the nonliteral sense. Mary Beth would not have had a change of heart about him, unless she had wanted him for herself and he'd spurned her, but that didn't seem to be the case. "Did you say honeymoon plans?"

"Yeah. She got married while I was in jail."

"Was that already planned?"

Luke tried to remember. "She was engaged, but

I don't think they had set a date. I heard they suddenly decided to forego a big wedding and just elope."

"Doesn't that strike you as very odd? Her best friend is brutally murdered, so she gets married and goes away on a honeymoon rather than sticking around to see if the murderer is convicted."

"Maybe Ginger's death made her worry about her own mortality, and she didn't want to waste what little time she had left."

Kelly made a face at him. "Is that coming from the reporter or the amateur shrink?"

"A little of both," he replied with a chuckle. "But the reporter's nose says something stinks about it."

"I agree. If we could find her now, she might be able to shed some light into the shadows."

"That's a real long shot."

"True, but you seem to be on a lucky streak this week, so maybe the odds are with us. Would you happen to remember the name of the man she married?"

Luke furrowed his brow for a moment, then brightened with a recollection. "Jimmy . . . Jimmy James, or Johns, something like that. It was two first names. We went out with them on a double date once, but that was months ago, or years, depending on whose frame of reference we're using. He was away at college most of the time that Ginger and I were together. Now that I think about it, whenever Ginger mentioned him, she usually referred to him as Mary Beth's fiancé rather than by name. I thought it was her way of keeping engagement rings on my mind. Sorry. I'm usually good with names, but I don't remember his."

"That's okay. There was probably an announcement in the paper."

Twenty minutes later, Kelly not only confirmed that Mary Beth Nevers had married Jimmy Joe Jackson, but that when they returned from their extended honeymoon cruise around the world, they planned to settle in Marietta, Georgia, where Jimmy was being made a partner in his father's car dealership. It was enough of a lead to give them hope that Mary Beth might still be around.

"I think you'll find this even more interesting," Luke said in a hushed voice, even though there was no one around to hear him. "The last piece of mine that was printed before Ginger's murder was the one in which I interviewed an FBI special agent regarding the profile that had been drawn up on the Lake Sidney Lanier rapist and added in a few assumptions of my own. Here, read it yourself and tell me what you think." He printed out a copy and handed it to Kelly.

She skimmed over the physical description that she already knew fit Luke in a general way. Based on the rapist's repeated routine, it was concluded that he loved his mother and resented his father, since he treated the victims with a twisted sort of respect, but left the scene in a condition that would ensure the husband's knowing what had happened. He seemed to be striking a blow at his own sex and their animalistic nature rather than the women he actually assaulted.

Though he carried a knife, he had never used it to do more than induce fear, and seemed to go out of his way to keep from causing his victims pain, including the act of penetration. Violent aggression was not his first choice. He was possibly a pacifist.

Since they were all married women, it was suggested that the rapist might be single and unable or unwilling to attract a wife of his own. Here, Luke had questioned if that meant that the ski mask was hiding more than the rapist's identity, perhaps an ugliness within.

It was further concluded that the rapist was a local man who knew the area, could blend in quickly and easily before and after the crime, and was able to keep track of everyone's schedules without anyone being suspicious of him. There was a strong possibility that the victims and/or their husbands were all acquainted with this man.

When she was done, Kelly let out a soft whistle. "It sounds to me like this could have been written about a lot of men, but the perpetrator might have felt like you were drawing an arrow right to his house."

"Exactly. It might have been the proverbial straw that broke somebody's back. By the way, the line in there about the pacifist was very effectively used against me."

"Do you think it would help to get a transcript of your trial?"

He shrugged. "I doubt it. I vividly recall every minute of it, and the only thing it would help do is convince you that I really was guilty."

By midafternoon, armed with copies of every article that was even remotely related to their research, they drove from the *Atlanta Journal*'s offices to Kelly's town house.

"I can't get over how much the city has grown," he said for at least the tenth time since they'd left Charming that morning.

"Actually, a lot of renovation and expansion was done in preparation of the ninety-six Summer Olympics that were held here."

"But these highways! How do you ever know which lane to be in?"

She laughed. "It's not so bad when you live here. Speaking of which, here's my exit." She was anxious to get to her telephone to see if they could locate Mary Beth, but she was also looking forward to seeing his reaction to the modern amenities within her home.

The moment she entered her front door, however, she completely forgot about showing off. As she set down her laptop and purse, she noticed a pair of men's loafers in the entranceway. A sports coat was draped over the back of a dining-room chair. On the pass-through counter between the kitchen and dining area was a used coffee mug.

"What's the matter?" Luke asked, noticing her

sudden change of expression as she looked around. Rather than answer, she took off up the stairs from the alcove, so he dropped their overnight bags and followed. He watched her grow more and more agitated as she checked her closet, then several drawers.

"Damn him! Damn him to hell!" she exclaimed when she entered her bathroom. "I'm going to kill him." She shoved Luke out of her way and marched to the phone next to her bed.

His first thought was that she'd been robbed, but her fury seemed to be directed at a specific male, probably the one whose toiletries were on the bathroom sink. "Does this have something to do with your ex-husband?" he asked while she waited for someone to answer their telephone. He noticed that there was no cord connecting the receiver to the main unit, but figured he could save that question for later.

She held up a hand to quiet him. "Is he there?" she demanded, and was clearly dissatisfied with the response. "Oh. Well, when did he—" The sound of the front door being closed distracted her. "Never mind. He's here." She slammed down the receiver and again had to push Luke out of her path as she tore down the stairs.

"Kelly, wait—" The warning he was about to issue was clearly a waste of time since she was already confronting her nemesis on her own.

"How dare you! I have tried to be tolerant. I have done my best to be patient with this new obsession you have with me, but now you've gone too far. You had better have one hell of an explanation—never mind, I don't want to hear it. Yes, I do. Talk!"

Luke smothered a laugh as he imagined her cocky ex-husband trying to get a word in while she ranted at him, and decided to spice up the action a bit more. Quickly, he shed all his clothes but his briefs and wrapped a towel around his waist. Padding barefoot down the stairs, he loudly called, "Hey, babe, what's taking you so—"

His sentence hung in the air as he reached the first floor and saw a nerdy-looking guy with short blond hair and glasses . . . and very red cheeks. Whoever he was, Kelly's tirade had clearly rendered him speechless. When the man spotted Luke, a sound came out of his mouth, but it was more of a squeak than a word.

Kelly scanned Luke from head to toe with a look of exasperation. Rather than being grateful for his attempt to help, she looked like she was about to turn her anger on him.

"Has every man on this planet gone completely nuts, or just the ones around me?"

Luke opened his mouth to explain, but she cut him off with a slashing motion of her arm and turned back to the nerd. "You first. Why are your things all over my house?"

Another squeak came out before he regained his composure enough to form words. "You . . . you gave me your key."

"To come in here and water my plants once a week. Not to move in and share my underwear drawer!"

The nerd took a deep breath, pushed his glasses up the bridge of his nose, and did his best to stand taller than his below-average height. "If you will let me speak without interruption for one minute . . ." He paused to make sure she would give him that much, then began again. "My condo was tented for termites this weekend. I would have called and asked your permission to stay here instead of a hotel, but you chose not to give me a number where I could reach you. I really didn't think you would mind. How was I supposed to know you were returning home unexpectedly . . ." He frowned at Luke. ". . . with *company*?"

Now it was Kelly's turn to be tongue-tied. "Oh. I, uh, of course I wouldn't have minded. I've just been under a lot of stress the past few days, and when I saw all your things, then added that to how, um, *insistent* you were the last few times we talked, well, I'm sorry. I guess I jumped to the wrong conclusion." She sighed and rubbed her forehead.

The nerd cleared his throat and held out his hand to Luke. "I don't believe we've met. I'm Bruce Hackett."

Without thinking, Luke raised his hand, and a tiny spark leapt between them.

"Damn static electricity," Bruce said with a nervous laugh and grasped Luke's hand firmly before he could pull it away. "I'm an old friend of Kelly's, and her attorney when the need arises."

Luke was so stunned by the fact that his electrical charge had not thrown the man across the room, it took him a second to remember the name he'd given Kelly's ex. "Duke. Duke McCoy. I'm a *new* friend of Kelly's." He glanced down at his towel as the handshake ended. "I can explain—"

"Don't bother, honey," Kelly quickly said, placing her hand on his arm with a meaningful look.

He felt another tiny spark when she made contact, but nothing drastic. Suddenly he remembered how she had shoved him aside upstairs without being shocked. What had happened to his strange power?

"Kelly's right," Bruce stated in a more assured tone than his flushed face suggested. "No need to explain anything. I'll be out of here in a few minutes. In fact, I left the office early to come by and move out. Actually, my building was habitable as of last night, but I had a late meeting."

Luke nodded with understanding as the attorney failed to hide his discomfort and nervousness with a flow of chatter. It occurred to him that something that he was saying was a lie. What part, he wondered, and how did it affect Kelly?

As soon as Bruce headed upstairs to gather his things, she whispered, "What happened?"

Since her gaze was on the towel around his hips, he thought she was referring to his impatient lover act. "I thought it was your ex and I fig-ured—"

"Not that. I realized what you were doing once my anger at Bruce cleared up. I'm talking about the electricity. Is it gone, or did you do something to get grounded just now?"

"I didn't do anything that I know of. But you touched me upstairs, too, and nothing happened to you then either."

"Maybe it has something to do with your physi-cal location."

He gave that some thought. "I was electrocuted in Atlanta, but when I came to I was outside of your cabin. If anything, I would think being here might increase the charge."

"Then maybe it's worn off on its own. Remem-ber how I touched you by accident yesterday, and it wasn't that bad, and how after you took the last bath you didn't glow nearly as much as you did the first time?"

"God, I hope you're right. It'll make everything a lot easier if I don't have to be on guard con-stantly."

Bruce came back downstairs hauling a garment bag, a large suitcase, and a smaller tote. A few minutes later he had finished collecting the last of his belongings and made a hasty departure.

"Is he always so nervous?" Luke asked.

She pursed her lips. "No. He's usually very to-gether. But I did attack him rather voraciously, then his seeing you half naked after I repeatedly told him I wasn't interested in a romantic relationship with him or any other man. Well, I'm sure it threw him for a loop. You see, he'd gotten it into his head that he was in love with me, and I was hoping it would wear off if he didn't see me for a while."

"Just so that I'm prepared in the future, are there any more men vying for your attention?" He meant to tease, but once the question was out, he realized that he truly wanted to hear her answer.

"I've never stopped to count. A few thousand, I guess." She smiled at his reaction. "I have a lot of male readers, some of whom are temporarily incarcerated, who seem to think that I'm as beautiful and sexy as my heroines. I think it's very interesting how female readers tend to fantasize about being the heroine in the book, but the men—"

"Did you notice how much luggage he had with him?"

She wondered if he'd heard anything she said. "What about it?"

"He said they were tenting his building this past weekend and that he could have moved back in last night. Why would a man need so much luggage for only two or three days?"

Kelly crossed her arms. "What are you getting at? Do you think I was right to begin with? That he had moved in here for more than a short stay?"

The instant her posture stiffened, he regretted mentioning it. "Naw. I'm just overly suspicious.

But I am beginning to think that you have a rather addictive effect on men, and it's not because of your writing."

That made her laugh. "Yeah, I'm a real siren. You'd better watch your step or I'll sing you one of my seductive songs and lure you to your destruction."

"Too late," he said, softening his expression. "I'm already bewitched, and I haven't read a single sentence of your writing." The fingers of his right hand combed into the golden hair along her temple and rested at the back of her head.

As he took a small step closer, her eyes widened with awareness, but she wasn't immediately certain what she wanted to do about it. The softness in her voice contradicted the indifference of her words. "If this is a test, I think it's safe to say you're no longer supercharged." He stroked her cheek with the thumb of his free hand. The tenderness of it made her sigh, but she stopped herself from giving in to the urge to touch him in return.

"Funny you should say that," he murmured. "I was thinking there was enough electricity flowing between us to light up Atlanta." His hands slid slowly down the length of her arms, then just as slowly, he brought her hands up between them.

As her knuckles brushed the coarse hair on his chest, she came to her senses. Abruptly, she freed her hands and backed up several feet. "You're right. There's plenty of electricity, or chemistry, or whatever you want to call it. I should know. I earn a living writing about the mysterious attraction that occurs between men and women. But I also know that it would be a major mistake to act on it."

"A *major* mistake? I think that might be exaggerating it a bit."

She took another step backward. "For you maybe. You have nothing to lose. Technically, you're dead. If I were in your shoes, I might find it very hard not to give into a great many temptations. After all, any second you could get zapped back into that electric chair. And maybe if I was a girl from the sixties, I'd jump into bed with you without a single thought about tomorrow.

"But I can't do that. Will is the only man I've ever been with and what happened between us is enough to stop me from rushing out and having sex for the sake of sex. If I ever get into bed with a man again it will be because of all the reasons that have nothing to do with electricity, like compatibility, intellectual equality, and emotional commitment."

"Two out of three's not bad," he said, trying to lighten the conversation.

"But it's not good enough for me. And don't try to tell me you have real feelings for me. If anything, your primitive male instincts have been triggered because two other men wanted me in your presence."

He felt her barb hit a sensitive spot and forced a grin. "Who's playing amateur shrink now?

Look, I'll admit that making a pass at you under the circumstances was out of line, if you'll admit, hmm . . ." He tried to think of something she was wrong about. "If you'll admit that you are as beautiful and sexy as any of your heroines."

She rolled her eyes and shook her head. "Go put your clothes back on, and I'll introduce you to some of the wonders of a home of the nineties."

He did as she ordered, taking their bags upstairs as he went.

Kelly let out the breath she'd been holding as soon as he was out of sight. She had just told one of the biggest lies in her entire life, and she'd gotten away with it. The truth was, every cell in her body was screaming for her to throw caution and prerequisites to the wind and jump into bed with Luke.

The hell with tomorrow. Live for the moment. Take a chance on discovering that all those great sex scenes she'd written over the years weren't only make-believe.

But the logical part of her mind had voiced an argument that was quite different from the explanation she'd given him. She was already half in love with Luke simply from spending time with him. Considering the way her insides melted when he touched her face, she knew without having to experience it that sex with him would finish her off. She'd be head over heels in love . . . with a man who could vanish in the blink of an eye. Then, where would she be?

Alone, as before, but with a hurt much greater than she'd ever felt because of Will. No, it didn't matter how good it would be with Luke, it wasn't worth the pain that was sure to follow.

"Kelly," he called down to her. "Come up and show me how this telephone works without a cord."

"Jezebel!" Gabriel roared. "That was a clear foul. We agreed to non-interference."

"I did not break the agreement," she insisted, though she didn't quite meet his eyes. "It was unfair of you to give him that electrical charge to begin with. I merely neutralized it."

"Hmmph. I suppose it won't make any difference in the long run. She'll keep him at arm's length just as well."

"Hah! That shows how much you know about women, especially women who've been without the company of men for some time. She'll give in before they return to Charming."

Gabriel rubbed his jaw. "Would you care to make a side wager on that?"

Jezebel inched forward. "What did you have in mind?"

"If you're right, the six-week time is halved to three. If you're wrong, it's doubled to twelve weeks. But it must be absolute unemotional fornication before they leave Atlanta."

"Unfair advantage. She's already emotionally involved. I'll agree to copulation without a commitment from him."

"Done. And *positively* no interference this time."

"On either side."

"Agreed." Gabriel pretended not to be pleased with the terms, when, in fact, he was quite satisfied. Even if Kelly's resolve to keep their relationship platonic dissolved, Luke's poison ivy rash was sure to enforce another night of celibacy, and by the time it was no longer a problem, they would be on the way back to Charming . . . with six additional weeks to fall in love and admit it.

"Ta-dah," Kelly sang out as she set the plate of little pizza bagels in front of Luke. "Five minutes from freezer to microwave to table. Are you amazed?"

"If they're as good as they smell, I'll be even more amazed. I had a frozen TV dinner once, and it wasn't worth the tin tray it came in. I thought it was a great idea, especially as a bachelor who hates to cook, but I swore I wouldn't eat another one until somebody figured out how to keep the food from tasting like metal."

He picked up one of the mini-pizzas and inhaled its spicy aroma at close range. "God, the last time I had decent pizza was in Detroit."

"In that case, we'll order the real thing for dinner, but these can be your appetizer." She watched him take one bite, swallow it, then decide they were good enough to hold off his hunger for the moment.

Since she considered the microwave the finest

invention of the century, she had saved it for last. Beginning in her bedroom, she had told him about portable, speaker, and cellular phones, answering machines, voice mail, beepers, and caller identification boxes; digital clocks and watches. In her bathroom was an adjustable shower head and a large Jacuzzi bathtub, which she promised he could try out later. Though she couldn't demonstrate one, she told him about the photosensitive panels in some public rest rooms that control water flow and flush toilets.

Downstairs, she showed him her office with its fax machine. Though she had thought the video cassette recorder and video camera would dazzle him, he only saw them as expected improvements over eight-millimeter home movies. The sound from her stereo system and the compact disc player impressed him, but not nearly as much as the remote control for the television.

While Luke finished off his appetizer, Kelly called information. Let it be easy, she prayed as the operator came on the line.

"Hi. I really hope you can help me. I'm trying to locate a woman who was my best friend in high school, but we lost touch with each other over thirty years ago. Recently I found out . . . well, suffice it to say, I'm getting my affairs in order and would truly love to see her one more time." She went on to tell the sympathetic operator what details she had about Mary Beth and hoped the gross distortion of the truth wouldn't come back to haunt her.

The operator was able to confirm that there were two Jackson car and truck dealerships—one in Marietta and one in Decatur. Kelly made a note of their phone numbers, then for the next ten minutes, she madly scribbled the numbers of every residential listing that could be Mary Beth's in those two areas of metropolitan Atlanta. All together, there were twenty-seven possibilities, including two with the last name Nevers.

"Just out of curiosity," Luke asked, "why did you make up that elaborate story?"

She finished making check marks next to the numbers she thought were the likeliest, then answered. "I don't have a phone book here to do the search on my own, and information operators usually just play you a computerized message based on the one request you called about. Computers have some wonderful capabilities, but they're still limited. I needed a human who would do a lot more for me than a machine. It wasn't entirely honest, but it worked. Now I have to think of what story I'm going to give Mary Beth if I do find her."

They exchanged ideas until they came up with one that sounded like it would get them in Mary Beth's front door, then Kelly started working her way down the list. She hit the jackpot on her eleventh try.

"Good evening. This is Kelly Kirkwood, with

the *Atlanta Journal.* I'm trying to reach Mary Beth Nevers Jackson, wife of Jimmy Joe Jackson, owner of Jackson Cars and Trucks. The receptionist at the dealership gave me this number."

"This is Mrs. Jackson."

"Great. I'm working on an in-depth piece about how Atlanta has grown from the point of view of wives of successful businessmen who have lived here for at least thirty years. Your name was given to me as someone I really must include. I can give you my personal guarantee that the intention of the article is entirely positive and would give your husband's business a free plug in several hundred thousand newspapers."

"What would you need from me?"

Kelly heard the suspicion in the woman's tone and tried to allay her fears. "A half hour of your time should do it. I could come to your home, or meet you somewhere for lunch if you prefer. Unfortunately, I'm on a very tight deadline, so it would have to be soon." There was such a long pause before Mary Beth responded, Kelly feared that she'd hung up.

"I suppose it will be all right," she finally said. "But I have to attend a board meeting at the hospital tomorrow and the women's auxiliary has their monthly brunch the next day. If you'd like to come to my house at three o'clock that afternoon, I could give you a half hour."

"That would be fine." She wrote down directions to the Jackson home in Marietta and thanked

Mary Beth profusely for her assistance. After she hung up, she filled Luke in on what he couldn't hear. "So, she's on guard, but agreed to see us Thursday afternoon."

"You're really quite an accomplished storyteller," he said with a grin. "I hope I'm never on the receiving end of one of your lies. I'd never be able to tell."

She immediately thought of the big lie she'd already told him. "I've had lots of practice," she answered with a light shrug.

"Storytelling? Or telling lies?"

"I refuse to answer on the grounds that you might throw it in my face later."

He winked at her. "Smart girl. So, what's next on your agenda?"

"Well, we probably should start by making up a new agenda. It doesn't make much sense to drive back to Charming until after we've talked to Mary Beth."

"What about the interview you were trying to set up with Reid O'Neill?"

Her eyes opened wide. "Geez, I almost forgot about that." She glanced at the clock. "It's not quite seven o'clock yet, maybe the drugstore is still open." Quickly, she called information, then O'Neill's drugs, and was relieved to hear a familiar voice. "Hi, Mr. Scanlon. It's Kelly Kirkwood. I'm in Atlanta for two days, but I'm expecting a message to be left there for me."

"As a matter of fact, one was dropped off just a bit ago, from Mr. O'Neill himself."

She weighed the time factor against privacy and figured everyone in Charming would soon know what she was up to anyway. "Could you read it to me, please?"

"Sure thing." There was the sound of paper tearing. "It says, 'Dear Mizz Kirkwood, I am most flattered by your interest in a poor, small-town boy such as myself. If you will call my secretary at the number below, she can arrange for us to meet at a mutually convenient time.'"

She wrote down the number he gave her and promised to stop in to see him when she got back. "We made it past the gate," she told Luke. "O'Neill is willing to talk to me. But I think it would be best to hold off until after we hear what Mary Beth has to tell us."

"I agree. So, what do we have on the new agenda so far?"

She made him wait until she got a pad and pen from her office. "Okay, tomorrow morning I call O'Neill's secretary for an appointment Friday, if possible. Thursday afternoon, we meet with Mary Beth, so sometime before that we need to work out our strategy on that."

"It would probably help if we went through everything we have so far, create a list of the people involved, draw up some theories, and make a separate list of outstanding questions."

"That's exactly what I was planning to do," she

said with a smile. She tore off the top sheet of paper that she had titled "Agenda," and applied her pen to the first line of the next page. "Let's see. We have the Ku Klux Klan—"

"Whoa! Back that horse up a bit. Do you think we could order that pizza first and work until it's time to pick it up? I'll think a lot better once my stomach knows more food will be coming. Actually, I'd think even better if I could get a cold beer to go with the pizza. It's been a while since I've had one of those, too."

"First of all, we don't have to pick it up. They deliver, and usually in less than thirty minutes; just another little bonus of higher technology. Unfortunately, they won't deliver alcoholic beverages, but I might have a bottle of wine." She got up and went to her refrigerator. What she saw inside made her take another look in the freezer. When she had gotten the pizza bagels out before, she hadn't been paying attention, but now she noticed several frozen food items that were not on her usual grocery list. Inside the fresh food section were a lot of items she might buy, but she knew she had removed all the perishable products before going to Charming.

"What's the matter?" Luke asked, joining her in the kitchen. "Why are you staring at your refrigerator like you've never seen it before?"

"Can you tell me why a man who was only planning to spend two or three nights in a place would stock this much food? Or why there would be a steak ready to cook when he got home if he was intending to move out this afternoon?"

He grimaced rather than give her the answer.

"What would you do if you were me?"

"Since he is an old friend, and I gather he's never exhibited any psychotic behavior in the past, I'd probably let him know that I thought he was lying about only being here for a few days. In fact, I'd probably check on whether his building was really tented first, then confront him again. Although, catching him today might have been enough to straighten him out."

"Geez, I hope so. Well, the good news is, he's a beer drinker, imported, of course, but there are four cold bottles in here, and that is what you wished for." She handed him a bottle and an opener, then got out the bottle of white zinfandel for herself. While she removed the cork, she directed his attention to the Italian restaurant menu held on the front of the refrigerator door with magnets. Beside that was the menu from her favorite Chinese restaurant. "It's all much better than anything I'd cook, so you can't go wrong."

"I'll stick with my first choice—pizza, with pepperoni and mushrooms."

She laughed. "That's my regular order." She called it in, and they carried their drinks back to the dining-room table. "Okay, where were we?"

"You were about to blame the Klan for my troubles, and I was about to point out the problem with that. An individual man raped and murdered Ginger, not a gang."

"True, but the murder and your frame-up could have been organized by a group of people. My theory on this one is you ticked off the Klan to begin with. Then you were unwittingly closing in on the real serial rapist, who very possibly might have been the son of the Imperial Wizard. You had an affair with a woman whose husband and brother were Klan members on top of that. I think they put their heads together and figured out a way to eliminate their number-one annoyance, namely you."

"You could be right, but who did the actual deed? Even if Junior was the rapist, he never seriously injured a single one of his victims. Murder wasn't in his profile."

"He could have become angry or frightened and strangled her on the spur of the moment."

"In that case, it wasn't a premeditated plan carried out by a group."

She twisted her mouth back and forth and wrote a few lines. "Okay, set Junior aside for a second. If there were more than one man involved, we'd have to find out which one was capable of cold-blooded murder for the protection of one or more of the others."

"Which also brings us to the scenario where an outside professional was hired. That one would be the hardest puzzle to figure out, almost impossible."

"Right. So, back to Junior. Maybe he was doing what he'd done many times before, only this time something went wrong and he killed Ginger. He might have gone to Daddy after the fact and solicited help to cover up his boo-boo."

"I like the sound of that one, at least from an investigative standpoint. Getting an unstable personality to brag about a crime they've gotten away with is not an impossible feat. But here's another possibility. The Imperial Wizard knew about his son's perverse hobby, and being one of those cold-blooded creatures, planned the whole frame-up for all the above reasons, raped and strangled Ginger himself, then simply used his power to ensure my conviction."

"Ooh, that one's not bad either, but if he was calculating enough to pull that off, I doubt if he could be easily convinced to fess up on his own. And last, but not least, let's not forget ol' Reid, the cuckolded husband. He could have enlisted the aid of the Klan or done the whole thing himself. After all, his power in this town is nothing to sneeze at either. I keep thinking about that call you swore you got from Ginger. If it was her, she claimed Reid had beaten her and she needed rescuing. In that case, he becomes the number-one suspect."

"And if we can verify that he inherited a fortune when she died, that would make the case even stronger. But I've played back that phone call in my head a thousand times, and something tells me it wasn't Ginger."

"Could it have been a man disguising his voice?"

"I suppose, but I really don't think so."

She let that sink in for a moment. "Do you realize what that means? If you're right, there was a woman accomplice. And that woman would know the name of the man who put her up to that phone call."

Luke nodded approvingly. "Now if she would just come forward after thirty-two years of silence and spill her guts to us, you'd have the ending for your book, and I could travel back in time, right the wrongs, and live my life the way I should have."

She smirked at him. "You still don't believe our investigation is going to make any difference, do you?"

"Not true. It could make a big difference. This time, instead of my being spontaneously combusted and transported through time, we could both end up dead."

Chapter Nine

"Now who's exaggerating?" Kelly asked.

"We went over this before, but I think it bears repeating. You're used to your safe, make-believe worlds, where you control all your characters' actions. I've done this kind of unofficial criminal investigation in the real world, and the one piece of advice I can give you from experience is that you can never forget that if you corner an animal, no matter how gentle it normally is, it might attack you."

She clucked her tongue at him. "And I told you, I intend to be very careful about what I say to whom."

"And I intend to keep reminding you that you're treading on very dangerous ground in unfamiliar territory."

"Fine." She took a deep breath and reviewed what she'd written so far. Her stomach definitely did not like being reminded that she could be get-

ting in over her head, but damned if she was
going to let him know she was a big chicken.

The arrival of their pizza brought a swift finish
to their review session.

"Would you like to watch one of my James
Bond movies while we eat?" Kelly asked.

"Absolutely. You get it ready, and I'll go find
some plates and napkins."

"That's okay. I'll get them."

"Kelly, please. You're clothing and feeding me.
At least let me try to be useful."

She had a wicked thought of exactly how she'd
like him to help her, but firmly quashed it. "Fine.
Paper plates are in the cabinet above the sink, napkins on the table, and a pizza server is in the left-
hand drawer."

He returned with the items she named, plus her
refilled wineglass, and another bottle of beer for
himself.

"Several actors have played James Bond, but
since you saw the first movie, I thought you might
get a kick out of seeing the last one that Sean
Connery did, *Never Say Never Again*." She checked
the label, then inserted the tape into her VCR.
"This one came out in 1983."

Luke chuckled and shook his head. Kelly had
made him so comfortable he was able to forget
his circumstances for long stretches of time. Thus,
it had taken him a moment just then to realize
that 1983 was in the distant past for her, even
though it was a future date to him.

He hadn't grasped the entire concept of home movies from Kelly's explanation, but as the commercial-free film began to run, his mind reeled as well. What an incredible time he'd been thrown into. He could spend the entire next year just discovering new things.

Having a woman as beautiful and bright as Kelly for a guide sweetened the pot even more.

Even if they did discover how to do it, why in God's name would he intentionally return to 1965, rather than remain in 1997?

His gaze drifted away from the television screen and onto Kelly's profile. If only she wasn't so dead set on righting wrongs of the past, he could be looking forward to an exciting future. After all, it was a wrong against him, not her. Shouldn't that make it his choice?

On the other hand, she had taken him in, fed him, clothed him, and was introducing him to the modern world. He hated to think how tough it would have been without her assistance. He clearly owed her and, at the moment, the only thing she wanted from him was his cooperation with her research. That and his dubious protection against all the bad guys surrounding her were the only paybacks at hand, so he would continue to go along with her for now.

In the meantime, he would try to figure out how to change her mind about his going back.

She must have felt him watching her for she glanced at him with a question in her eyes. He smiled and returned his visual attention to the movie, but his mind remained on their difference of opinion. He assured himself that he wasn't being entirely selfish about this; he was thinking of her welfare as well. She really was playing with fire and didn't seem to have an appropriate amount of fear about it. If he could convince her to give up this mission, he might be saving her from danger, even death. Why, he'd be a genuine hero!

So, back to the original question. What action on his part would show Kelly that they should forget about the past, drop the investigation, and move forward with a new plan?

As if by divine intervention, the answer appeared on the television screen, as Agent 007 drew the woman of the moment into his arms and kissed away any doubt she had about him.

Could he change Kelly's mind with his kisses? Could he distract her with his touch enough to make her forget about solving the mystery and concentrate on more pleasurable pursuits? Could he satisfy her so well, she would want to keep him around awhile?

Seduction to achieve a goal was not a very chivalrous thing to do, but if the end result also benefited the lady, surely it was justified.

She as much as admitted to wanting him, though she was hung up on the idea of getting a commitment before having sex. Well, he'd never lied to a woman about his preference to remain unattached, and he wouldn't start now. He'd just have to find another way to convince her that a passionate affair would be good for her even without promises about the future.

And it definitely would be good for her, considering what she'd told him about her unhappy marriage and limited physical contact with the opposite sex. She really deserved to know that making love with a man could be enjoyable. In fact, if he helped her get over her bad experience, he would be performing another good deed!

Then again, considering the number of men openly declaring their love for Kelly with no success, a direct approach would probably fail for him also. He knew from his own experience that sometimes the best seduction was when the lady thought it was all her idea.

He smiled as a plan began to form.

Kelly ordered her heart to stop racing. This was absolutely ridiculous. Her body was behaving as though it were anticipating a night of glorious passion. Even the very practical part of her mind was betraying her with images of Luke's naked body—which she had already seen often enough to recall it in splendid detail. Of course, she hadn't actually seen him aroused, but she could imagine—

No! She had to stop thinking about how his hands had felt as they slid down her arms. She had to stop wondering how it would have felt if she had allowed him to kiss her.

It probably would be easier to keep her mind off such agitating thoughts if they were watching a movie she hadn't seen a dozen times. It definitely would be much easier if Luke didn't keep glancing at her with that look that said he'd rather be watching the movie with her curled up next to him, her head on his chest, his fingers running through her hair.

Or was that also her overactive imagination?

She considered having another glass of wine to put her fantasies to sleep, but decided that could be risky since she'd already had three and another could lower her inhibitions as well. She really needed to keep her wits about her if she was going to successfully resist the temptation Luke represented.

Fortunately, he was a gentleman. When she backed away from his advance before, he instantly accepted her decision. No whining or begging or lies to get her to say yes, just acceptance of her decision . . . as it should be. And thank goodness for that, because if he so much as moved one inch in her direction, she was afraid all her good reasons for keeping their relationship plantonic would fly out the window.

Why, oh why, did his electrical charge have to go away? She was so much safer when his touch would have killed her.

The movie finally came to an end, and, though every nerve in her body was on full alert, it was late enough for her to claim exhaustion after their long, busy day.

"I'm beat, too," he said, stretching his arms as he rose from the sofa. "Where would you like me to bed down?"

She stopped the answer in her head from coming out of her mouth. "The guest room upstairs is already made up, and it has its own bathroom. If you need anything, I'll be right across the hall." She felt a flush warm her body as soon as the words were out and tried to conceal it with a quick getaway. "Good night."

He caught her hand as she tried to hurry past him. "Wait. There's something I need to say."

She paused, turning her body back toward him, but keeping her face slightly averted.

"Is everything all right?" His one hand moved to more fully envelope hers while the other gently touched her chin to get her to look at him. "You seem a bit jumpy."

His thumb stroked the back of her hand as if to soothe her, but anything that involved his touching her was going to have the opposite effect. She tried to ease away, but he held her firmly. "I'm fine, really."

"I don't believe you," he said, continuing the slow circular motion with his thumb. "I think you're still upset about what happened before, and I think we need to talk a little more about it so that you can get a peaceful night's sleep without worrying that I'm going to sneak into your room and pounce on you."

"I wasn't thinking anything of the sort!" she retorted with a forced smile. "In fact, I can honestly say, I already trust you more than any of the other men in my life. I'm probably just edgy about . . . about having to wait a whole day before we can interview Mary Beth. Yes, that's probably it."

He gave her a skeptical look, but said, "Okay, if you're sure, because it's very important that you believe you're safe with me. No matter what that judge said, I never forced myself on a woman."

Now she felt bad for making him worry. "I believe you, Luke. I swear, I'm not afraid of you."

"Thank you. For your belief, your trust, and your honesty. But I want to be completely honest with you as well. You are, without a doubt, the most incredible female I've ever met. When I told you that you epitomized my fantasy woman, I was dead serious. You're beautiful and sexy, but also intelligent, strong, creative, self-sufficient, and generous beyond comprehension. I can't help but want something more intimate to develop between us.

"Simply holding your hand right now is more exciting than—well, let's just say I've done a lot more with other women and didn't feel this good. But if holding your hand once in a while is as much as you'll allow me, I'll settle for that and be a happy man. Unless and until you give me a sign that you want more out of this strange relationship of ours, nothing else is going to happen between us. Okay?''

His speech took away what little common sense she had retained. She was ready to give him the sign he'd asked for right now, but all she could manage was a helpless expression and a bob of her head. He smiled and, as he slowly lowered his head, she parted her lips and closed her eyes. Instead of the expected sensual kiss, however, he gave her a brotherly peck on her forehead.

"Good night, sweetheart," he murmured in her ear, then walked up the stairs.

It took Kelly several seconds to remember to breathe, and when she did, all she smelled was the essence of Luke. She knew she was a lost cause in that moment. It was only a question of how long she could hold herself back, knowing exactly what she wanted, knowing it was readily available, yet knowing it couldn't possibly have a happy ending. At least he had left the timing up to her.

In a bit of a fog, she checked the front-door lock, turned off the lights, and dragged herself up the stairs to her room. Only when she pulled back her comforter and top sheet did the fog lift. Another smell filled her nose and this one outraged her. "Damn, damn, damn him!"

Within seconds, Luke rushed into her room, shirtless and pulling his jeans up over his hips as he entered. "What's the matter?''

Despite her anger, she was momentarily distracted by his open zipper and the glimpse of white briefs below his navel. Geez, she was behaving like one of the heroines in her novels! "I'm sorry. I didn't mean to disturb you." She turned back to her bed and began stripping the linens.

"I'll be more disturbed if you don't assure me that I'm not the one you were cussing at."

She yanked a casing off a pillow, then threw both across the room. "This has nothing to do with you. I just never seem to realize how naive I am until I get smacked in the head. I knew Bruce's things were in here, but it didn't register that it meant he *slept* in here, in *my* bed, instead of the guest room."

"Are you sure—"

"Oh boy, am I sure. Not only did he leave plenty of his cologne behind on my pillowcase, but it's mixed in with another very distinctive odor that I might not have recognized if not for the obvious stain on the sheet." She abruptly turned her back on the bed and tightly hugged herself. "Why would he do such a sick thing?"

Luke came up behind her and wrapped his arms over hers. Without saying a word he passed his strength to her and when she began to relax, he turned her to face him and hugged her close, gently rocking her until she was completely calm again. "If you'll tell me where the clean sheets are, I'll take care of this for you."

She shook her head as she lifted it from his

chest. "I don't want to sleep in here tonight. If you don't mind, I'll switch rooms with you."

Though he assured her he could do it himself, she insisted on helping with the linens. A few minutes later, they exchanged bags and said good night again.

As she was preparing for bed, it occurred to her that if she'd stayed in her room she could have soaked in the Jacuzzi until all her muscles unclenched, but it was too late for second thoughts. Luke was probably already settled in . . .

No, she wouldn't think about him lying in her bed, stretching his nude body against the clean sheets. It was bad enough that she was aware that he slept with nothing on. Dwelling on thoughts of Luke in her bed was just as frustrating as thinking about Bruce and what he'd done, in a different way of course.

She got into bed and began her nightly ritual of brushing the knots out of her hair. Though it was usually a very calming activity for her, it didn't work tonight. "*Ow*," she squealed out loud when she yanked so hard on one tangle that tears filled her eyes.

A heartbeat later, there was a knock at her door. "Kelly? Are you okay?"

"I'm fine. Except for being stupid."

"May I come in?"

She sighed. It was impossible to put him out of her mind if he wasn't even out of sight, but she didn't want to be rude. She thought about getting under the covers, but her big nightshirt covered her so well, it seemed silly. "Sure. Come on in."

He opened the door, walked straight toward her, and declared, "You've been crying."

Her eyes quickly took in the fact that he had at least slipped on his running shorts. "Oh, no, I—" Before she could tell him about how she'd pulled her hair, he was beside her on the bed, holding her close and whispering soothing baby-talk into her ear. He obviously thought she was still distraught about Bruce. It was so charming, she decided to postpone the explanation.

"I'm here," he was saying. "And as long as I am, nobody is going to hurt you."

She could have written that line, she thought, but it still felt good to be on the receiving end of such words when they were said so sincerely. It also felt very, very good to have his hands running up and down her back.

It would feel even better if she'd earned his concern honestly. "I wasn't crying," she murmured, then made some space between them. "I was brushing my hair and pulled on a tangle, but I thank you for trying to comfort me in my moment of distress anyway."

He grinned and gave her a little more space. "Well, then, thank you for giving me an excuse to hold you." He picked up the hairbrush. "May I?"

Unable to resist his pleading look or the offer, she turned to give him free access to her locks. They were both quiet for a while, except for an occasional deep breath on his part or a sigh of appreciation on hers. When he set the brush down and massaged her neck and shoulders, she decided he must have some telepathic abilities on top of all his other attractive traits, for it was precisely what she was wishing he would do.

"I once knew someone with long hair—not as long as yours though—and she had to put it in a hair net at night to sleep. Is that what you do?"

"No," she answered, picking up her Scrunchie. "I just twist it into a knot with this. Or if I want waves the next day, I sometimes braid it." She started to gather her hair into a tail to demonstrate, but he stopped her.

"One more minute, please. It's just so beautiful." He urged her to face him, then threaded his fingers into the sides of her hair. Bringing the two sections forward, he draped them over her breasts. "I can almost imagine you riding a horse, wearing nothing but your hair."

"Geez, I hope you're imagining that it's summertime," she said with a nervous laugh. Oddly enough, she felt flattered by the suggestive comment that she would have considered lewd coming from another man.

His gaze snared hers and held it until she stopped fidgeting. "Actually, I was thinking of autumn and how the colored leaves would look dull next to you." His hand cupped the back of her neck as his mouth moved closer to hers. This time she kept her eyes open, yet she was still unprepared for what he did.

A centimeter away from a kiss, he suddenly stood up and headed for the door. "I'm sorry. I promised I wouldn't do anything like that, and—"

"Luke, please."

He stopped, but didn't turn around.

"Don't go."

Chapter Ten

"I have to," he said, still keeping his back to her. "If I'm going to keep my promise I have to get out of here now."

Her head was swimming, whether from the wine or rushing hormones, she didn't know, and no longer cared. "You said I'd have to . . . How big of a sign do you need?"

"To keep me from feeling like I'm taking advantage of you at a weak moment . . ." He turned around, and she couldn't help but see the physical sign he'd been trying to hide from her. "For me to walk back to that bed, it would have to be a really big sign."

Her body clamored for her to make a move, and she thought of what she could do, but shyness slowed her down. "Would you close your eyes for a second?" He did, and she turned off the lamp next to her bed. The light coming from his room was more than enough. Taking a deep breath for courage, she pulled off her nightshirt—she couldn't go so far as to remove her panties—then sat with her legs folded beneath her, and arranged her hair over her breasts the way he'd done before. "Okay, you can open your eyes."

The reward for her efforts was his sharp intake of breath and a whispered, "Wow."

Still, he didn't come to her. "You need an even bigger sign?" she asked in an uncertain tone.

He slowly shook his head. "No, the sign's perfect. I just thought I'd send up a prayer of thanks while my brain is still functioning." He finally walked to the side of the bed and stroked her cheek. "I have no idea what I ever did in my life to deserve you, but I promise I'll do whatever you need to make sure you don't regret this."

He bent down and lightly touched his lips to hers. A tiny spark passed between them, and he grinned. "I guess there's still a little of that charge left."

"Actually," she said, rising to her knees and snaking her arms around his neck. "I was hoping for more than just a little electricity from you."

The slightest pressure at the back of his head brought his mouth back to hers with serious intent. It was the kiss she'd expected the first time, and the second, and the third, yet it was still so much more than she'd imagined any kiss could be. His lips were soft and warm and seemed to fit hers as though they'd been formed to come together this way.

She was so absorbed in the way he was alternately nibbling and caressing her lips that she barely noticed how they came to be lying down on their sides. Although she had blatantly offered herself to him, his fingers concentrated on arousing her arm and back. At the same time, his leg and foot moved over hers, making her aware that he intended to make love to every inch of her body with every inch of his.

Just when she thought she'd have to ask for more, his tongue slipped between her teeth to play inside. She responded to the deeper contact with a low moan and a shift of her hips that brought their lower bodies into contact.

Up to that instant, his actions had all seemed controlled, almost practiced, but the animal within him suddenly broke out. His hand captured her bottom and kneaded it as he pressed his erection hard against her most sensitive spot, moving with exactly the right rhythm to bring out the animal in her as well. Instead of making love to her mouth, he now ravished it. It no longer mattered who they were, where they came from, or where they would be tomorrow.

He was man, and he wanted to possess her in the most primitive way.

She was woman, and she wanted his possession more than anything she'd ever wanted in her life.

Although she had seen him unclothed numerous times, she had yet to touch his hard, lean body the way she'd fantasized. Her hungry fingers slid up his arm, explored his chest and shoulder, and trailed down his back.

His reaction to her touch was a muscle spasm so violent that he nearly fell off the bed.

"What happened?" she asked, seeing that he was clearly suffering from some discomfort. "Did I scratch you?"

The growling sound that came out of his throat was a combination of pain and frustration. "You didn't do anything wrong," he said through clenched teeth. "It's the damn poison ivy rash." He rubbed his backside with the heel of his hand. "It was almost completely cleared up and hadn't bothered me all day, so I didn't think to put on any calamine tonight." He flinched again and tried to rub a spot on his back. "I'm sorry. I've got to take care of this."

Kelly sighed as he hurried out of the room. She couldn't have made up an aborted love scene this outrageous if she'd thought about it for a month. Her body was going to take a few minutes to catch up on the change of plans, but it would readjust. It always had before.

She put her nightshirt back on and went across the hall where Luke had already stripped off his shorts and was smearing lotion on his bottom. She tried not to think about the fact that she still hadn't touched that part of him. "Can I help?"

"I've been managing for days by myself," he grumbled.

"Don't get snotty with me, fella. I didn't push you into that bush."

He looked appropriately sheepish. "Sorry." He handed her the pink bottle and a ball of cotton. "Yes, I would appreciate it if you could get my back."

She poured some lotion on the cotton and dabbed it on the few spots she could see on his lower back. "I'm surprised you're still itching. The rash is almost completely cleared up."

"I know. But there are a few spots . . . one of which became more sensitive as the skin stretched . . ."

"Oh. I hadn't thought of that." She bit her cheek to keep from giggling. "I guess they're right when they say scratching it only makes it worse."

He laughed and his grumpy mood lifted instantly. He turned around and gave her a firm kiss. "You're incredible, you know that?"

She kissed him back, then said, "I was recently thinking the same thing about you."

"I really am sorry about this." He kissed her again, slower and for a longer time. His hand eased up from her waist and found her breast. As soon as his palm brushed across the nipple, it hardened into a peak, and he tightened his fingers over her fullness. He took his mouth from hers and whispered into her ear. "Just because I'm temporarily out of commission, doesn't mean we can't do something for you."

"Mmm. That sounds wonderful. But you know what?" She gently moved his hand off her breast.

"After all this time, I either want everything or nothing."

He twisted his mouth to one side. "Well, maybe if we had a rubber—"

She shook her head. "No such luck. In fact, now that you bring it up, I guess I was being stupid about that, too. I wasn't even thinking about the consequences. That shows you how out of practice I am."

"Hush. I like the fact that you're out of practice. And that you want to wait until we can have everything. I'll take care of it tomorrow."

Her cheeks warmed and she lowered her eyes. Making advance plans to have sex sounded so cold. Somehow a spontaneous roll in the hay after a couple of glasses of wine could be chalked up to temporary insanity. But arranging for it a day ahead of time, like it was just another item on their agenda, well, it no longer felt right. In fact, now that her mind was clearer, she wondered what had made it seem so right earlier.

Luke tipped her chin with his finger. "Where'd you go just now?"

She forced a smile. "Never-never land. Peter and Tinkerbell said hi."

He didn't buy it. "Are you sure we're okay?"

"*We're* absolutely copacetic. But very tired. So-o-o if you're comfortable now, maybe we could try the good-night routine again and see if it takes this time." She rose on tiptoes and kissed him lightly. "Good night."

He stopped her before she could leave the bathroom. "We don't have to sleep in separate beds."

"I think it would be best, under the circumstances. There's no telling what that darn electrical current could make us do when we're sound asleep in the middle of the night."

"Right," he said with a lopsided grin, but the confidence had gone from his voice. He gave her another soft kiss and let her go.

He had no idea what had happened, but he instinctively knew it was more than a simple postponement of pleasure.

Somewhere in the middle of his calculated seduction, the rug had been pulled out from under him. Instead of entrancing her with his masterful technique, he found himself being entranced. He was suddenly as impatient as a teenager, without the least bit of control, then, just as abruptly, even that was taken away from him.

His plan had been to bind her to him with passion, but when she walked away just now without the least hesitation, he was the one who nearly fell to his knees to beg for the privilege of sleeping in the same room with her.

It was beginning to look like he had caught the same mental illness as Will Kirkwood and Bruce Hackett had.

Perhaps Kelly really was a siren who lured men to their destruction.

He replayed that conclusion in his head, recalled the picture of her posing for him on her bed, and chuckled softly. She might be luring him to destruction, but dear God, what a way to go!

Kelly awoke the next morning with fresh resolve. All the reasons she'd originally had for keeping Luke at arm's length made even more sense after last night's near disaster. No more wine for her until he was on his way back to his proper time and place!

In the meantime, she decided that they would have a brief discussion about it this morning, then she would figure out a way to keep him so busy today, he wouldn't have time to think about . . . *it*.

She could hear the shower going in her bathroom, so she went downstairs, started the coffee, and returned to take her own shower before he emerged.

By the time she dried her hair, put on some makeup, and joined him downstairs, it was nearly ten o'clock. "Good morning," she said cheerfully and headed straight for the coffeepot. "I hope you slept well." While her hands were occupied, he came up behind her, slipped his arms around her waist, and kissed her neck.

"Good morning, and not as well as I might have under different circumstances. I showered this morning, and I'm very pleased to announce that there isn't a single trace of the rash left . . . anywhere."

She felt her pulse quicken beneath his lips and had to remind herself why he had to be discouraged. *I do not need another unhappy ending in my life!* Right. Stiffening her posture, she eased out of his embrace. "We have to talk."

Luke ran his hands through his hair with a frustrated sigh. "If man had to choose the one sentence he most dreads hearing from a woman, I think that would be it."

As she took her coffee to the table, she tried to put him at ease with a little humor. "I can think of a better one. How about, 'Honey, I'm pregnant.' That one sure scared the hell out of Will."

Returning to his chair across from her, Luke studied her face with narrowed eyes. "I thought you said you were a virgin when you got married."

She took a sip of coffee to wash down the emotions that always rose when she thought about babies. "I was. I got pregnant six years later. But only for about two and a half months."

"What happened?" he asked quietly.

"Miscarriage. It wasn't any big problem, just one of those things."

"And you never got pregnant again?"

She let out a dry laugh. "That would have been kind of tough. Will and I were down to having sex about once a month before that. My getting pregnant at all was completely accidental. Afterward, he never touched me again. Like I said, the idea of fatherhood scared the hell out of him. I guess he thought having a baby would mean he'd have to grow up himself."

Luke reached over and covered her hand with his. "I'm sorry."

She shrugged and tried to withdraw her hand, but he held it more firmly. "Luke, I—"

"No. Let me say something first. You're acting like what you just told me doesn't mean anything to you, and yet, I could almost feel your heart breaking. Not only did your husband stop showing you physical affection, he stole your natural right to be a mother."

"*What?*" She needed to hear him repeat those words so that she could decide if he was being a macho-pig or an intuitive genius.

"You told me that women's rights were expanded along with those of other minorities, but if your husband refused to have sex with you, and you wouldn't consider an extramarital affair, then he was taking away your freedom of choice about whether to have children or not."

She decided he was a genius, and she truly resented him for voicing such a painful truth. Subconsciously she had probably always felt that way, but for whatever reason, she had successfully repressed it. Now, with his amateur shrink act, he had peeled back the heavy, protective curtain and forced her to look directly at her loss.

He released her hand and leaned back. "I shouldn't have said that, should I? Minding my own business has never been one of my strong characteristics."

His worried expression made her forgive him

for being right. "You weren't out of line. It was my own fault for bringing it up. And speaking of accepting blame—"

"Uh-oh."

She swallowed hard and began again. "Last night . . . don't get me wrong, I mean, I find you incredibly attractive, almost irresistible, but I have to resist. If I hadn't had that wine maybe my mind would have stayed clear about . . ."

"You've changed your mind," he said, succinctly summarizing her intended speech. "Okay."

"Okay? Just like that?" She had arguments ready to present. Why wasn't he demanding an explanation?

"Of course, just like that. I already told you, the decision is yours. I have no interest in making love to a woman who doesn't want me."

"It's not that I don't—" She stopped herself from talking in circles. He'd agreed, and that's all she wanted out of this discussion. Right? She listened for a confirming answer, but none came.

Luke took her hand again and squeezed it. "Really, it's okay, but I get to say one more thing and then we drop it. Your ex-husband was a jerk. Any rational man, myself being in front of the line, would consider it a privilege to father a child with you." He gave her a moment to let that sink in, then released her hand. "Now, what's on today's agenda?"

She could barely believe she was off the hook so easily, but she knew better than to press her luck. "Well, first I have to make that appointment with Reid O'Neill's secretary. Otherwise, we've done as much analyzing as we can do at this time, and we can't visit Mary Beth until tomorrow, so I thought we could be tourists today."

"Sounds good to me. Where are we going?"

"I thought we could have lunch in Underground Atlanta." His strange expression reminded her that he wouldn't know what that was. "It's a historical site that was part of the underground system used by escaping slaves. About eight years ago, it was developed into a mall. You'll understand when you see it.

"From there, I thought we could go see the Martin Luther King, Jr., National Historical Site. After that you'd have a choice of the High Museum of Art—it has a great Renaissance exhibit—or I could take you to see the Cyclorama at Grant Park. That's this enormous circular painting of the 1864 Battle of Atlanta. The Atlanta Zoo is there also. On the opposite side of town is Six Flags Over Georgia, if you like amusement parks."

"Six Flags was getting off the ground the last time I was here. I like amusement parks, but I'd rather see some of the other places first. Yes to the Underground. And absolutely yes to the King site. I'll pass on the museum, but a visit to the park sounds great. I always meant to see the Cyclorama, but never quite got around to it, and I do love a good zoo."

"Really?" she said with some surprise. "Me,

too. I'm practically one of the family, I'm there so often. Watching the animals sometimes helps me give unusual traits to my characters. Did you ever see Stone Mountain? I don't remember when it was completed."

"If you're talking about the carvings of the Confederate heroes, they had just restarted work on the project last year, I mean, in sixty-four. There was a lot of excitement generated about it. How did it turn out?"

She smiled. "You'll have to see it with your own eyes, but it's best to visit at night. So that's where we'll finish up."

Once that was decided, Kelly called O'Neill's secretary and was able to schedule an appointment at one o'clock on Friday, but only if she would agree to come to his home for lunch. She let the woman know that her assistant would be accompanying her.

They were halfway out the door when she remembered to grab her cap for him to protect his scalp from the sun.

Kelly had suggested lunch in Underground Atlanta because of the number of choices Luke would have. It hadn't occurred to her how fascinated he would be by all the shops. He insisted on going inside every one, no matter what they were selling. Every few seconds he would pick something up or point to it and ask her about it. For the next hour, she found herself giving him a crash course in commercial marketing.

From time to time, she would glance around to make sure no one was listening too closely to their odd conversation. That was probably the only reason she noticed the man.

"Don't turn around right away," she told Luke. "But I think we're being followed."

He continued to study the aviator-style glasses with the mirrored lenses he had in his hand. As he tried them on and looked in the mirror on the counter, he said, "White male, brown hair, mid-thirties, wearing a light blue T-shirt with the words 'Hard Rock Cafe' across the front and a pair of blue jeans with a rip across the left knee. I spotted him about fifteen minutes after we got here." He grinned at his own reflection. "These are so hip!"

"The word is cool, and they're the perfect answer to hiding your eyes." She motioned to the sales clerk. "We'll take these." As she paid for the glasses, she murmured to Luke, "So, you agree that he's following us?"

"Why do you think I've made a point of going into every single store? He's either a tail, a purse-snatcher, or a pervert. But I figure we're better off pretending we don't notice him so that he doesn't get sneakier on us. How about lunch now? I'd love a big juicy cheeseburger smothered in onions with a mountain of french fries on the side!"

"Geez, your cholesterol count is going to go through the ceiling."

"My what?"

"Never mind. It's just another one of those things we health-conscious people of the nineties have to worry about."

The man did not follow them into the restaurant, and he was nowhere in sight when they came out. They continued to keep a lookout for him as they went to Kelly's car, but either he'd grown bored with his game or he had gotten sneakier as Luke feared.

The Martin Luther King, Jr., National Historic Site was a beautiful place for solemn contemplation, but as they stood looking across the pond that surrounded the tomb, Luke suddenly grasped Kelly's hand and squeezed. "Don't look now, but our friend is back. He's wearing a cowboy hat and changed into a plaid shirt, but I recognize the jeans. Same rip. I'd say we have the answer to one of our questions. He's not only tailing us, he's probably a pro."

Kelly raised her brows and whispered, "You mean like a hit man?"

He smothered a laugh. "No, I mean like a private detective, although not a very good one. He must have changed his clothes while we were eating."

"But how did he know where we were going?"

"My guess is he followed the car. That's undoubtedly how he got to the Underground."

She could not resist a surreptitious glance around to see the man for herself. "Then he had to have been waiting outside my town house for us to leave. Why didn't we see him?"

"He's probably driving a very inconspicuous car—unlike us—and we weren't looking for a tail before. Now we will."

The contents of her stomach objected to her sudden nervousness. "Why would someone be following us?"

"Good question. My first answer would be that your ex-husband hired him. Second guess would be your weird attorney friend. Third, maybe your preliminary snooping has already caused someone to worry."

She shook her head. "I can't believe either Will or Bruce would go to such an extreme after we made it clear to both of them that we were having an affair. What more could they possibly hope to learn by having me followed? As to your third supposition, I'm sure I haven't said anything to anyone that might raise suspicions about what we're up to."

"Maybe someone who works at the newspaper noticed which articles we were pulling and passed the information along to someone else. Someone who could be negatively affected by your digging up dead bodies."

She gave that some thought, then shook her head. "That's too far-fetched. Besides, I didn't see anyone getting particularly nosy, and you can't just tap into someone else's microfiche the way you can a computer."

His eyes widened. "You can do that?"

"Yes, but that's another lesson. Look, whoever this guy's working for, he's giving me the creeps. If you're ready, I'd really like to get moving and see if we can lose him on the next leg."

He squeezed her hand again. "Don't worry, babe," he said in a bad Bogart imitation. "With you at the wheel and me riding shotgun, even Sam Spade wouldn't stand a chance." He finished it off with a wink that made her giggle. "Now, we're going to leisurely walk to the car and take a really long time pulling out. Hopefully, we'll see what kind of car he's driving. He can't change vehicles as easily as he changes clothes."

Before getting into the Camaro, they made a show of spreading a map out on the hood and studying it until Luke saw which car the cowboy got into. "God, most of these cars look the same—like boxes on wheels. No wonder we didn't spot him. He's driving one of those boxes, a white one. Okay, fold up the map and get in slowly. If he has any brains, he'll pull out in front of us to throw us off, and maybe we'll get a chance to get a better look at the car and license plate."

Since she was completely inexperienced with this sort of thing, and he seemed to know what he was doing, Kelly followed his instructions precisely. To her delight, the cowboy behaved exactly as Luke predicted, and she was not only able to identify that it was a Toyota Celica, but they got his license plate number as well.

Luke wrote it down as she drove toward the exit. "Great. Now, which would be easier for you, trying to shake him on side roads or the expressway?"

She grinned. "I'll take the high road any day. Fasten your seat belt, *babe.* It's the law now." By the time she was on I-75 again, the Toyota managed to maneuver into a position behind her. For a few minutes, she maintained the speed limit in the far left-hand lane, occasionally checking the rearview mirror.

Suddenly Luke sat forward and gaped at a sign. "Did that say Atlanta-Fulton County Stadium?"

"Yes. It's off the next exit. Wasn't that here when you were?"

"What baseball team plays there?" he asked excitedly.

She glanced at him curiously. "The Braves. Why? Do you like baseball?"

"Like doesn't begin to describe—"

Abruptly, she pressed the accelerator to the floor and cut across all three lanes of traffic, barely avoiding an accident, and making the exit ramp by a hair.

"Holy sh—" Luke released his death grip on the dashboard as she slowed down to make the turn at the end of the ramp. "What the hell was that?"

She winked at him. "A strategic maneuver with an ulterior motive. Please note that the Toyota is no longer behind us."

He scanned the area, then took a calming breath. "And the ulterior motive?"

"Since you like baseball so much, we're going to go by the stadium and see if there's a game tonight."

"That would be great. You can't imagine how much I had been looking forward to the Braves moving to Atlanta. I was a big Tiger fan in Detroit, so I really missed not being able to see a big league game here. The Milwaukee team was scheduled to start playing at this stadium in—"

"Nineteen-sixty-six," she said before he could. "Of course, that was the second move for the team; the first being from Boston to Milwaukee in 1953."

"That's right," he said with some surprise. "What about Hank Aaron? Did he stay with the Braves or did he get traded?"

"He stayed with them through the 1974 season, then went back to Milwaukee with the Brewers. But in that last year in Atlanta, on April eighth, he hit his seven hundred fifteenth home run, breaking Babe Ruth's record, which, by the way, did not make certain white supremacists all that happy. I believe the abuse he and his family had to take were part of his decision to leave."

Luke was staring at her with narrowed eyes. "Did you say the Brewers? I never heard of them."

"Yes. In 1969, both the National and American leagues expanded to twelve teams with two divisions, eastern and western. One of the teams was the Seattle Pilots, who then moved to Milwaukee in 1970 and changed their name to the Brewers."

Luke shook his head. "I'm in shock."

"Over what part?"

"The part where a *girl* is telling me baseball facts. How do you know that stuff?"

She smiled. "My dad was a big fan. I'm an only child. The more I knew about the game, the more time he spent with me. I couldn't help but be a fanatic about the game. You should see me play *Jeopardy!* I've got the sports category licked." She realized he had no idea what *Jeopardy!* was, and added, "It's an extremely popular television game show. Trivia—little-known and generally useless facts—is very big with my generation."

He made a face at that. "So-o-o . . . who won the World Series in . . . 1945?"

She clucked her tongue at him. "Too easy. In both 1935 and 1945, the Detroit Tigers won over Chicago. and for your information, they also took the championship in 1968 and 1984. Are you impressed?"

"Hell, I found a girl who likes baseball. I'm in love!"

"Uh, uh, uh, I warned you about that falling-in-love-with-me business."

"Well, maybe I'll get to meet your father one day and thank him for filling your head with useless facts."

"I doubt if you'll be around long enough to

meet my dad." A period of static silence followed that statement until she spotted the stadium entrance that could take her to the advance ticket sales window. "Cross your fingers," she told Luke as she came to a stop. "Why don't you stay here? I'll only be a few minutes."

It was closer to twenty when she returned with two tickets and a brown paper bag. "There's a game tomorrow night, Atlanta versus the San Diego Padres—another one of those teams added in 1969—and I couldn't get box seats, but we will be behind the Braves' dugout. I figure we'll have plenty of time Friday morning to drive back to Charming for our lunch appointment. And this is for you," she said handing him the bag.

He pulled a baseball cap out and laughed when he saw the embroidered words, "Detroit Tigers."

She was delighted by his reaction. "They had hats for every team, but I thought you might like that one best."

He tossed her cap in the back seat, put on his new one, and checked himself out in the mirror.

"You should still trim your hair before we go see Mary Beth tomorrow," Kelly noted. "I could do it for you in the morning."

Remembering how he had pleaded to keep his hair intact during the electrocution, he leaned back in his seat and grinned. He had had his juicy cheeseburger and fries for lunch, he was being chauffeured around in a sports car by a beautiful woman, and he was going to see a baseball game tomorrow night. He didn't care what the hell she did to his hair.

From the stadium, she drove to Grant Park. They both stayed alert for any sign of the white Toyota, but she seemed to have successfully lost him for the moment.

"You didn't warn me that she's an ex-race car driver!" Evan Dillard complained to his client.

"Hmmph. That doesn't sound like her. Are you sure he wasn't the one driving?"

"I can tell the difference between a man and a woman."

"Hmmph. Considering what I'm paying you, I certainly hope so. Did you learn *anything* worthwhile?"

"Depends on what you call worthwhile," the private investigator replied. "You said they were lovers, but I didn't see anything that confirmed that. Based on lights going on and off last night, I'd say they slept in separate rooms. And all the time I watched them today, I only saw him take her hand once, and that was more like to get her attention. No kissy-face like new lovers usually do."

"Do you have a theory?"

"Yeah. You said she's famous and has money. I think she's hired herself a bodyguard. I definitely recognized an attitude of protection and surveillance about him."

The client laughed out loud. Kelly wouldn't hire

a bodyguard even if she knew someone was stalking her. She treasured her privacy too much. She and this Duke fellow had made sure he believed they were lovers, but if that were the case, why separate bedrooms? And if her houseguest wasn't a bodyguard or a new lover, what was he to her? Once that question was answered, he could figure out how to get him out of the way.

Still, it would be much better for him if the man *was* a bodyguard. "I think you're wrong about him being a bodyguard, but in case you're not, isn't there some way you could verify that?"

"Sure. I could show his picture around. See if he's local. If he's a pro, he should have prints on file somewhere. It wouldn't be too hard to pick up a set off her car and look for a match."

"Good. Do that. And keep following them. I want to know who Duke McCoy is, and what he's doing with Kelly. She's very vulnerable right now and I wouldn't want anything to happen to her." *At least not without my being directly involved.*

Chapter Eleven

"I swear I'm not making this up! People were lined up on both sides of the street, watching this guy in a girl's majorette outfit do cartwheels down the center line with cars whizzing by him on both sides, and every time he turns, the little skirt flops down and he's got this red ribbon tied around his pri—, uh, private parts."

"Stop!" Kelly pleaded, wiping a tear from the corner of her eye. "I've got to catch my breath."

"But I haven't told you my elephant story yet."

"Don't you dare," she said wagging a finger at him. "Eat your high cholesterol dinner before it gets cold."

As she watched him heap a chunk of butter and a spoonful of sour cream on his baked potato, she decided she couldn't remember the last time she'd laughed so hard or so long. It had all started when they were watching the monkees in the zoo and Luke was reminded of a funny story he had cov-

ered back in Detroit when he first started out as
a cub reporter. The more she laughed at his stories, the more outrageous they got. At least half a
dozen times she asked his permission to incorpo-
rate one of his tales in her book.

She glanced at her watch to make sure they
were still on schedule. Knowing what was coming
later, she had kept Luke moving from the Cyclorama, through the zoo, and on to dinner. It was a
casual-style restaurant that she chose because it
was only a few minutes from Stone Mountain. The
only thing he cared about was being able to order
a thick steak.

In the back of her mind, she still wondered
about the man in the white Toyota, but that concern was pretty much shoved aside by thoughts
of what a good time she'd had with Luke all day.
She was fairly sure that she had never met a man
with whom she had so much in common. From their
careers to the toppings on their pizza to their love
of baseball and zoos, they could have been
hatched from one mold.

And they say *opposites* attract!

Of course, she'd probably get tired of being
around someone who thought like she did all the
time, and liked all the things she did. It would
probably be too much of a good thing. Perhaps,
if he wasn't quite so handsome, and charming,
and funny, if he had a few flaws, his perfection
might not get on her nerves right away. Perhaps
if he wasn't quite so considerate of her feelings.

But he was the poster boy of consideration. Not once did he bring up her change of heart about their relationship. Not once did he do a single thing that could be called flirtatious. He had accepted her decision, and that was that. They were friends. Who had everything in common. Friends whose physical attraction to each other almost set the bed on fire last night.

"Are you feeling all right?" Luke asked.

She blinked at him. "Yes, why?"

"Your face got very flushed a second ago. I was worried that something didn't agree with you."

She shook her head, shrugged, and took a sip of iced tea. Something wasn't agreeing with her all right, but it wasn't the food. It was a little something called celibacy. She wondered what he'd say if she told him that. It was easy to blame her wanton behavior last night on too much wine. What could she blame it on today? Too much laughter?

As they were finishing their meal, a family with a little baby girl was seated at the table next to them. Instead of quickly looking away, as she usually did, Kelly watched the mother prop the child up in her infant seat so that she could see everyone around her. Unexpectedly, the baby looked right at Luke and smiled. He wiggled his fingers at the child and she kicked her legs excitedly in response.

"Did you ever have any children?" she asked him.

He shook his head while swallowing the last bite of steak. "Never married."

She smiled. "You don't have to be married to have children, you know."

He raised one eyebrow and with more than a touch of sarcasm, said, "Really? Are you the same woman I was talking to over coffee this morning?"

His remark confused her for a moment, then slowly, she made sense of it. He probably hadn't meant to say anything earth-shattering just then, but it had that effect on her nonetheless. She motioned to the waitress for their check as her mind sorted out the new awareness.

She wanted a baby. Her husband had not. Now she had no husband and no prospects on the horizon. She was already thirty-one and would soon be closing in on the age when it would no longer be easy or safe to give birth. Thus, she'd previously come to the old-fashioned, narrow-minded conclusion that she would never experience the joys of motherhood. Why hadn't she thought of this on her own?

The waitress brought their check and Kelly handed her a credit card, which launched a brief explanation of the use of plastic and the economy's growing dependency on credit.

Luke's expression darkened. "Do you have any idea how much money you've spent today?" He snorted. "Today? How about, since I landed on your doorstep."

"I told you, it's not a problem."

"Well, it's beginning to feel like a problem to me. I need to find a way to start paying you back."

She clucked her tongue at him. "That's ridiculous. Change places with me for a minute. What if I landed on your doorstep instead? Wouldn't you do as much for me?"

His response was held up while the waitress returned and Kelly signed the charge slip. By the time they'd left the restaurant, however, he had his answer ready. "Yes, I would do as much for you. But can you honestly say that you wouldn't feel at all obligated to pay me back in any way?"

"Of course, well, I mean, I would . . . Okay, you win. We'll figure out a way for you to pay me back. How fast can you type?"

He chuckled. "At least as fast as you can think up the sentences."

"That's it then. You can be my secretary slash research assistant, at a rate of pay . . . commensurate with your living expenses." She unlocked the Camaro's doors with the remote on her key ring.

"Have you ever hired a secretary slash research assistant before?" he asked with a skeptical look as he got into the passenger's side.

"No, but I always thought it would be nice to have one."

"Not good enough. Keep thinking."

"Are you a neat painter? I wouldn't mind changing the colors in my town house."

"And when would I do this job? While you're sticking your nose into everyone's business in Charming?"

"Oh. Okay, so I'll keep thinking."

The parking area for Stone Mountain was nearly full when they pulled in. She had hoped it wouldn't be too crowded, but it was a clear summer night and obviously a lot of people had had the same idea she had.

"Now you get to see why I brought the quilt," she told Luke as she got it out of the back.

As soon as he caught sight of the enormous carvings on the stone wall, he stopped walking. "Good God. It's incredible!"

She gave him a nudge. "As they say, 'you ain't seen nuttin' yet.' Come help me find an empty spot on the grass."

Not long after they were settled, the show began. Symphonic music poured over them as brilliant beams of colored light danced in the air.

"How are they doing that?" Luke asked in utter amazement.

"Laser beams and computer technology. There's a whole industry developed around special effects like this. Just watch."

And he did, with his mouth agape most of the time. The truth was, Kelly didn't really know how they made it look like the horses were galloping or how it appeared that Jefferson Davis's chiseled mouth formed words. She thought it was more wondrous not knowing how the magic worked.

She had experienced this magic several times in the past, whenever someone from out of town was visiting, but tonight, seeing it through Luke's eyes, made it seem brand new for her as well. Without stopping to analyze her actions, she reached over and tucked a strand of hair behind his ear.

He glanced at her, and she smiled. That was all it took, a touch and a smile, and everything changed again.

Wordlessly, he shifted position so that she was seated in front of him between his thighs, and as he wrapped his arms around her, she relaxed against his chest . . . and sighed with utter contentment.

They remained that way, gazing up at the stars, long after the show ended and most of the audience dispersed. The only people left were lovers, savoring a few more minutes of wonderment. As if the laser beams had illuminated a dark spot in her mind, Kelly made a monumental decision in those minutes, but she decided to wait until they got home before sharing it with Luke.

When she suggested it was time to leave, she sensed his reluctance and understood. After all, they had enjoyed a beautiful day together and, as far as he knew, it was now over. If she told him of her decision, she was certain it would cheer him up again, she just wasn't all that certain they'd make it out of the park without getting arrested.

They were both quiet on the drive back to her

town house, and she used the time to mentally rehearse her speech. As they entered her neighborhood, he suggested she drive around the block to see if their tail had returned ahead of them. Since they couldn't see the man or his car, they put him out of their minds for the night.

When she turned the engine off in her driveway, Luke asked, "Do I need to apologize for something?"

"Why would you think that?"

"I had a great time today. I thought you did, too, but you seemed to have tensed up and— Did I misread a signal back there? I wouldn't have held you if I thought—"

She pressed her finger to his lips. "Hush. If I hadn't wanted you to hold me, I would have told you. If I seemed tense, it was only because I was thinking. Now, I'm all finished thinking, so let's go inside so I can tell you what it was about."

Her words took the frown off his face, but left the confusion. Taking his hand, she led him inside to the couch and sat down. "I've changed my mind," she stated simply. His expression softened a bit more, but he was clearly waiting to hear the rest before giving in to a smile.

"I told you I didn't want to have sex for the sake of sex, and that part's still true. But the part about my needing an emotional commitment, well, that's changed. The fact is, you can't make me any promises, even if you did fall in love with me. However, I think we like each other a lot and that, plus the physical attraction, well, I've decided that's enough."

He leaned toward her for a kiss, but she stopped him. "Wait. There's more. I know I don't have to tell you this, but it would be deceitful of me not to. I thought of a way you can pay me back for everything, for as long as you're here."

His frown returned. "If your intention is to drive me nuts, you're succeeding. How did we go from having sex to my payback?"

Her cheeks flushed, but she got the words past her embarrassment. "Sex is the payback."

His mouth opened and closed twice before he could respond. "Are you saying you want to pay me for . . . *servicing* you? Like a gigolo? I don't know whether to laugh or be insulted. First of all, that offer doesn't fit your personality. Secondly, after last night, you know very well how much I want to, *ahem, service* you, without having to be paid for it."

She had gone this far, she had to finish it. "Yes, I know, that's why I feel safe in making you this . . . um, proposition. You see, it's not just the sex, although I'm pretty sure I'll enjoy that, it's the . . . the fringe benefit you could give me."

"Kelly, there are several parts of my body, my brain being one of them, that would appreciate it if you would get to the point sometime soon."

She swallowed hard, took a deep breath, and looked directly into his eyes. "I want you to get me pregnant." While he absorbed that shocker, she continued. "You gave me the idea over dinner, and this morning you said you'd consider it a privilege. Well, I'd consider it a privilege to be impregnated by a man with your mental and physical characteristics. Women have babies without husbands all the time. True, it's not really my style, but I could adjust, and people don't care about whether a child is legitimate or not anymore." Tears filled her eyes as she finished her plea. "I want a baby very badly, Luke. Will you give me that gift before you leave?"

"Good God," he murmured. "You're serious."

She sniffled and swiped at her eyes. "Perfectly."

"When was your last period?"

She was thrown by the abruptness of the question, but she answered. "Last week."

"Are you regular?"

"Yes, but—" She stopped talking as he suddenly rose and headed for the stairs.

On the second step, he turned and snapped his fingers at her. "What are you waiting for? You're probably ovulating while you're sitting there. Come on, Miss Kirkwood, we better get to it. I wouldn't want you to think you weren't getting your money's worth. You might have to give me some help though. I've never tried performing under pressure before."

"You're angry."

He marched back and glared down at her. "You're damn right—no, I'm not *angry*. I'm *pissed*! And why shouldn't I be? How would you like it if I looked you straight in the eye and said, 'I don't really want you to put your filthy hands on me, but I'd really like your egg, so I guess I'll have to put up with the rest of you.' Huh, Kelly? How would that make you feel?"

Her bottom lip quivered and she tried to bite it to make it stop, but that only made it worse. The tears that she had held back before suddenly burst forth, and she bolted up off the couch. "I'm sorry," she cried as she ran up the stairs.

Luke slumped into the spot she'd vacated. What had just happened?

It was clear that one of them had lost all their marbles, but he wasn't sure which one.

He wanted her, *a lot*, yet, instead of carrying her off to bed at her request, he yelled at her.

She wanted him—at least he thought so—but her personal morals were in the way of their having a good time. So, she came up with a way to circumvent her guilt, give him a way to pay her back for her generosity, and possibly wind up with the one thing she seemed to want most in the world.

When he put it that way, there wasn't much question about which one of them was crazy. He soothed his bruised ego by reminding himself that they'd almost made love last night, before she thought about making babies, and assured himself that if she wasn't extremely attracted to him, she wouldn't have asked for his help in such a personal matter.

Was what she had suggested so much worse than his plan to seduce her into forgetting their so-called mission so that he could stick around? At least she had come right out and told him about her ulterior motive, where his plan had been one of deception. Of course, he knew by this morning that it wasn't a workable plan. To seduce someone, you have to be the one in control, and if anyone held the reins in this house, it was Kelly.

Suddenly he remembered the thought he'd had last night about how the best seduction was when a lady thought it was all her idea. This may not have been how he'd planned it, but it sure as hell had the same result.

Gathering his misplaced mental marbles, he headed up the stairs to try to repair the damage he'd done.

The door to the guest bedroom was closed, so he knocked lightly. When he heard no response, he said her name, but she still didn't answer. Not willing to accept silence, he tested the doorknob and, when he found it unlocked, he eased the door open part way.

Kelly curled up in a fetal ball and pulled the covers over her head. "Go away."

Instead of obeying, he sat down on the bed beside her. "I want to talk to you," he said and stroked the part of the mound that he assumed was a shoulder.

"I don't want to talk to you now. I'll be fine in the morning. Talk to me then."

Her command would have been much easier to take seriously if she didn't make him think of the big tortoise they'd seen playing peek-a-boo at the zoo. "Sorry, can't wait till morning. You see, I have these sperm that get all dressed up in tuxedos to take this very special egg to the prom . . ."

That got her attention. She flipped the covers off and sat up with a growl. "Is that what you came in here for? It wasn't enough that I made a total fool of myself downstairs, you had to come up here to make fun of me some more? I suppose now you'll add me to your repertoire of nutty stories you tell at cocktail parties!"

And that got him right back. "God, no, Kelly. I was only trying to make *you* laugh. Stupid idea, huh?"

She laid down on her side with her back to him. "Just go away."

He sighed loudly, got up, and walked out, closing the door softly behind him. Two seconds later he came back in the door and sat down beside her again. "I want to talk to you."

Glaring at him over her shoulder, she asked, "What are you doing?" His face was a picture of contrition.

"I'm starting over. In case you didn't notice, my first try was a dud."

She rolled her eyes, clucked her tongue, then gave in. Propping pillows behind her, she scooted up against the headboard and nodded for him to speak his piece.

"I acted like an ass, and I'm sorry."

"There's no need to apologize. I obviously insulted you. I didn't mean to, but I see how you could have taken it that way. I am not angry with you, if that's what you think. I'm angry at myself, but like I said, I'll be over it by morning."

"Why are you always so willing to take the blame for everything? Wait. Don't answer that. You're making me forget what I intended to say. You caught me off guard downstairs, and I reacted from my gut. There is nothing I want more than to finish what we started last night, and if the result was a baby, well, like I said, I'd consider it an honor that you chose me to help.

"Maybe it would help my case if you kept in mind that only this morning I had to switch gears from planning a night making love to you to hands-off completely. You've got me spinning in so many directions, I don't know which way you want me to go."

"You're right. And I'm really sorry."

He took her hands in his. "And there you go taking all the blame again. At least let me share it. There was nothing wrong with your proposition. Only the way I reacted to it. Everything you said was perfectly logical. I would have probably come to the same conclusion if I were in your shoes."

She cocked her head at him. "Is it possible that you were surprised to hear *logical* thinking from a woman? So surprised, that instead of reacting with typical male logic, you became *emotional*, like a woman?"

His mouth curved up on one side. "You mean like a yin-yang balancing act?"

She shrugged. "It's an explanation I could live with."

He gazed deeply into her eyes until he was certain she meant that. "Then here's to yin," he said and softly kissed one side of her mouth. "And yang." He placed another kiss on the opposite side.

She framed his face with her hands and held him still. "May they have a beautiful meeting somewhere in the middle."

As their mouths came together to seal their new understanding, Luke slipped off his shoes and stretched out alongside her. After a moment his lips moved along her cheek to her ear, and his hand rested on her lower stomach. "I really am looking forward to making a baby with you . . . if you're sure that's what you want."

His warm breath against her neck made her shiver, and she covered his hand with hers. "I'm sure," she whispered back into his ear.

"And you're not going to change your mind in the morning?"

"Uh-uh. No more mind-changing."

"That's good. Because I've heard that this job doesn't always get finished with one try."

He nipped her earlobe and the shiver shot all

the way down her spine. "Mmm. Yes, I've heard
the same thing. Sometimes it takes a lot of work."

"It could probably run into overtime."

His tongue traced a line down to her collarbone
and she raised her chin to give him freer access.
"You might have to keep at it morning, noon,
and night."

He shifted his body so that he was hovering
over her, then slowly lowered himself so that yin
and yang were meeting as they were meant to.
He rolled his hips against hers and a spear of
pleasure made her gasp.

"I . . . can tell . . . that you're definitely . . . up
to the job."

"Whatever it takes," he said, repeating the
movement that kept taking her breath away. "I
intend to satisfy you even if I have to do it
over . . ." Again he made her gasp. ". . . and
over . . ." Again. ". . . and over."

She whimpered aloud as her whole body con-
vulsed with an unfamiliar sensation, and he
quickly gave her his mouth so she could take
some part of him into her to accompany the
feeling.

She drew his tongue into her mouth and caressed it with her own. If it were possible, she
would absorb every part of him into every part
of her, just like this. Her hands moved over him,
desperate to touch bare flesh, and again, he gave
her what she needed before she understood it
herself.

In one swift movement, he pulled off his T-shirt and tossed it to the floor. Then he sat very still while she examined his offering.

You may not have the practical experience, she told herself as she slid her hands over his shoulders, down his arms, and back up, *but you do have the book knowledge. He might even appreciate a little experimentation.*

Ever so slowly she let her palms glide over his chest, not quite touching at first, just close enough to move the hairs. When she could see that he liked that, she switched to exploring at closer range with her fingertips, carefully avoiding his nipples. The way they contracted anyway revealed how anxious they were for attention, so she outlined them with her nails and rolled the hardening peaks between her fingers.

His sharp intake of breath was her confirmation that she was indeed doing it right. Encouraged, she replaced her fingers with her lips and tickled him with her tongue and teeth until he grasped her shoulders and gently forced her back.

"Enough," he said on a heavy exhale and rose to his feet. "I'd like you to do something else for me."

She thought she understood and undid the top button on his jeans.

"Not that," he said with a grin and backed up. "Not yet anyway. First, I'd like you to do what you did last night, only more."

She was willing to do whatever he liked, but

she had no clue what that was. "Can you be a little more explicit?"

His smile broadened. "Actually, I can be very explicit. I want you to pose for me, like you did, only with nothing on at all. Just you and your hair. You have no idea how much that excited me when I opened my eyes and saw you . . . like that. It was like having a *Playboy* centerfold come to life, only better. None of the women I've ever seen in that magazine are anywhere close to being as beautiful or sexy as you are."

Never in her life did she imagine she'd be flattered by a man comparing her to a *Playboy* bunny, but she was much more than flattered. The idea of posing nude for him, seductively exhibiting herself for the sole purpose of inciting lust in him was surprisingly arousing to her. "All right. I'll be your centerfold model, but only if you'll be my photographer. That means no touching, only pictures, *pretend* pictures, that is."

He hadn't expected her to go along, let alone improvise. He was absolutely delighted. "Is it okay if I sit?" She nodded, and he moved the rocking chair to the foot of the bed. He also took the opportunity to unzip his jeans to give himself more room to grow.

As he sat down, she outlined the rest of the game. "You have to close your eyes, as if you were the camera itself. The lens can only open when I say 'click,' then it has to close again after five seconds, so I can get ready for the next picture. And you don't move from that chair. Agreed?"

He nodded and casually leaned back, as if this wasn't the most mind-blowing thing a woman had ever done for him.

"I'm not going to start until you close the shutter," she reminded him.

He closed his eyes and wondered just how aggressive she could get if he kept encouraging her.

Kelly felt a twinge of unease as she started undressing, but firmly squelched it. This was her chance to do all the nontraditional things her heroines always got to do, to freely explore her sexuality without fear of rejection or abandonment. This could be . . . no, it *was* every woman's fantasy. With that in mind, she kicked off her panties and posed on the bed with her hair covering all the essential parts.

"Click."

He raised his eyelids and mentally photographed every delectable inch of her. When she repeated the trigger word a few rapid heartbeats later, he obediently closed his eyes again.

The way he practically devoured her with his eyes gave her the courage to be a little bolder with each pose. By the fourth shot, she pushed all her hair behind her and lifted her breasts, tempting him to replace her hands with his. He almost came out of the chair on that one, but then she said, "click," and he fell back again.

She soon discovered that the sensuous posing

was at least as arousing to her as it was to him. Her heart was racing, her breath was shallow and erratic, and she was getting very, very damp between her legs. And here she thought she was doing this to turn *him* on.

By the eighth pose, the game was becoming more frustrating than satisfying. She was more than ready to move on, and she had no doubt that he was also.

As he opened his eyes for the next picture, he saw her on her knees, with her bottom facing him. Breaking her own rules, she peeked over her shoulder at him and she ran her tongue over her upper lip. He didn't know whether to laugh or cry, so he pounced.

She squealed and rolled to her back a second before he landed on top, grasped her wrists, and held them over her head.

"*That* was cruel," he said and nipped the tip of her nose.

She giggled and squirmed beneath his weight.

"You think you're funny, huh? That's doubly cruel. In fact, I think that makes you downright bad. And do you know what happens to bad girls?"

She stopped squirming and narrowed her eyes at him. "Don't even think about it," she warned sternly.

"Bad girls get spankings," he said with a lascivious eyebrow wiggle, just to let her know he was still playing.

"Your zipper is scratching me," she said, hoping to distract him. "Why don't you finish getting undressed now?"

He grinned, seeing right through her ploy. "You do it for me." She tried to free her hands, but he held tight. "Uh-uh. Use your feet. After some of those poses, I'm sure you're flexible enough."

She didn't think it was possible, but if it kept his mind off spankings, she was willing to give it a try. Bending her knees up on each side of him, she discovered that she actually could hook her toes into the waistband of his jeans and maneuver them down his thighs and past his knees. The bigger surprise was the effect the contortion had on her. "*Mmm*," she moaned as she repeated the exercise to de-brief him.

As her moist flesh rubbed directly against his already pulsing erection, he went completely rigid. "Don't move," he muttered through clenched teeth.

"You're not itching again, are you?"

"No. I'm just . . . too close. Just don't move."

"You mean like this?" She purposely disobeyed, pulling her knees all the way up to his ribs, stretching and exposing her entrance more fully to him. He groaned, and she tilted her hips to entice him even more. "I'm close, too, Luke, but I don't want to wait. *Please.* I want to feel you inside of me, *now*!"

On that word he surged forward, filling her with his heat, explosively releasing his tight control, and carrying her with him on a wild ride into space. She clung to him as they soared higher and higher. Whirling and spinning faster with each ragged breath until they crashed headlong into the sun itself.

Gabriel steeled himself against the triumphant sound of Jezebel's laughter. He had been so sure she couldn't win this one! Sometimes he wondered if it was really necessary to give humans quite so much free will. Just look where it's taken Luke and Kelly.

"Half of six is three," Jezebel sang out. "And they've already used up part of the first week. Luke Templeton is practically mine, Gabriel. Why don't you save yourself the next two weeks of aggravation and give up now? I'll go easy on you, I swear."

"He still has plenty of time," the archangel returned in a much more confident tone than he felt.

Ah, well. He'd done as much as he could do. And he knew that Jezebel had not interfered. Kelly made that choice entirely on her own. Now Luke's fate was entirely in her hands.

Gabriel could only pray that Luke did not succeed with his plan to distract her from their mission.

Chapter Twelve

Kelly had no idea how much time passed before she came back down to earth, but when she did, she still had a hard time breathing. Luke's full body weight was on her chest. "Luke?" she whispered and gave his shoulders a nudge. He stirred and took a long, deep breath, which only made it worse for her. "Please, I can't breathe."

He lifted his head and blinked down at her as though wondering how she'd gotten there. Finally full awareness set in, and he quickly rolled off her.

As she filled her lungs, he brought her hand to his lips and kissed the palm. "I'm sorry. That wasn't how I wanted it to go the first time." He glanced down at the tangle of clothing around his ankles and shook his head in bewilderment.

As he finished undressing, she turned onto her side and smiled. "You mean you didn't plan to pass out on me?"

He made a face. "I didn't pass out. Well, not

completely. I just . . . hell, I don't know what happened to me. It never happened like that before."

She arched one brow. "Is that good or bad?"

He chuckled and quickly kissed her. "Oh, it was definitely good, but I wasn't referring to the big finish, I was talking about how soon we got there. This first time I meant to concentrate on making it good for you. Instead, everything was for me."

"Not true at all," she countered. Recalling how easily his ego had been dented before, she determined to give it a boost. "I have a confession to make."

"I'm all ears."

"I've written hundreds of erotic love scenes, without having a whole lot of, um, *hands-on* experience."

"I believe you." He kissed her briefly. "But it didn't show."

She giggled shyly. "Thank you. But what I wanted to tell you is, I never . . . experienced . . . um . . . the big finish."

Cocky male pride filled his eyes. "And now you have?"

She nodded. "Twice, if you count the little one at the beginning. And you know what? It was even better than my imagination."

He laid back and folded his hands behind his head. "Aah, then my work here is done."

She promptly rewarded him by hitting him with her pillow. "Smart-ass!"

In a heartbeat, he had her pinned on her back again and was straddling her hips. "I haven't forgotten that I owe you a spanking."

"Oh no, master," she begged, batting her eyelashes at him and trying not to laugh. "Not that. I'll do anything you say, just spare me that."

He pretended to give her plea some thought, then pulled her up off the bed with him. "All right. You may bathe me. In the magical whirling pool. We'll postpone the spanking for the moment. But if you misbehave again . . ." He shook his index finger at her in warning.

She caught his hand and closed her mouth around his finger, sucking on it as she slowly drew it out again. "Misbehave? I wouldn't think of it."

"God help me," he murmured and led her into the master bath.

While the Jacuzzi filled with hot water, Kelly pinned her hair up so that she wouldn't have to deal with drying it when they were done playing. Thinking that he might enjoy the entire stress-reducing experience, she lit the twelve-colored candles, one of which was vanilla-scented, that lined the back of the tub and started her favorite New Age tape. When the tub was full, she turned on the jets, turned off the lights, and bowed slave-style to Luke. "Your bath awaits, master."

He nodded with satisfaction. "It's good to see that a few things from the sixties caught on. Candles and mystical music. All we need is some good weed."

"That's still around, too, but not in this house. I could get you a beer if you want. There was one left."

He drew her into his arms and smiled down at her. "No thanks. I'm so high on you right now, I don't need anything else." As he dipped his head for a kiss, his hands slid down her back and cupped her bottom, urging her to rise on tiptoes.

She felt his sex stir and her body responded in kind. She would have been happy to forget the bath and go back to bed, but he gently ended the kiss and helped her step into the tub.

The groan of intense pleasure that he emitted as he sank down into the bubbling water made Kelly laugh until he held out his hands in invitation. She knelt down between his thighs and placed her hands on his chest, but he turned her around and made her lie back against him.

"It's time to find out what makes Kelly feel good," he said in a suggestive tone. His wet hands glided up and down her arms and gently massaged her shoulders. "Tonight, when we were at Stone Mountain, sitting like this, do you know what I was thinking about?"

"Riding with the rebel cavalry?" she asked in mock innocence.

"You're close," he said with a chuckle. "Riding was definitely on my mind. Remember how I had my arms around your waist, like this?" He encircled her, and she nestled into his embrace. "I kept telling myself to be content with holding you, but I kept thinking about moving my hands, just a few short inches."

Very slowly, he showed her what he meant until her breasts rested in his hands. As he learned the feel and shape of them, he said, "I have a confession to make to you now. I love long hair on a woman, but this is my real weakness." He kneaded her flesh, alternately squeezing and caressing. "Now that you've given me permission, I may have a hard time letting go."

She chuckled softly at the image that created. "That could become a problem."

He kissed the top of her head. "You have no idea how inventive I can be when I set my mind to it. The question is whether *you* like my hands on you like this." He covered her fullness and pressed her flesh upward. He opened his hands again and brushed his palms over her puckered nipples, and she inhaled deeply. "You seem to like this, but I don't read minds. You're going to have to tell me." He lightly pinched the peaks, then continued to toy with them as he repeated, "Tell me."

"I like."

"What?"

"Your hands on me."

He kissed the top of her head again. "Good girl. Do you think you'd like my hands on any other part of you?" She nodded and he moved his hands up to her shoulders and neck. "Here?"

She closed her eyes as he pressed his thumbs along the muscles. "Mmm-hmm."

"How about here?" His fingers walked down her arms and interlaced with hers, and she nodded again. He went on, stroking her thighs, her hips, and her stomach, each time asking for her approval and receiving it.

Finally his hands returned to her breasts and he felt her quickened heartbeat. "You seem to be getting excited about something. Is there anywhere else you'd like me to touch?" he murmured against her ear.

"Mmm-hmm."

"Show me."

She reminded herself that this was her opportunity to be as wanton as she chose and, covering his right hand with hers, she boldly dragged it down over her stomach and pressed it between her legs.

"Very good. Now tell me, do you like my hand just covering you like this, or do you prefer this?" He slipped his middle finger between her curls and found the heart of her need.

Her response was a frustrated moan as she pressed her head back against his shoulder and grasped his thighs to brace herself. He clearly knew her body better than she knew it herself. With expert manipulation, he catapulted her to the very edge of climax in a matter of seconds, then abruptly withdrew his hand.

"You didn't answer me," he reminded her.

Breathless and dazed, she could only nod.

"I guess I'll have to repeat the question. Which do you like better? This?" Again he cupped her entire sex with his hand, and she sighed. "Or this?" His finger stroked her clitoris, and she moaned for him. "Or maybe you prefer this." He slipped two fingers inside, scissoring them back and forth and pressing against a spot on the upper wall that caused an eruption that vibrated through her entire body.

"Easy, honey," he whispered as he continued to apply pressure to the erogenous zone until her body stopped quaking. "You should probably take a breath now," he said with a smile in his voice.

"Holy shit!" she exclaimed after she exhaled.

His chest shook with laughter. "Not exactly the words I was hoping for, but they'll do."

She swiveled around and gaped at him. "How did you . . . *What* did you . . . I had no idea. There really is a G-spot! Can everybody do that? I mean—

"Sh-s-sh," he sounded and kissed her softly. "Analyzing it takes the magic away." He watched her working to hold back the next question and grinned with comprehension. "Yes, you may use it in the book."

She didn't bother to ask how he knew what she

was thinking. "Thank you, but, you know, you may have to do it a few more times for me to be able to describe it in words."

And he didn't bother to voice his amazement at how quickly she had gone from an old-fashioned girl to a seductress, but he took a moment to thank God for his good fortune.

She inched upward for a kiss and became aware of the strong effect his act on her had had on him. Her fingers closed around his erection and tested the strength of it, but a moment later he moved her hand to his chest.

"Not yet. It's still your turn."

She cocked her head at him. "In that case, I should be allowed to have whatever pleases me, right?" He warily agreed. "Well, what would please me most at this moment is to touch you, so don't interfere."

"I'm beginning to notice a real bossy streak in you," he said, pretending that he didn't like it. She scraped her fingernails down his chest, being sure to catch both nipples, and he stopped complaining.

She moved her hands to his lower body and explored every masculine millimeter. She guessed from the death grip he had on the edges of the tub that he couldn't take much more, so she brought it to an end in a way she hoped would surprise him.

As her fingers kept him on that edge, she straddled his hips and guided him to her opening. In one long, slow slide, she absorbed the length of him into her body, then shifted her hips in an easy rocking motion that barely made a wave in the churning water.

With each forward movement, Luke felt Kelly clench her vaginal muscles around him. He was torn between the need to rock with her and the selfish desire to see if she could do it all on her own. Then he lost the chance to decide as she brought his hands up to her breasts and pressed them there while her mouth took hungry possession of his.

A heartbeat later he lost another battle to make it last. Although this time was not nearly as explosive, it seemed to go on forever as Kelly's talented muscles continued to pulse around him long after he was spent. Finally she relaxed against him with a sigh.

"Again?" he asked simply, wanting to be reassured that she was at least as satisfied as he was.

"Mmm," was all she could manage.

"Do you think we'd drown if we just went to sleep right here?"

"We could drain the tub," she mumbled sleepily. "Cover ourselves with towels."

"Sounds good to me."

"Of course, the mattress on my bed is softer."

"And a lot less cramped. Not that I don't like you right where you are. But by morning, I'm not sure I'd be able to get up."

She lifted her head and gave him a kiss and a smile. "Well, we certainly don't want to do anything that would prevent you from *getting up*." She contracted her muscles one more time as she slipped away from him.

Once the spell was broken, they wasted little time moving from the tub to the bed, and a few minutes after that, they were both sound asleep.

When Kelly opened her eyes again, she saw Luke propped up on his elbow watching her. She smiled, and he kissed her.

"Good morning, beautiful. I was giving you five more minutes, then I was going to resort to drastic measures."

"Oohh, if that's anything like what you did to me last night, maybe I'll go back to sleep." She stretched her entire body and decided that every part of her felt absolutely lovely.

"I'll give you a hint," he said, raking his gaze over her body. "It's something we didn't get to do last night."

She frowned at him. "If you're going to start that spanking business again . . ."

He laughed and kissed her nose. "No spankings . . . at the moment. What I had in mind was a little less . . . active. I'll give you another hint. It would start like this." He pressed his lips to the curve of her neck, wet the spot with his tongue, then lightly sucked. From there he used his tongue to trace a line down between her breasts, made a large, damp circle around one, then drew smaller and smaller circles until his tongue found the center. Molding both breasts in his hands, he licked and nibbled on the nipple, then sucked the whole peak into his mouth.

Kelly whimpered as she felt the pull all the way

down to the base of her abdomen. Threading her fingers into his hair, she gently urged him to release her. "Please stop. For now. I love it, but I really need to—"

He sat up and grinned. "Sorry. I got carried away. Go ahead."

Rising, she caught sight of the clock. "Good heavens! It's almost noon. You should have gotten me up as soon as you woke. We have an appointment with Mary Beth in a few hours, and we still have to trim your hair."

"Are you hungry?" he asked as she headed into the bathroom.

"Starved. Why don't you see what Bruce left behind?"

"Yes, ma'am," he answered with a salute and went to find a pair of shorts.

Kelly was considerably more comfortable a few minutes later. As she was rinsing her face, she couldn't help but notice that the eyes in the mirror were sparkling back at her. Why, she looked like a twenty-year old girl again!

Thinking that she might get hair all over her when she gave Luke his trim, she decided not to get dressed yet. She was about to throw on a nightshirt when she remembered the pretty black peignoir set hanging in the back of her closet. Slipping on the satin robe made her feel even sexier than she already did and, after tying the belt, she loosened the top just enough to give Luke a glimpse of cleavage.

She gathered up her hair-cutting scissors, a comb, and a towel, and headed downstairs. To her surprise, two glasses of orange juice were on the table, coffee was brewing, and Luke was making scrambled eggs with bits of ham. "Can I keep you?" she asked, giving him a hug from behind.

He grinned at her over his shoulder. "I've had a few thoughts along that line." He set down the spatula and turned to her. His eyes widened when he noticed what she was wearing and that her hair was brushed out. "Wow." He pulled her close for a long kiss. "Aah. You brushed your teeth. And I so liked your morning breath."

She gave him a little shove. "Smart-ass. I was going to help, but for that you can serve me." As she sat down, she made sure that the skirt of the robe fell open to reveal her crossed legs.

It took him a moment to get his mind back on cooking, but in a short time, he brought one plate of eggs and two cups of hot coffee to the table. "Will there be anything else, madame?"

She scanned him from top to bottom before answering. "Not at the moment. You may be seated."

"I would, but you're in my seat." He grasped her elbow and raised her to her feet. Before she understood what he was doing, he sat down in her chair and pulled her onto his lap. "Much better." He scooped up a forkful of eggs and brought it up to her mouth. "Open wide."

She obeyed, then fed him a mouthful. She had

never been a fan of love scenes that revolved around food, but he quickly helped her to revise her thinking. Each time it was her turn to feed him, his hands roamed, over and under the satin robe, without actually taking it off her.

"I'm full," she said when he tried to feed her the last bite.

"So am I," he said and tilted his hips upward to clarify exactly what part of him was full.

She watched him put the eggs in his mouth, then slowly pull out the empty fork, and realized she was going to have to be the strong one. "It's after one o'clock."

"And?"

"And we're supposed to see Mary Beth at three."

"So?"

"So, it's a bit of a drive. I better cut your hair now."

"Do you actually know how to do that?"

She smiled. "Baseball was my dad's favorite pastime, but he was a barber for a living. I spent so much time in his shop when I was growing up, I couldn't help but pick up a few skills."

"Okay, but you probably should get off my lap first."

"Oh." It was only then that she realized he was no longer holding her there, and she quickly got moving. After draping the big towel over his shoulders, she wet his hair and started on the front.

She had only taken the first snip when he untied her belt so that the robe fell open in front of his face.

He leaned forward and kissed her navel, and she was very, very tempted to give in, but as his mouth moved lower, she found her strength. "Do I need to remind you that I have scissors in my hand?"

He looked at her with complete innocence. "You could put them down."

"Then we'd be late."

"We could cancel." His hands slipped behind her and urged her to come closer.

"Luke!" She backed up and closed her robe again. "You know we can't do that. It's very important that we talk to Mary Beth."

He sighed and sat back. "Okay. I'll be good." She bent forward to take another snip and the top of her robe gaped open just enough to tease. "If I didn't know better, I'd think you were doing this on purpose."

"The only thing I'm doing on purpose is trying to give you a nice haircut." She watched him close his eyes rather than be faced with temptation, and she felt a thrill of feminine power. How very lovely it was. And how very lovely of him to allow her to experience it without automatically trying to steal it away.

Because he was letting her get away with it, she continued to tease him with seemingly innocent glimpses of bare skin and sensual touches as she circled around him, while her conversation remained strictly business. "I left it pretty long on top to help hide the burn. It's healing nicely, but you'll still probably want to wear a hat when you're outside."

She combed through his shortened hair one final time, then satisfied that she'd done a very professional job, and he looked quite different, she took the towel off his shoulders and dropped it onto the floor with his sacrificed curls. "Don't get up yet. Let me dust you." Taking a clean kitchen towel, she lightly brushed it over his neck and shoulders, his back and chest, his stomach, his thighs—

"That's it!" he exclaimed and yanked the towel out of her hand. "You asked for this!" With just enough roughness to momentarily startle her into submission, he grabbed her by the waist and pulled her facedown across his lap.

She squealed in surprise as she fell forward. When she tried to wriggle out from his grasp, she found herself firmly trapped. "Luke! This isn't funny." He gave her protruding bottom a light smack that didn't hurt at all, but she kicked in protest anyway.

"Be still or the next one gets harder," he warned, and she stopped squirming immediately. "You obviously have to be taught a lesson," he said in a tone that suggested that he was going to get great enjoyment out of being the teacher of that lesson. Keeping one arm braced across her shoulders, he ran the other one down her back and legs to the hem of the robe, then gathered the satin as he brought his hand back up until the lower half of her body was bared to him.

"Such a pretty ass," he said, tickling her lightly with his fingers. "It really would be a shame to mark it with big red handprints."

"Luke—" Another light swat hushed her again.

"The thing is," he continued, as he went back to tickling her, "you must be punished for such blatant misbehavior. Refusing to let me play with you, then purposely arousing me is a serious offense, young lady."

"I could give you another bath . . . later tonight," she offered hopefully.

His fingers never stopped moving over her as he considered that, only now they roamed lower, down the backs of her thighs and up between. "No, I don't think that would make us even for what you've done. You see, you've put me in a state of considerable discomfort with no intention of easing it. Only something equally diabolical will suffice."

"We're really going to be late if—"

He slapped her a little harder. "What I have in mind will only take a minute or two, then we'll get ready to go. But you have to remain very still and quiet. Here, try this." He lifted his arm from her shoulder and offered it as support for her head. "Better?" She mumbled and he accepted that as her response.

The hand on her backside now eased down to where her thighs pressed together. "Open," he said, and she parted her legs a little more. "More," he ordered and inserted his fingers into the valley.

Her body spasmed as he swiftly found her nerve center and fully awakened it. Within seconds, she could feel her body temperature rising as liquid heat rushed to aid him in his work.

232   *Marilyn Campbell*

"Very good," he proclaimed as he withdrew his hand. "'That didn't even take a full minute. Okay, you can get up now."

She thought she misunderstood. "What?"

He turned her and helped her sit upright.

It took a moment to balance out from the rush, but when she did, she still didn't understand.

"Now we're even," he said, grinning at her. "We're both thinking about sex, our bodies are primed, but there's no time to do a good job of it."

Thinking one could solve such a minor dilemma, she smoothly turned and straddled his hips. As her one hand verified that he was ready for her, she brushed her lips over his and murmured, "There's nothing wrong with a quickie in the kitchen."

His thumb easily found her button and pressed it. "No, there's nothing wrong with a quickie, except that if I gave you that, it wouldn't be much of a punishment, would it?" He stopped touching her and took her hand away from him. "Now that you know how good a climax can be, it's going to be nearly impossible for you to wait until we get home later to have one."

"Hah! That's ridiculous. As soon as I get off your lap, the feeling will start to fade, and my whole mind will be on our interview with Mary Beth."

"That might be true, if I didn't intend to keep after you all day, just to make sure you can't get sex off your mind."

She made a face at him. "I have a tremendous

amount of self-discipline when I'm working. I simply won't allow you to distract me."

He gave her a quick, hard kiss on the mouth. "You'll allow it, because you'll be thinking about this: the best sex you'll ever have in your life is when you're kept on the very edge . . . for *hours* . . . without being able to come."

Since she couldn't contradict him from experience, she got up. "I'd better clean up this room."

He caught her hand before she walked away. "One more thing." He stood up and put his whole body into kissing her senseless again.

When he released her, she smiled up at him. "You really are very, very good."

"So are you, sweetheart." He placed her hand over his erection so that she could feel the spot of wetness she had caused.

Her feminine power swelled once more, and she gave him a squeeze. "Does that mean two can play this waiting game of yours?"

He laughed and shook his head. "I'm beginning to wonder which one of us is really going to be punished today. You go on up and get ready. I'll clean up down here."

Dillard waited until McCoy finished playing Susie Homemaker before leaving his hiding place on the fenced-in patio. The closed vertical blinds over the sliding glass door made it difficult to get any clear pictures, but he was fairly sure his client would be satisfied with what he did manage to shoot through one narrow separation.

There was no question now about the couple being intimate. Nor did he have any question why his client wanted the lady. He had practically had an accident in his pants just from watching.

However, he still wasn't sure they were actually *lovers*, in the traditional sense. Not only didn't they act all lovey-dovey in public yesterday, the guy cooked for her, then cleaned up the mess, as though he were her employee. Of course, he supposed some men might do that sort of thing to be able to fool around with a woman like that, but his gut told him this was something else.

He returned to his original thought that McCoy was Kirkwood's hired bodyguard. Maybe, besides providing security against crazy fans, they decided he could guard her body personally as well. At least it was something he could check out. He had no trouble lifting the guy's prints off the car door, and if he was lucky, his pal at the county lab would be able to positively identify them in the next day or two.

Meanwhile, from what he just witnessed, Kirkwood and her playmate wouldn't be going anywhere for a long while. He figured he had time to drop off the prints, get the roll of film developed, and make a dozen calls or so.

Chapter Thirteen

Despite Luke's attempts to distract Kelly every few minutes, they managed to be on their way shortly after two o'clock. Before heading to Marietta, however, Luke suggested they drive around the block again to see if the white Toyota was parked nearby.

"He must have given up," Kelly said. "Or maybe we simply bored him to death with all the sightseeing yesterday."

"I don't get it, but he doesn't seem to be interested in our travels today. Let's keep our eyes open though, just in case he really was smart enough to change cars."

As they were leaving her neighborhood, Kelly decided they'd better get gas and pulled into a station.

"What are you doing?" Luke asked as she got out of the car.

"It'll only take a minute," she assured him, but

his curiosity demanded she explain about self-service and paying by inserting a credit card into a slot at the pump.

"What if you needed your windows washed or your oil checked?"

"Some places still provide that service, but it usually costs extra. It's faster to do it yourself anyway."

He wasn't sure he liked this advancement until he realized how quickly they were ready to be on their way.

Mary Beth had given excellent directions to her home; it was only the traffic that made it seem like a long trip. At no time, however, did they notice anyone following them.

"Well, this is it," Kelly said as they pulled into the brick-paved circular driveway of the Jacksons' large home. "Remember, let me do the talking."

"Sure thing. But I have to tell you something important first."

He looked so serious, she was afraid to hear what he had to say.

He leaned over, close to her ear, and said, "You remember what I did for you in the tub last night?" His hand snaked beneath her skirt before she could think to object. As he massaged her through her panties, he added, "Tonight I'm going to do that again, only my tongue will be involved at the same time." Seconds later, he got out of the car, waiting for her to join him.

"You're going to be sorry for that," she muttered as she walked past him to the front door.

"Wait. I forgot the hat."

"Too late now. Just try not to let her see the top of your head."

"I forgot the sunglasses, too."

Kelly gave him an exasperated look. "And here I thought you were trying to distract *me*!"

He was almost embarrassed, but not quite. "So it backfired a little. What do you want—" The front door opened, ending any last-minute change of plans.

"Good afternoon."

Kelly smiled at the attractive brunette in the doorway. She looked ten years too young to be Mary Beth, but a nod from Luke told her otherwise. Money was such a miraculous preservative. Walking quickly to the door, she shifted her notebook and purse to her left hand and held out her right. "Mrs. Jackson? I'm—".

She was cut off by the audible gasp and shocked expression on Mary Beth's face as she gaped at Kelly then Luke and back to Kelly. She began to sway and Luke hurried to catch her.

"You . . ." She stared at Luke and shook her head. "You can't be him." Then her gaze darted to Kelly and her eyes filled with fear. "And you can't be her." She shrugged off Luke's support. "Is this some kind of sick joke?"

Kelly opened her mouth to protest, or at least explain who they were, but Luke was faster.

"I'm very sorry we've upset you, Mrs. Jackson. We were afraid if we explained over the phone, you wouldn't agree to see us. My name is Duke McCoy. My uncle was Luke Templeton. I'm told I strongly resemble him."

Mary Beth nodded slowly as she continued to stare suspiciously at him. "Strongly resemble does not begin to describe the likeness. For a moment there, I thought I was looking at a ghost. Except for the hair. It's the exact same color and texture, but you wear it shorter than he did. It might not have been such a shock if I had not been looking at old photographs only last night."

She abruptly shifted her attention to Kelly. "But that does not explain you."

Again Luke replied before Kelly could get a word out, which was just as well, since their original plan had clearly been tossed to the wind.

"This is a good friend of mine, Kelly Kirkwood. She's an author. I'm sure you've seen some of her books."

Mary Beth's expression altered instantly as she recognized the name. Now she was anxious to shake hands with her. "Oh my, yes. Of course I have seen her books. I have a few of them inside. My friends are going to be absolutely pea-green when they hear that you visited me personally. You are such a talented writer! Please forgive me for not recognizing you, but over the phone I thought you said you were a reporter."

"Actually, what I said was—"

"Why are we still standing out here in this heat?" Mary Beth suddenly asked and stepped aside. "Please come in and let me get you a cold drink." As she led them into a contemporary, yet formal living room, she said, "It is not quite the cocktail hour, but those stuffy old board meetings get me so thirsty, I suppose we do not truly need to pay attention to the clock now, do we?"

Kelly glanced at Luke, in hopes that he understood what that meant. The woman's speech pattern seemed oddly stilted, as though she had taken elocution lessons to lose her southern accent, but they didn't quite take.

"A beer would be great if you have one," he said with a broad smile. "If not—"

"Oh, I have anything you could possibly think of," she said and touched a button on the wall. A mirrored panel slid away and revealed a completely stocked bar. "Please make yourselves at home. What can I get for you, Miss Kirkwood? I could whip up a pitcher of strawberry daiquiris."

Luke was giving her a meaningful look that she thought she understood, and though she really would have liked a diet soda, she said, "That sounds wonderful, but please call me Kelly."

"Only if you'll call me Mary Beth." It was clear a moment later that Mary Beth had already "whipped up" the pitcher of daiquiris before they arrived.

As she found a beer and a frosted mug for Luke,

he said, "I want to apologize again for misleading you about our visit, but I was afraid—"

"Water under the bridge and all that. Just start fresh." She brought the pitcher of daiquiris, glasses, and Luke's beer to the coffee table on a silver serving tray. As she poured for her and Kelly, she asked, "So, how did the two of you meet?"

Though the question was totally irrelevant, Kelly wanted this woman to think of them as friends, so she smiled and turned to Luke. "Why don't you tell her, honey? You always tell that story so much better than I do." She pretended to share a confidence with Mary Beth. "I'm the writer, but he's the talker. Does it for a living."

"Really? What is it you do, Duke?"

Luke gave Kelly another look that she had no trouble translating, and she fluttered her lashes at him.

"I . . . uh . . . I'm a state senator. In Michigan." Kelly choked on the first sip of her drink, and he solicitously patted her on the back. "I didn't know Kelly was anybody special when I met her at one of my fund-raisers. Just thought she was one of those women who go to those things to meet wealthy men. You know the sort."

Mary Beth thought that was very humorous. Kelly aimed a mental dart between his eyes.

"Anyway, to make a long story short, she finally makes her way through the crowd to meet me and somebody bumps into her. She spills her champagne down the front of my pants, and without thinking, tries to brush it off . . ."

By that time, Mary Beth was giggling like a schoolgirl with her first crush, and Kelly was taking slow deep breaths.

"When she realizes what she's doing, she looks up at me with the pinkest cheeks you've ever seen and, I've got to tell you, it was like I was hit with two thousand volts of electricity." He affectionately stroked Kelly's cheek, and it was all she could do to keep from smacking his hand. "We haven't been apart for more than a few hours since."

"O-o-oh, how romantic," Mary Beth said. "That is almost exactly the way it was for your uncle and my friend, Ginger. It is truly amazing how much you look like her, Kelly. Of course, nothing like he resembles Luke, but there is enough of a likeness that you made me think of her when I first saw you with him."

Kelly blinked at her. "I'm sorry. Did you just say I look like Ginger O'Neill?" The sip of daiquiri turned a bit sour in her stomach.

"Not identical, mind you, but there are similarities. I think you might be taller than she was, but she also had a very . . . *womanly* figure. I was always so skinny. Her hair was a little darker red and only came down to her shoulders, but she wore it straight like yours. Would you like to see the pictures I was talking about?"

"I'd like that very much," Kelly said with a

smile that evaporated as soon as Mary Beth left the room.

"I *talk* for a living?" Luke whispered. "That was the best you could do? You really put me—"

"Shut up."

He jerked back from her snarl. "You can't be mad about that story I made up. It was no worse than the one you—"

"I don't care about the story. Why didn't you ever mention—" Mary Beth's reappearance forced her to smile again.

She set the open album on the table in front of Kelly, and Luke scooted close to be able to see at the same time. He took advantage of the opportunity to put his arm around her, but a glare from Kelly made him withdraw.

"I only have those three pictures of the two of them. Had I known at the time . . ." She sighed and drained her daiquiri glass. As she refilled it and topped off Kelly's, she said, "I believe you were going to tell me the real reason for this visit."

Kelly's mind was busy digesting the fact that the woman wasn't mistaken. She and Ginger O'Neill had more than a little in common. They could have been sisters.

When Kelly failed to speak, Luke continued to improvise. "One day after Kelly and I got to know each other, I told her about my having an uncle who had been electrocuted for a crime that he swore he didn't commit, and it gave her an idea for a new suspense novel. Naturally, the final version would be fictional, but she thought it would help if we could do a little research about the actual case. And that's why we're in Atlanta." He gave Kelly's back a nudge to get her to jump in.

She pulled her gaze from the photographs, then pretended to take a long sip of her drink. By the time she set her glass down, her brain was back on track. "We were able to get all the basic facts from old newspapers, but I was hoping to get some more personal information. As you know, I write *romantic* suspense. I read that you were her best friend, so I thought you might be able to help me with Ginger and Luke's characters."

"Well, I don't know. It has been a very long time. Water under the bridge and all."

"Yes, I understand. But I'm not going to be quoting you or anything like that. No one would ever know I spoke to you. In fact, no one will even be able to tell who the story is really about by the time I'm finished with it. I'm just looking for some general impressions from you. Like, do you think they were really in love, or was Luke just taking advantage of a young, confused girl?" Luke's posture stiffened, but she ignored him.

Mary Beth's eyes glazed a bit as she called up old memories. Before she answered, she finished another glass and refilled it. "Ginger was young, compared to Luke, but I don't think she was ever confused about anything. Just because she was my friend doesn't mean I was blind to her faults. She wanted to get out from under her parents' rule, and marriage was the best solution at that time. Oh, she could have had any number of young men, but she wanted financial security. When Reid O'Neill offered his hand and promised her the world, she grabbed it like it was the brass ring at a carnival.

"The only problem was, she was bored with him in a month and had trapped herself in a town too small to get away with any, ahem, extracurricular activities, if you know what I mean. I could never understand why she did it. If she had just waited a few years, she would have had enough money of her own to marry for love and live wherever she wanted, like I did."

Kelly leaned forward. She was about to get the answer to one of the big questions on their list. "Why would she have had money if she had waited?"

Mary Beth took another swallow. "She had a trust fund. I think it was from her paternal grandmother. About a half-million dollars, which was an awful lot of money back then. Anyway, she couldn't touch it till she was twenty-one."

"So, let me see if I understand correctly. Ginger inherited a fortune when she turned twenty-one, right before she met Luke. Then she left her husband to go to him. Could Luke have known she was wealthy and purposefully seduced her?"

She laughed. "I don't know if he knew about the money, but if anybody did any seducin', it was Ginger on him. The first time she saw him, she started makin' plans for a new future. Besides, even if he did know about the money, I don't think it was as important to him as it was to her."

"I gather you liked him," Luke said trying to add more positive light to the interview.

"Oh yes. He was handsome and funny and had such strong opinions on so many different subjects. Ah'd really hoped he woulda asked her to marry him, but Ginger just couldn't pin him down. Confirmed bachelor, Ah think."

Kelly noticed that the not quite refined diction was slipping and took back the lead. "Was there any truth to his claim that he didn't know she was married?"

"He didn't," Mary Beth stated flatly. "Ginger made me swear not to tell him until she had him completely hooked. That's what she used to say. But with all her shenanigans, she couldn't even get him to say he loved her."

Luke cut in again. "So, do you think that's why she went back to her husband? Because she got tired of waiting for m-my uncle to get off the fence?"

She laughed again. "Heavens no. Ginger would have stayed with Luke indefinitely . . . at least until another man came along who *would* marry her. Her husband couldn't, um, how should Ah say this, um, make her happy when the lights went out, and apparently Luke was quite talented in that department. She would have stayed with him, even without the weddin' ring, rather than go back to sleepin' with Reid O'Neill if that's all there was to it."

Recalling one of her theories, Kelly asked, "Did someone threaten her or Luke's life if she didn't return to Charming?"

Mary Beth cocked her head. "What a strange question. No, Ah don't believe so. It was the trust fund she went back for. There was a clause in it that she hadn't been aware of before. If she was found to be behavin' in an illegal or immoral manner prior to her thirtieth birthday, the monies reverted to the estate, which her father controlled.

"Did Ah mention that her daddy and Reid were lodge brothers? Well, they were, and good friends, too. So, Ah suppose, in a way, Ginger was threatened, because he told her if she didn't return to her husband and be a dutiful wife, she would end up penniless. No matter how handsome or *talented* Luke was, he didn't have money. She made her choice, and money won.

"What happened to the money when she died?" Kelly asked, trying not to appear too anxious for the answer.

"Her husband inherited it, of course, though that was hardly comfortin'. Poor man was devastated over losin' her so soon after getting her back."

"So devastated that he ran right out and built an empire," Luke muttered. "It was all about money, then."

Mary Beth squinted at him. "What did you say?"

"Nothing," Kelly replied. "We had just had some theories— Tell me, in one article, it sounded like you didn't believe Luke was guilty. What made you change your mind?"

Mary Beth's alcohol consumption was finally having a visible effect on her. Kelly had to repeat the question before the woman could answer, and when she did, her cultivated speech pattern slipped further into the back woods.

"Ah didn't change mah mind. Ah don' know who did that terrible thing to Ginger, but Ah was never convinced that Luke did it . . . no matter what that jury decided."

She put her finger to her lips and leaned forward. "But don't tell Jimmy Joe Ah said that. He'd have a conniption."

Kelly leaned toward her and spoke in a conspiratorial voice as well. "Why is that?"

"Because of the trouble Ah almost caused when we got back from our honeymoon. It was the only time in all our years of bein' together that we had such a terrible fight."

"They changed your deposition, didn't they?" Luke interjected.

Worry filled her eyes. "Ah did not say that."

"It's all right, Mary Beth," Kelly said in a soothing tone. "No one will ever know we talked to you. We were just very confused about why you left the country prior to the trial."

She fussed with her hair and put on a phony smile. "Why, Jimmy Joe's daddy won that fabulous trip around the world, an' he wanted us ta have it as a weddin' present, but the departure date couldn't be changed. We had ta git married and go right then. Jimmy Joe simply would not wait no longer for me ta be his wife. An' everybody promised me mah deposition would be as good as if Ah was in court mahself."

She was beginning to mumble her words now as well, and Kelly had to prompt her to go on. "And by the time you came back . . ."

"They had executed Luke. Ah wasn't supposed to know that they changed mah words, but Ah found out by accident, and when Ah tried to say somethin' about it, well, like Ah said, Jimmy Joe went kinda crazy on me."

She looked pleadingly at Luke. "Y'all do understand, don't you? There was nothin' Ah could do that would have made a difference. They said the evidence against him was overwhelmin'. They would have found him guilty whether Ah'd testified in person or not."

Kelly focused on how often she kept using the collective word "they."

"You could have contacted his parents," Luke said in a frigid tone. "It might have helped them to know that someone believed in his innocence."

She hung her head and shook it. "Wouldn't have made no difference. He was already gone. Water under the bridge."

"Did you know Junior Ramey?" Luke asked quickly, before she nodded off.

Mary Beth raised her head, but her eyes remained downcast. "Yes, of course. We all graduated from high school together."

"We?"

She nodded. "He always had the biggest crush on Ginger—most of the boys did—but once, in tenth grade Ah think it was, she agreed to go to a movie with him. You see, he was also gonna inherit lots of money one day, so she thought he might be her answer. But she couldn't stand the sight of him. Even in the dark theater, she new what he looked like. How could someone who looked like her be seen in public with a creature like him? No matter how much money he would have when his daddy died, it would simply be too embarrassin'."

Kelly had to restrain herself from reacting to that important bit of news. "I read that Junior was later arrested for breaking into a woman's home. Do you think he might have actually been the Lake Sidney Lanier rapist all along?"

Mary Beth frowned and shook her head. "Naw. He was always extremely shy with girls, and when he did speak to one of us, he was very polite and respectful. Ah remember thinkin' that he would have made someone a good husband . . . if he hadn't been so hard to look at."

"Do you know where he is now?"

Mary Beth held up a finger, then stood up and

walked over to a desk on the opposite side of the room with more grace than an inebriated condition warranted. "Now Ah know why Ah saved this," she said and brought a thin booklet back to Kelly. "When our class had their thirty-year reunion, they made this up, so everyone would know what everyone else was doin'."

Luke looked at the booklet without crowding Kelly this time. When Kelly found the paragraph about Beauregard Ramey, Jr., she and Luke received another shock. Junior Ramey was still living in the area and was managing the O'Neill's store in Buford! The plot was getting muddier by the minute.

Kelly made a note of Junior's home address and phone number, then asked, "Just one last question, if you don't mind. Do you think the Ku Klux Klan could have been involved in Luke's frame-up and Junior's being let off on the attempted rape charge?"

Mary Beth's head popped up; she looked panic-stricken. "I did not say that. I *never* said that!" She rose to her feet and rubbed her arms as if the room temperature had suddenly dropped. "You had better leave now. Jimmy Joe will be home soon, and he would not like it if he knew I had had company here this afternoon. He gets very unhappy when I socialize too much."

Not wanting to run into Jimmy Joe any more than Mary Beth wanted them to, they thanked her for her time and were pulling out of the driveway minutes later.

"Are you thinking what I'm thinking?" Kelly asked as she drove down the street.

"Considering all the thoughts bouncing around my head right now, I'm sure some of them would match up with yours."

"First, Ramey. What Mary Beth said about him could tie in with the profile of the rapist, but when you add in unrequited love for Ginger . . ."

"He sounds guilty as hell, on all counts."

"But now we know for sure that Reid had something huge to gain from Ginger's death."

"He got all that money and his revenge against me personally. So, we still have two prime suspects, either of whom probably had the clout to have me framed. Back to square one."

"I was in that store in Buford," Kelly said. "That's where I bought your clothes. Ramey might have even been there when I was there."

"It doesn't sound like you could have missed him if he was there. It would probably be best if you didn't go back there again though."

She shot a sideways glance at him. "Why? Because he might think I'm Ginger and try to kill me again?" She pulled into the parking lot of a shopping center, came to a rough halt, then lashed out at him. "What kind of game are you playing with me?"

Chapter Fourteen

The attack was completely unexpected. All Luke could think of was his discarded plan to seduce her so that she'd want to keep him around, but nothing had happened in the last hour to make her aware of that. "Wh-what are you talking about?"

"You did your damnedest to get me to cancel this appointment and now I know why. It wasn't sex. You didn't want me to find out about Ginger, did you?"

His voice raised in defense. "I have no idea what you're getting at, but maybe you'd like to explain about some of those leading questions you were asking. I thought you were convinced that I was innocent."

"I was! Until I found out that I'm Ginger's mirror image, and you just happened not to mention it. What did you do, search the country for a big-breasted redhead who was gullible enough to believe anything you said just so you could have some more sack time with your dead lover?"

He grasped her shoulders and gave her a shake. "Listen to yourself! You're talking crazy."

She knew he was right, but she wasn't entirely wrong. "So what? You lied to me, and I don't understand why."

He loosened his grip on her shoulders but didn't let go. "Tell me how I lied to you." She looked away. "Kelly, how can I explain if I don't know why you're upset? Do you think I lied to you about being electrocuted and traveling through time?"

She sighed and shook her head. There was too much evidence backing up that part of his story.

"Do you think I lied about not committing the rapes or Ginger's murder?"

Again she shook her head. She believed in his innocence even more so after listening to Mary Beth.

"Then what?" he begged, guiding her face back toward him.

She met his eyes, then lowered her lashes, and quietly spelled it out for him. "I thought you wanted me. But it was only because I reminded you of her."

He was stunned. "How in God's name did you come to that conclusion?"

She huffed. "I'm very logical, remember? I saw the photos. I heard what Mary Beth said about how it was love at first sight for you and Ginger, and how—"

"Excuse me, but if you were listening to Mary Beth, you would realize she was talking about *lust* at first sight, not love."

"What's the difference? The point is when you were with me last night and this morning, it was *her* you were thinking of, and that makes me feel like . . . like . . ."

"Like you have no value as a woman?" Luke finished for her. "Kind of like how you made me feel last night?"

He had a point; she just wasn't ready to give in to it. "Did you, or did you not, tell me I epitomized your fantasy woman?"

"Yes, I did, and you do."

"And that woman was Ginger O'Neill."

He threw his hands up in exasperation. "I told you—no, I believe I *confessed* to you last night, what my weaknesses are when it comes to women. I don't see why you're upset now. I was electrocuted, and by some weird miracle, I got *dropped* at your cabin. I didn't pick you out of a lineup of women because you resembled Ginger."

"I know that," she admitted, though it put a large dent in her accusation.

"So what if I'm attracted to a certain . . . appearance? Aren't there certain physical characteristics that attract you to a man?"

She was losing ground and knew it. "But I look so much like her."

"Only in a very general way," he said, stroking her cheek. "Do you remember what I said the first day? About you being *different* from any of the women I knew?" She grudgingly acknowledged that she did. "That wasn't a lie. Yes, when I got a good look at you I noticed the similarities, but on every single physical aspect, you bested her. What was more impressive to me, however, was what I heard coming out of your mouth, and how you thought and acted.

"You heard Mary Beth, and she was Ginger's best friend. She was shallow, self-centered, money-hungry, and needed a man to lean on."

Kelly clucked her tongue. "If she was so bad, why did you—" She rolled her eyes. "Never mind. Big boobs, long red hair, who cares about her personality."

He shrugged sheepishly. "What can I say, I'm a man, and most of the women I knew were like her. But I must have known that what attracted me to her wouldn't last because I couldn't bring myself to ask her to marry me."

Or tell her you loved her, Kelly added to herself, recalling what else Mary Beth had revealed.

"What it all comes down to is this. I'm attracted to you for more than the obvious reasons. If I wasn't, I wouldn't have cared if you only wanted me for my sperm. And if you were really only interested in me for the purposes of pregnancy, it wouldn't matter to you that you look like a former lover of mine. Face it, Kelly. If we didn't have feelings that go beneath the surface, we wouldn't be able to hurt each other. I like *you*. And you like me. Okay?"

"I guess, but it still gives me a strange feeling."

He eased back into the passenger seat. "I see. Well, I don't know what else I can say. Do you want me to move out?"

"No! Of course not."

"Do you want me to go back to keeping my distance?" When she didn't answer immediately, he sighed. "I don't suppose it has occurred to you that you weren't the only one who took a punch in the gut back there."

"What do you mean?" she asked, her mind still on his previous question.

"I may not have asked Ginger to marry me, but I was pretty crazy about her. I wasn't exactly doing cartwheels the day she told me she had a husband and preferred to go back to him. But today, I found out her reason for leaving me wasn't even that good. She chose *money* over me."

Kelly covered his hand with hers and gave it a sympathetic squeeze. "I'm sorry. You're right. I was only thinking about *my* feelings. But now that we're talking about yours, there was something you said that I thought you might need to examine. You haven't said much about your parents, but from what you have, I've gotten the feeling that you were close. Aren't you curious about whether they're still alive?"

He slipped his hand away from hers and looked

away. "Even if they were, they'd be in their late eighties. My showing up now would hardly be a blessing, unless they were wishing for a heart attack.

"I have thought about contacting my sister, though." His expression softened with memory. "She was the basis for my cover story to Mary Beth today. Shirl's married name was McCoy, and they'd had three daughters before I moved away. Finally, while I was in jail, she had a baby boy. That's why she couldn't be here for the trial.

"Anyway, that's how I came up with the idea of a nephew; I really do have one out there some-where about my age. But then I thought about how old Shirl would be now—sixty-four—and I decided to forget it. If you're right about my hav-ing to go back, what good would it do anyone for me to pop in for a few hours then disappear again? Nobody in their right mind would believe my story anyway."

"I did."

He grinned. "I'm not sure we've established your sanity yet, Miss Kirkwood."

"Smart-ass," she muttered with a smirk. "Just for that, maybe we'll skip the Braves and go to the opera instead."

He perked up instantly. "I almost forgot about the game. What time is it?"

"A little after five, and that means rush-hour traffic. The game doesn't start until seven, but it's clear on the other side of town. How do you feel about a picnic dinner in the car along the way?"

Since he didn't want to miss one minute of the game, he was willing to go along with anything that would get them there on time.

Picking up a full chicken dinner without leaving the car led to a discussion of the drive-thru window development, from fast food, to banking, to funeral homes.

Again Luke was struck by the awareness that everything in the nineties seemed to be geared to high-speed living. "Everyone seems so obsessed with doing things faster and saving time. What are they saving it for?"

"Is that a rhetorical question, or are you asking my opinion?"

"Opinion, please."

"I'd have to say we're saving time on mundane things in order to have time to do whatever we individually find interesting. An awful lot of people now set aside time to exercise or work out every day—organized aerobics classes, body-sculpting with weights, jogging, skating, there are even clubs for walking. Like I've already mentioned, we've become a lot more health-conscious in the last decade.

"But I also think a great number of people put the additional time into their careers. Most of the women of my mother's generation never worked outside of the home. Now, most women do, even when they have small children. A lot of the time-saving is aimed at helping working mothers juggle personal responsibilities with a career."

"What about you? Are you planning to be a *working* mother?"

The possibility that she might be a mother of any sort someday gave her a warm feeling. Of course, there was that little matter of getting pregnant to begin with. Her hand touched her stomach. Could it have happened last night?

"Hello? Is anybody home?"

Kelly smiled. "Sorry. I was just thinking— Yes, I'll continue to write, but that doesn't require me to leave the house on any regular basis. In fact, there are a number of companies that are making it possible for their employees to work at home in a variety of jobs. Computers really are changing the way we live."

The rest of the trip to the stadium was more relaxed once the air was cleared. Halfway there, Kelly thought to turn on the radio and chose a station he might like.

"Hey!" he exclaimed as "Louie-Louie" resounded from speakers all around him. "I know that song! It's by The Kingsmen. It was a huge hit last year."

Kelly laughed. "By last year, I assume you mean 1964, but it's been recorded by different groups several hundred times since. Wasn't there some big scandal around it that made it so popular?"

"Oh yeah. The rumor was that the lyrics were purposely garbled to hide obscenities. It was banned in Indiana, but the FCC couldn't confirm the rumors because they couldn't understand the words at any speed."

She shook her head with another chuckle. "Wait until you hear some of the lyrics to today's songs. Anything goes, from the 'f' word and chants to the devil to the virtues of cop-killers."

"That doesn't sound like progress to me," he said, making a face.

She shrugged. "Personally, I think it's taking the right to freedom of speech over the top, but I don't have to listen if I don't want to. A large audience has tuned into stations like this one that only play what they call 'oldies.' "

"Put Your Head On My Shoulder" by Paul Anka, came on next and the mood in the car shifted with the melody.

"This is one of my favorite slow-dance songs," Luke said and started to hum quietly.

"Do you dance?" she asked, thinking how long it had been since she'd slow-danced with a man . . . since her wedding day, a lifetime ago.

"I do okay." He graduated from humming to singing the words. As the second chorus began, she couldn't resist making it a duet. By the third, they were pretending to serenade each other.

"That wasn't bad," Luke said, applauding their vocal efforts when the song ended. "Maybe we could be like Sonny and Cher! 'I Got You Babe' was number one the week before I got the chair. One of the guards used to constantly switch stations on his radio looking for it. I must have heard it a thousand times. Whatever happened to them?"

"They broke up. I think it was back in the seventies."

He frowned. "Oh. That's too bad. I thought they had a really different sound together."

"She went solo and sang her way to fame and fortune and multiple cosmetic surgeries, and did some movies. He went into politics in California."

His brows raised. "Another one?"

She nodded. "Clint Eastwood, too."

He shook his head in bewilderment and went back to singing along with the radio.

They arrived at the stadium early enough to get a good parking space, buy a program and souvenir book, and observe the players warming up. Kelly's heart swelled as she watched Luke. He looked like a little boy, sitting on the edge of his seat, wearing his Detroit Tigers cap, and studying the program. Would their child look like him? Or her? Or an interesting combination of the two?

She realized that her thoughts had brought her back to an earlier question of Luke's. Did she want him to go back to keeping his distance, or not?

As if he read her mind, he leaned close and whispered in her ear. "I don't know if it will make any difference to you now, but last night, when I told you it had never happened for me like that before, that was the God's truth. One of my, um, *talents*, was that I never lost control with a woman, and that includes Ginger." He leaned back so that she could see the sincerity in his eyes.

"Really?" she asked unnecessarily.

He grinned. "Yep. You're the first woman who made me forget my good manners."

Her mouth curved into a smile, and she gave him a brief kiss. "Thank you."

"All better?" he asked hopefully.

"All better. In fact . . ." She drew his head back down so she could whisper in his ear. "I once wrote this scene where the couple had sex in the passenger seat of a sports car, and I've always wondered if it was actually possible."

He burst out laughing, much to the amusement of the people around them, and as the baseball game began, their personal game was restarted.

At the end of the top half of the first inning, he repaid her tease with a reminder of what he'd told her in the Jacksons' driveway. At the end of the bottom half, she simply said the words, "peacock feathers." Each time it was his turn, he managed to make her blush, and with every one of her suggestions, she managed to make him increasingly uncomfortable in his fitted jeans.

It occurred to her that he was speaking from extensive experience, where she was drawing solely on her imagination, but in the end, the result was the same. They were both wired for action by the time the last out was called.

With a tight grip on Kelly's hand, Luke wove his way through the departing crowd as though demons were chasing them. Between speed-walking and laughing, she was breathless by the time they reached her car, but instead of letting her get in the driver's seat to drive quickly away, he dragged her around to the passenger's side. Before she realized what he was up to, he opened the door, sat down, and pulled her onto his lap.

"Was the door open or closed in your scene?" he asked, frowning at the length of her legs still outside the car.

Chuckling, she said, "Closed, and it took place in a driveway without a horde of spectators."

"Your windows are tinted so dark, no one could see inside. But if you don't get your legs in here so I can close the door and turn this light off, I swear, I'll start making love to you just the way we are."

Considering the state he was in, she didn't put it past him, so with a little effort, she swiveled on his lap and put her feet in the driver's seat. The instant he closed the door, he assaulted her mouth with his own. There was nothing romantic or gentle about the way his tongue overpowered hers or the way his hand groped at her breast. He wanted her hard and fast, with no further preliminaries or games.

And she wanted him the same way.

But the logistics of the scenario were just difficult enough to slow them down to a point where Kelly's modesty awakened. "I can't do this," she said, breaking the kiss.

"Sure you can," he said, applying a rhythmic pressure between her legs with his hand. "Straddle me, one knee on each side. If I push the seat back—"

"Stop," she said, grasping his wrist to prevent

him from further clouding her mind. "Please. All I can think about is people walking by with kids and seeing the car rocking and knowing what we're doing in here. Besides, my heroine was a petite little thing, not at all like me. I think someone my size is more suited to having sex in the back of a van."

Chuckling, he held her face between his hands and kissed her soundly. "If anything, sweetheart, you should envision yourself in the back of a limousine. Not because of your size—which could not be more perfect—but because that's what you deserve." He took a ragged breath that helped him regain some control.

"Weren't you the man who told me the best sex was when you had to wait for it?" His groan was another form of flattery. "Hey, at least *you* don't have to drive home."

"That's right," he said with a grin and eased his hand up to her breast. My hands will be free and you won't be able to do anything about it."

She playfully slapped his hand away. "You mess with me while I'm driving, and I guarantee you I'll stop the car and make you get out and walk. By the time you find your way there on your own, you'll have forgotten what we were going to do when we got there."

"Party pooper." He pretended to pout, but helped her to maneuver into the driver's seat.

Whether due to her threat or his common sense, he behaved himself all the way to the town house. When she turned into her neighborhood, he reminded her to drive slowly around the block to see if they were still being spied upon.

"I don't understand it," Luke said when they finally pulled into the driveway. "But I guess he got what he was after in one day." He leaned closer and his expression changed. "Which means, we're alone, in a driveway, in a sports car. Just like your scene." He wiggled his eyebrows. "Want to try again?"

"Not unless you can wiggle your nose and turn this car into a limo. Personally, I'm ready to cash in on that promise of yours, and there's a room upstairs that would make a much better setting for it than this car."

"Sold," he said, and gave her a kiss. "Last one up the stairs has to serve breakfast in bed tomorrow."

He made a dash for the front door as she got out of the car more leisurely and dangled the keys from her hand.

"Smart-ass," he muttered and headed back toward her with a threatening look. She giggled and escaped him by circling the car, but he still caught up to her at the front door.

Her laughter ended when he caged her with his body and pressed his mouth to hers. As she wrapped her arms around his neck, his hips moved against hers, letting her know that the long car ride hadn't eased his discomfort one bit.

With a little effort, they managed to get the door unlocked and opened, but making it up the stairs was completely out of the question.

* * *

Dillard lowered his binoculars and stepped out from behind the tree. He wanted some of whatever McCoy was taking. Talk about going at it like rabbits! They were making him so horny, he was ready to take care of himself. And he would, if he had to spend another night in his car, but now that the happy couple were home and tucking each other in bed for the night, he was going to go home for a few hours himself. Hopefully, his wife would remember who he was. Maybe if he was good enough, she'd even agree to switch cars with him tomorrow so he wouldn't have to worry about them spotting him again.

As he walked the three blocks to the shopping center parking lot where he left his car, he congratulated himself on his good luck. When he'd returned that afternoon and saw the car gone, he was afraid they'd given him the slip again. After losing them yesterday, he didn't want to tell his client he'd done it again.

They probably only did some more sightseeing anyway, and what he accomplished was a lot more worthwhile. By tomorrow afternoon, he would probably have some solid information to pass on and justify the retainer he'd been paid.

If luck stayed with him and the computers didn't crash, by tomorrow afternoon, he could know as much about Duke McCoy as he did himself.

Chapter Fifteen

"Now I know why it's called ram-it-up-against-the-wall sex," Kelly said when she could think again.

Luke raised his head and grinned. "I never heard it called that, but it certainly fits." He supported her hips as he separated their bodies, and she lowered her legs. "Once again, that wasn't exactly what I had planned."

She brushed her nose over his, Eskimo-style. "But once again, it was incredible."

He stepped back and scanned himself with some amazement. His pants were around his ankles . . . again. He bent down to pull them up, and as he did, he tucked her discarded panties into his jeans pocket.

"I believe those are mine," she said as she smoothed down her skirt and rebuttoned her blouse.

Giving her a wink, he said, "Not anymore. Are you hungry?"

"Starved," she admitted and followed him to raid the refrigerator.

They spoke only with their eyes as they ate sandwiches and washed them down with the last of the wine and beer. When they were finished and Kelly assumed they would be heading to bed, he surprised her once more.

"Do you have any records?" he asked.

"Of what?"

"The kind of music we were listening to today."

"Oh, I thought you meant *records*, like files. No, I don't have any oldies, but I've got some CD's you might like."

"Would you put something on? Something slow."

Choosing the new Mariah Carey album, she waited for it to start to adjust the volume as he turned off most of the lights.

"May I have this dance?" he asked, formally holding out his hand.

She glided into his arms as if she'd done it a hundred times before. "How did you know?"

He kissed her temple as his body molded to hers. "It was written all over your face when we were in the car before."

"And here I thought I was such a master at hiding my feelings."

His hand slid up and down her back. "I'm glad you can't hide them from me. It makes it a lot easier to please you when I can see exactly what you're thinking."

For a while, they simply moved with the music, and it was quite obvious that he was better than an "okay" dancer. But with their bodies pressed so close together and the sensual way his hands continually roamed over her, Kelly's thoughts soon turned to a more intimate kind of dancing.

Without her needing to say a word, he stopped swaying and led her up the stairs to her room. Strains of the love song drifted up, maintaining the slow pace, as Luke undressed Kelly, then himself.

After arranging her hair behind her so that he had a completely unobscured view, he lightly ran his hands from her neck, over her breasts, and down her hips. "You are, without a doubt, the most beautiful woman I have ever known. And I'm not just talking about the package, but what's inside."

She returned his compliment by caressing his chest and stroking his erection. "I didn't know how much I could enjoy being with a man. Thank you for showing me."

He grinned and eased her backward until they reached the edge of the bed. With a touch, he guided her to sit, then lay back while he hovered over her. He captured her mouth for an intense but brief kiss, then said, "Thank me later."

She closed her eyes and inhaled deeply as he kissed his way down to her breasts, made exquisite love to them, then continued downward. He more than fulfilled his promise to drive her mad with his mouth and hands before satisfying them both once more.

It was morning before she remembered to thank him, and then there wasn't enough time to do it the way she wanted to. After she gave him a hint of what she had in mind, however, he was happy to take her rain check.

By midmorning, their bags were repacked and they were ready to return to Charming for their lunch with Reid O'Neill. After Mary Beth's reaction to seeing the two of them yesterday, despite Luke's haircut, Kelly thought about changing her appearance a little. However, since her photo was in the back of all her books, that didn't make much sense.

"But don't you take any chances," she reminded Luke. "You wear both your hat and glasses at all times while we're in public in Charming. And make sure you have a pad and pen. Remember, you're supposed to be my assistant."

"Got any great ideas to explain why I would keep on a hat and sunglasses indoors?"

She pursed her lips as she gave the problem some thought. "A brain tumor. If you had recently had surgery, they would have shaved a portion of your head, which would explain the hat, and the glasses would be because your eyes are still sensitive to light."

He rolled his eyes. "I'm beginning to worry about the condition of *your* brain. Are you sure there's nothing I can say to talk you out of doing this? It was one thing to interview Mary Beth, but going to O'Neill's home . . . that's the lion's den."

"I'm well aware of that, and if I could go around town asking questions without him finding out, I would do that instead. But that's not an option in a town as small as Charming. I need his stamp of approval first. Once he's agreed to the biography, I'll have *carte blanche* to interview whoever else I choose. I just have to play to his ego and avoid any mention of his murdered wife."

He sighed loudly and shook his head.

"You don't have to go with me."

"Like hell I don't," he said, frowning. "Not only do you need someone to watch your back, I wouldn't want to miss seeing that son-of-a-bitch's face when he gets a look at you. Maybe we'll luck out, and he'll think Ginger's come back from the dead to haunt him. He might even blurt out a full confession and save us a lot of trouble."

She made a face at him as they headed for the car. "You are such a smart-ass. No wonder they executed you."

Highway construction on the outskirts of Atlanta delayed them so long, they had to go straight to the O'Neill estate without stopping at the cabin.

The first thing they noted when they arrived was that there were several more cars than one would expect to find in the driveway of an elderly, single man. Hannah greeted them at the front door with the same barely polite stiffness

Kelly had experienced previously. From the grand foyer, the housekeeper led them to the library.

"Miss Kelly Kirkwood and her associate, Duke McCoy," Hannah announced in the doorway. "Lunch will be on the table in five minutes." She then stepped out of the way so that Kelly and Luke could enter.

Their curiosity about the number of cars outside was satisfied as soon as they walked into the library and saw four men instead of only one. The three facing them were at least in their seventies and the fourth, a younger man, judging by the small amount of gray in his dark hair, had his back to the door, perusing the bookshelves. As Luke had hoped, Kelly's appearance momentarily stunned at least two of the elderly men.

The shortest, a man with very little hair and drooping eyelids, quickly collected his thoughts, stepped forward with a forced smile, and extended his hand. "How do you do, Mizz Kirkwood? Reid O'Neill. I can't tell you how flattered I am to have you in my home."

As Kelly shook his hand and explained about Luke's "recent surgery," Luke scrutinized the aged face and body of Ginger's husband. His voice and demeanor exuded the reknowned southern hospitality, but Luke's intuition told him the man was very tense about this appointment.

"As it turned out," he continued, "I had to have a business meeting this morning, so I hope you don't mind that I'm killing two birds with one stone, so to speak. Allow me to introduce my associates who will be lunching with us." He motioned toward a tall, husky man with a full head of thick, white hair and a mustache to match. "This is a longtime friend and colleague of mine, Beauregard Ramey."

He graciously kissed Kelly's hand and said in a gravelly voice, "My friends call me Beau. I hope you will, too."

As he gave Luke a quick, firm handshake, his friendly expression vanished. He clearly disliked not being able to see Luke's eyes. Though Ramey had aged, Luke immediately recalled seeing him in the courtroom beside O'Neill every day of the trial. The other man may have been there as well, but there was nothing distinctive about him to be certain.

"And this is my company's treasurer, Andrew Chapman," O'Neill said, then spoke to the man who seemed more interested in reading the titles of the books on the shelves than turning around to meet the guests. "Junior?"

Luke heard Kelly's sharp intake of breath on hearing the nickname and discreetly gave her a warning nudge. As Junior joined their circle to be introduced, he kept his face turned to the side, so that his scarred flesh was partially concealed. Luke gave Kelly points for being able to give him the same warm smile that she had offered the others.

If Junior noticed a similarity between Kelly and

Ginger, he gave no indication of it. Then again, if he had committed the crimes they suspected, Junior Ramey was a master of deception.

"And I believe that brings us right up to the minute that the little general ordered us to report to the dining room." As he showed them the way, he said, "I may own this house, but General Hannah runs it. Don't know what I would have done without her all these years without a wife to take care of me."

O'Neill walked to the head of the long dining-room table and directed Kelly to take the seat to his right with Luke at her side. The other three men sat opposite them, and Luke got his first good look at Junior Ramey's grotesquely disfigured face. It was even worse than he'd imagined.

A chilled cucumber soup and selection of crackers was at each place, but before anyone could taste, Andrew Chapman recited a prayer of thanksgiving. Throughout the first course, O'Neill and Beau Ramey asked Kelly and Luke superficial questions about their backgrounds and how they liked Georgia. It helped that they had just spent two days sightseeing.

"You look so familiar," Beau said, narrowing his eyes at Kelly. "Do you have family in these parts?"

"Not that I know of," she replied with complete innocence. "I'm originally from Scranton, Pennsylvania, and I'm pretty sure all of my relatives have been in that area for generations."

Beau was clearly not satisfied with that answer. "Is Kirkwood your family name, or a pen name?"

"Actually, it's my married name." She made him wait a second before giving him the information he was really looking for. "My maiden name was Quinn and my mother's maiden name was Fitzsimmons."

Beau seemed to be searching for another logical reason why Kelly looked familiar, but Hannah's entrance with a rolling cart distracted him.

With a swift efficiency, she served a grilled chicken caesar salad and corn bread to each guest and departed again. Luke had thought the watery soup seemed like an odd choice, but the less than manly fare for the main course disappointed him. He wondered if there was a fast-food drive-thru on the way back to the cabin.

"As you can tell by the menu," O'Neill said in a slightly annoyed tone, "I don't even have a say about what foods are served at my own table. Thanks to the collaboration of Hannah and my family physician, the only time I even get to look at barbecued pork ribs or fried chicken in this house anymore is at our annual Fourth of July picnic." For the next quarter hour, he regaled Kelly with highlights from past picnics.

Hannah was clearing the table before Kelly was able to politely commandeer the conversation. "That's a wonderful story, Reid. In fact, it would make an excellent opener for your biography."

Luke caught the quick glance that passed be-

tween O'Neill and the senior Ramey, and knew
without hearing another word that Kelly would
not be getting a green light on her project. No
matter how good the reason sounded, they
couldn't allow anyone to dig up the past.

"Why don't you tell me what you have in
mind," O'Neill said, as though he was actually
interested.

"Americans love stories about self-made men,"
she began enthusiastically. "From everything I've
heard, you'd be the perfect subject and with my
clout in New York, I'm sure we could put together
a proposal that would practically guarantee an
auction. I hope you don't mind, but, just to get an
idea, I mentioned the possibility to my agent, and
I'm not exaggerating when I tell you he flipped for
it. He thinks we could get seven figures easily."

"S-seven figures?" Reid repeated with no little
surprise. "My life story could bring in over one
million dollars?"

"Oh, at least one. And then, of course, the
movie deals are on top of that. By the way, did
you know that my last book is being made into
a movie?"

Luke had to bite his cheek to keep from laughing out loud. She was really good. He watched
the eye movements and subtle body language
among the three older men and could easily guess
at the translation. O'Neill no longer wanted to
turn Kelly down flat. Ramey was reminding him
of whatever they had discussed and decided be-

fore, and Andrew was siding with Ramey, no matter what his opinion was.

"I am certainly flattered, Kelly," Reid said with another side glance at Ramey. "And you seem to be a very honest, straightforward woman. However, I have heard of instances where someone grants an interview and their words are all twisted around by the time it goes into print. I myself have not experienced such treachery, but with all the people who would be involved in such a grand endeavor, I might not be so fortunate this time."

"I can offer a guarantee," Kelly quickly countered. "I can have it written in the contract that you would have approval of the final edited manuscript before it goes to the typesetter. Your story is so inspirational. Just think of all the young people you could influence. Besides that, a biography would give you the rare opportunity to share your thoughts and opinions with the entire world."

That lure even caused Ramey's brows to raise in speculation, but it wasn't enough to completely sway him. When O'Neill appeared to be out of objections, Ramey stepped in. "Pardon me for entering into a conversation that is clearly none of my business, but I feel there is something that Kelly should know. Reid and I have been friends most of our lives, and no one on God's great earth would be happier to see his life story become an inspiration to our young people. But there have been some dark times in his life, painful events that no man should have to relive, particularly not in public."

"I assure you, I understand," Kelly told him with great compassion. "Any delicate matters would be treated with discretion. It's not as if I'm some tabloid reporter purposely looking to dig up dirt to discredit him."

"Were you in the O'Neill store in Buford recently?"

Since it was the first time Junior had spoken, Kelly was momentarily taken aback. She had to force herself to look at him directly as she answered. "Um, yes, I was. Why do you ask?"

"You were asking one of my employees questions about Mr. O'Neill. Is that what you would do if he agreed to this . . . biography?"

"Well, yes. Other people's impressions and anecdotes are usually included, but as I said before, Mr. O'Neill would have final approval, so he could eliminate anything that didn't please him."

Although Kelly looked and sounded as though she were perfectly calm, Luke could see her wringing the linen napkin on her lap. They were seated too far apart for him to give her a reassuring pat. She was doing a great job of selling her idea; the problem was the only one interested in buying didn't appear to have the freedom to do so.

Hannah returned with coffee and tea service and dessert. Luke looked at the angel food cake and single scoop of rainbow-colored sherbet and decided long life wasn't worth it if it meant eating like this all the time.

Kelly continued to answer every objection with a confident assurance that everything would be handled with utmost care, but Luke could tell that she knew it was hopeless. What really amazed him was how well she was holding up under Junior's eery one-eyed stare. If Mary Beth had been correct about his having been infatuated with Ginger, he had to be doing mental backflips over Kelly, but, other than the unbroken stare, he gave no indication that he was affected by her presence.

O'Neill finally put an end to Kelly's misery. "I want you to know that I have never had such a wonderful offer from such a lovely woman, but I'm afraid my answer is going to have to be no. As Beau said, it would cause me too much pain to talk about certain events of the past, nor do I really want folks to be bothered with questions and interviews on my account."

"But I—"

"I'm sorry," he said, firmly cutting Kelly off. "That's my decision. And I hope that I am judging your integrity correctly when I say I do not expect to hear that you have gone ahead with this project on an unauthorized basis. That would truly disappoint me."

Kelly rose gracefully. "I wouldn't think of disappointing you, Mr. O'Neill, but you have truly disappointed me."

*   *   *

"I don't get it," Beau said as soon as the guests were out of the house. "Why would a successful author of love stories be so danged anxious to write a biography about a businessman? There has to be something more to it."

"I do hope your suspicions are correct," Reid said with a shake of his head. "For that was a hell of a lot of money I just turned down."

"Talk is cheap. There's no telling what the actual numbers would have been had you agreed." Junior let out a soft snort that got his father's attention. "Speak up if you have an opinion, son. That's why you were invited."

"Bullshit. I was invited because of my vested interest in Mr. O'Neill's past, and if you two aren't going to say it out loud I will. We were looking at a ghost today, and I don't believe for one minute that her being in Charming or her generous offer are purely coincidental."

"For once we agree," Beau said. "But it wasn't just her appearance that bothered me; it was also the fact that her assistant was so well disguised."

Reid frowned at him. "You didn't believe her explanation about his having brain surgery?"

"I might have, if that was the only odd thing about her being here, but putting it all together—"

Junior snorted again. "I've only got one good eye, but apparently I see better than the two of you together. Didn't either one of you notice the words on his baseball cap?" He gave them a moment to recall it before revealing the answer. "Detroit Tigers." When that didn't ring any bells for the older men, he spelled it out for them. "There was once a reporter who kept sticking his nose—and his dick—into other people's business. I'll give you three guesses what city that man was from."

Reid's droopy eyes widened with fearful awareness. "I had completely forgotten that detail. It was so many years ago."

"Well, I haven't forgotten," Junior said in a low voice. "I remember every single detail. The question is, was he purposely giving us a clue about why they were here, or was it an oversight on his part?"

Andrew Chapman spoke for the first time since the benediction. "The Lord works in mysterious ways, gentlemen. Perhaps it was a warning from Him that once again, there is an enemy in our midst."

Beau's expression hardened. "Then we must prepare ourselves to deal with that enemy."

"I don't think we should act in haste," Reid said with a fretful look. "Circumstances are much different today."

"You're quite right," Beau told him. "We should investigate the matter further before taking action. Mizz Kirkwood's a writer. Perhaps she's written something about what she and that assistant of hers are really up to. Junior, perhaps you'd like to take a peek inside that cabin she's been staying at. Seems I recall that you once had a taste for entering women's homes uninvited."

Junior would have been annoyed with his father's attempt at humor, if his suggestion hadn't caused a streak of excitement to race through his lower body. This woman reminded him so much of Ginger—

"Just a look around," his father warned, correctly guessing at the train of Junior's thoughts. "When *no one* is home."

Junior acknowledged the instructions, but that didn't mean he couldn't fantasize about doing it his way.

"Okay," Kelly said as they drove away from the O'Neill estate. "I got the same impressions as you. But how do you figure Andrew Chapman into the picture?"

"He's the Kludd," Luke answered simply, then elaborated. "The chaplain. Every meeting of the Klan opens with a prayer, and I think this was a private, but official, meeting of the powers that be, or at least the powers that were back then. His presence seems to confirm the theory that my being framed was a group effort."

"But it doesn't answer who actually raped and killed Ginger."

Luke sighed. "You know damn well who the rapist was at that table. He may only have half a face, but you had to have felt him staring at you the whole time. In that twisted mind of his he probably had you strapped down on the—"

"*Okay!* I felt it. But that doesn't mean he killed her."

"What the hell difference does it make? It was one of *them*. And they're still alive, and still dangerous. I don't want to see them do to you what they did to Ginger. You've just had your hands tied as far as doing any further investigating in this area. And we did as much as we could in Atlanta. It's time to forget it."

She frowned. "I can't. I'm writing a book about it, remember?"

"Then write the book. It's supposed to be fiction, so make it up. Just pick someone to be the actual murderer and get on with it. I'll help however I can, but there is nothing to be gained by pushing those guys into a corner."

Kelly was quiet for the rest of the short trip, but as they pulled up in front of the cabin, she asked, "Do you think I was wrong about your having to go back to 1965 to prevent Ginger's death or at least see to it that the guilty man was prosecuted?"

He stroked her cheek. "I think you're mistaken about why I was sent here. In spite of all our efforts, we don't really know that much more than what I'd suspected to begin with. After facing those men today though, I am certain of one thing. Even if I knew, without a doubt, who killed Ginger and framed me, it wouldn't make any difference. In 1965, they had all the power, and I had none. My knowledge would not have stopped them from doing exactly what they'd planned."

"I'm not sure I agree, but go ahead."

"What I'm getting at is this, if they hadn't gotten me one way, they would have done it another. I don't think my being sent here was a temporary reprieve. I think it was a full pardon, because there was no way I could have changed what happened."

She was almost convinced. "I'm not going to argue the point anymore. *But* if you suddenly get hit by a bolt of lightning, or a live electrical wire accidentally falls on you, and you get zapped back there, will you at least promise to *try* to save Ginger and set things right?"

"Deal," he said with a smile, then leaned toward her for a kiss.

Rather than kiss him, however, she said, "I still think we're missing something important. Why do I look so much like Ginger?"

"Please don't tell me we're back to that again."

She smiled at the worried look in his eyes. "I'm not upset. I'm curious. It's too weird to be a complete coincidence."

"Maybe the whole thing was God's way of making O'Neill remember what he'd done and giving him a scare. Or maybe you're the payback for my aborted relationship with Ginger."

Kelly cocked her head at him. "What did you say?"

He groaned. "Ah, you're not going to get mad again, are you? I didn't mean—"

"No, no, it's okay. But you triggered an idea, and whether it's true or not, it would work into my book beautifully. Come on. I have to write this down while it's bubbling in my head." She bolted from the car into the cabin, and he followed with their bags a minute later.

She was already scribbling on a lined pad when he entered, so he sat down across the table from her and patiently waited for her to fill him in.

"Ginger was murdered on July 9, 1965, right?"

"Right."

"And I was born on April 25, 1966." Her eyes were bright with excitement.

"Okay." He had no idea what she was getting at.

"If you count backward nine months from my birthday, you get July 25, 1965, which means I was conceived shortly after Ginger's death. Don't you see? I could be Ginger reincarnated."

Chapter Sixteen

"*Reincarnated?* Like in the Buddhist religion?"

He was looking at her so oddly, she laughed. "Yes, but Buddhists aren't the only ones who believe in the possibility of reincarnation today. In fact, it's even gaining credibility in the medical community as a possible answer to certain psychological problems, such as depression, and unexplained pain and illness."

"If you say so," he said, but his expression remained doubtful.

"Anyway, it satisfies my curiosity about the similarity in our appearance, and it will fit into the story perfectly. Think about what all of you said to me. You were in deep lust over Ginger, but something kept you from asking her to marry you. Now here I am, physically similar to Ginger, but—in your words—better on every score. Sort of the new, improved version of Ginger, which could be partially accounted for by the mere fact that I was born in a time period when women are expected to be more."

He glanced heavenward and pretended to be talking to God. "Are you listening to this? I wore myself out trying to convince her that I wasn't thinking of Ginger when I was with her and now I'm supposed to believe she *is* Ginger."

Kelly chuckled and gave him a playful slap on the hand. "Stop it. I didn't say you had to believe it, only that it makes sense in a strange sort of way. Besides, you, of all people, should be willing to believe that anything is possible. Now, please understand, as much as I enjoy your company, I have to do some work. So, go away."

He rose from the chair with a grin. "It would be a lot easier to go away if we were at your town house."

She looked up at him, then looked around as though she just realized the cabin only had one room and no television. "Oh. I suppose it would, but I really like the secluded atmosphere here and the fact that there are no phones. I'll tell you what. If you'll find some way to occupy yourself for a few days while I write up the detailed outline of the story, we'll move back to Atlanta after that."

He walked around behind her and kissed the top of her head. "We can stay here as long as you like, just so you don't make me sleep on the couch."

Tilting her head back, she drew him down for

a soft kiss. "The only way you'll be on the couch is if I'm on there with you."

He gave her one more brief kiss, then moved away. "You know, I always thought I'd like to try my hand at writing a novel. This looks like the perfect opportunity." He picked up one of her books that were sitting on the desk. "And I'm going to begin by familiarizing myself with what makes a bestseller today."

She smiled as she noted which one he'd chosen. She couldn't wait to see his reaction to the steamy sex scene in chapter five.

Dillard frowned at the evidence spread out on his kitchen table. His friend at the forensic lab was pissed with him for making him drop everything and risk his job for the sake of a joke. The only problem was, it wasn't a joke.

The fingerprints he'd lifted off Kelly Kirkwood's car were a perfect match with a convicted murderer named Luke Templeton. A comparison of the photos he'd taken of Duke McCoy and Luke Templeton's mug shots also seemed to confirm that they were one and the same man.

But Luke Templeton had been executed at the age of thirty-five in August 1965. Exactly thirty-two years later, he seemed to be back. That might be possible based on the information he'd uncovered about the electrocution. If, instead of being spontaneously combusted, Templeton had fooled everyone and had somehow actually escaped, he could still be alive today. However, he'd be sixty-six years old, and the man putting a big smile on Kirkwood's face couldn't possibly be that old.

That morning, he'd followed the couple all the way to Charming, where she had been staying prior to her recent visit to Atlanta. That was another factor that fit perfectly into the puzzle without giving him a whole picture. Why was she in Charming, the site of the murder for which Templeton had been executed? The second big question arose when he learned whose home they had driven to. Why would they be visiting the husband of the woman Luke Templeton had murdered over three decades ago?

Rather than stay on their tail in a location that would make it nearly impossible for him to remain unnoticed, he'd returned to Atlanta to find out whatever he could about Duke McCoy. Unfortunately, the conclusions he came to made no sense.

He had called his client, as he had promised to do, but instead of giving him any information over the phone, he made an appointment to meet with him personally the next morning, explaining that he had some interesting photos for him to see. Hopefully, after a good night's sleep, he'd know what he was going to tell the man.

"There's nothing to eat in this refrigerator," Luke complained. "I knew we should have stopped somewhere on the way here."

Kelly set down her pen. "I guess we could drive into town and pick up some groceries before the store closes."

"Is there a decent restaurant where we could eat first?"

She pulled her brain the rest of the way out of her story and gave him her full attention. "As a matter of fact, there is, but I don't think we should spend a lot of time in Charming. Or Buford for that matter. I don't want to risk bumping into Junior. How about a drive around to the other side of Lake Lanier? We'll eat and buy groceries over there. I'm ready to stop for today anyway."

Junior knew everything was going to work out for him as he watched the black Camaro drive away. Thinking that Kelly Kirkwood seemed like the kind that might go out to dinner rather than cook, he had decided to hide in the woods behind the cabin for a while. His patience had paid off.

He was somewhat surprised to find the doors locked against him, but he figured that was her big-city fear coming into play. It was such a waste of time when the windows had no latch on them. He was inside in a matter of seconds.

There was still sufficient light from the setting sun for him to get a good look around. He kept in mind his father's orders to make sure he left everything exactly the way he'd found it.

From a quick tour of the cabin, it was clear that her assistant was living here with her, which did not please Junior one bit. He'd been daydreaming about coming out here while she was sound asleep one night. It would be so dark, she wouldn't be able to guess his identity. He imagined himself becoming her secret dream lover who only comes to her under the veil of night.

It would be like having Ginger all to himself again.

The man with the Detroit Tigers cap, whoever he really was, was in the way. Just like the other man from Detroit had been.

He couldn't resist taking a moment to inspect her clothes, and when he found where she kept her lingerie, he had to touch the panties and bras, slide them over his skin, and imagine how they would look pulled tightly against her womanly flesh. He wondered if her pubic hair was reddish gold or dark brown like Ginger's. He could never forget what a surprise that had been when he finally got to see it. His eyes closed so that he could savor the memory of rubbing his face in those precious curls after having waited so long.

It was more than he could bear. He wanted this woman, even if she was only an imitation of Ginger, and one day soon, he would figure out a way to have her. But for now, he was forced to accept a substitute. Choosing one of the plainest pair of white panties in the drawer, he made himself at home on her couch. Seconds later, he had convinced himself that his nylon-covered fist was actually Kelly Kirkwood's lush body.

When his fantasy came to a pleasant finale, he was very tempted to leave the soiled panties behind so that she would know he'd been there and would soon be back for the real thing, but his father's words echoed in his ears, and he got control over the urge.

All daydreams and fantasies swiftly fled when he began looking through the papers on the table. As soon as he realized what Kelly Kirkwood's new book was truly about, he cursed himself for not bringing a camera. He would have much preferred to hand his father photographs rather than be the bearer of this bad news.

One piece of paper intrigued him more than the rest, however, and he committed the handwritten words to memory.

"Reincarnation? I think you've gone completely loco this time, Junior!"

Most of the time, Junior merely resented his father, but when he yelled at him like he was still six years old, he really despised the old man. "As usual, you weren't listening to me. I didn't say *I* thought she was reincarnated. That's what was written on the paper. It does seem to explain why she's so interested in the Luke Templeton case. You should have seen all the newspaper articles she had copies of, including a couple on me."

"Is that right? So she must have recognized your name when you were introduced. I'm surprised she didn't go screaming from the house."

"Why? According to the articles, I was completely vindicated. But if you think the idea of reincarnation is loco, wait till you hear this. The book she's working on has a man being wrongly accused of his lover's murder and sent to the chair. When they throw the switch, he seems to have been spontaneously combusted, but in actuality, he travels forward in time. Guess where he lands?"

"At a cabin being rented by the reincarnated lady author?"

"Bingo. Sort of makes you wish you could have gotten a good look at Duke McCoy without the hat and glasses, doesn't it?"

Beau huffed and shook his head. "What you're suggesting is totally outrageous, to say nothing for being downright blasphemous. There is no such thing as reincarnation or time-travel.

"What we have here is a beautiful woman with a very active imagination. As far as I'm concerned, we have the answer we were looking for. She's doing research for her new book, which is based on the Luke Templeton case, but the names, dates, and locations are all different in the story she's writing. As long as it stays that way, and she sticks to her agreement not to go around bothering people with questions, she's no threat to us."

"What about her assistant being in disguise and the Detroit ball cap?"

"I'm afraid we all fell victim to our overly suspicious minds. We should have known that a woman in her position could not afford to be involved in anything more devious than secretly acquiring information for her next book. I'm sure he's exactly who and what she said he is."

Junior was very disappointed with that verdict, but he kept his opinion to himself.

Beau grasped his son's arm and held tight. "You stay away from her, do you hear me? She's too well known for you to be messing with her."

"What if she keeps snooping around?"

Beau released Junior with a tired sigh. "If she becomes troublesome, we will discuss the matter again, but until such time, you will put her out of that perverted mind of yours." As he watched his son leave, he hoped he'd sounded convincing. In truth, he still felt there was something more going on around the author lady, but he couldn't have Junior mucking things up until he found out exactly what it was.

It wasn't that late when Kelly and Luke returned to the cabin, but the busy day had taken its toll on them. They had had a nice dinner, bought enough groceries to last them for a few days, and had enjoyed a leisurely drive along the lake. Falling into bed together was the only thing left on their minds.

As Kelly put the food away, Luke lit two kerosene lamps and opened the windows to let the cool night breeze flow through the cabin.

"What happened to the screen for this window?'' Luke asked as he opened the one that he had come through when he first arrived.

''What's wrong with it?'' she asked without looking.

''It's missing.''

She gave him a doubtful glance and walked over to the window to see for herself. ''It was on this afternoon when I closed up.'' She poked her head outside and saw the screen on the ground. ''It must have fallen off. I'd better go out and put it up, or we'll be attacked by mosquitoes.''

Luke insisted on doing the little chore and realized what was bothering him about the screen when he started to replace it. In order to climb in before, he had had to loosen several wing nuts that kept clamps pressed against the corners of the screen to prevent it from simply ''falling off.'' He quickly reattached it and went back inside.

''Don't touch anything for a minute,'' he told her as he turned on the two electrical lamps in the main room and the light in the bathroom.

Kelly watched him with wary eyes. ''What is it? What's wrong?''

''I don't know. Hopefully, nothing. But it's highly unlikely that the screen came off without some human assistance.''

Her breath caught in her chest. ''You think someone was in here while we were gone?'' She immediately recalled the sick feeling she'd had when she discovered that Bruce had been sleeping in her bed.

"Take a good look around. Try to remember where everything was when we left. Where's your computer?"

She checked the bags that they had yet to unpack. It didn't appear that they'd been gone through, and the laptop was still in its case, exactly where she'd left it. "There isn't much of value in here. The computer, my printer, and the generator are pretty much it. Maybe it was just a drifter looking for food and when he saw what little was in the fridge, he felt sorry for us and left."

"Do you have any money or jewelry?"

"No jewelry except the watch and ring I'm wearing, and I had my cash and credit cards with me. Anyway, wouldn't a thief have dumped drawers out or something?" Again remembering how Bruce had put his clothes next to hers, she checked each of the drawers in the bureau, then shook her head. "It doesn't look like anything's been touched." As she turned back to Luke, she noticed him frowning at the papers and files on the table. "What is it?"

"The few things of value are still here. Nothing seems to have been taken or searched, and no notes or mementos were left behind. That probably means it's safe to assume it wasn't a drifter, thief, or any obsessive fan, friend, or ex-husband."

"So-o-o, what conclusion are you coming to?"

"After today's lunch, it wouldn't have surprised me if someone had come out here to check up on what you were working on, but I can't tell if any papers have been moved. And the more I think about that, if one of them had read the information on this table, we probably would have been greeted by a circle of men in white hoods when we got back. Of course, the other possibility is the man who followed us around Atlanta. Maybe he—"

"That's enough," she said, holding up a hand to stop his speculations. "I think all this cloak-and-dagger stuff has got us jumping at our own shadows. The fact of the matter is, when I put the screen back on the other day, I probably didn't secure it very well, and when I shut the window earlier, I must have jarred it out of place. Now, I would be more than happy to go over this entire cabin with a magnifying glass if there was even one indication that someone had been inside, but there isn't. And frankly, I had something more interesting in mind for tonight."

She headed back toward the kitchen counter to finish putting away the groceries, but he caught her around the waist as she passed and pulled her close.

"By any chance, did the interesting something have anything to do with the baby oil you tried to discreetly slip into the shopping cart?"

She smiled up at him, pleased to see that he'd switched mental gears so easily. The lascivious grin on his face also told her he'd read chapter five of her book. "You get the lights and open the sofa bed while I make sure all the cold food is in the fridge." She was putting away the shopping bags when he unexpectedly barked at her.

"Kelly! What the hell is this doing here?"

She turned around to see him pointing at her gun where she had last put it—beneath the sofa cushions. With an embarrassed shrug, she admitted, "I put it there when I still thought I needed protection from you, and I guess I forgot about it. You can put it away."

"You *forgot* about it? Dammit, Kelly. You don't just *forget* about a gun. What if someone really had broken in here tonight, and found that thing. He could have gone out and killed someone with it, all because you *forgot* about it."

"Whoa, boy! Calm down. Just put it wherever you'd like, and I promise to be more careful in the future."

He crossed his arms defensively and glared at the weapon. "*You* put it away. Somewhere that I won't accidentally find it again."

"All right," she said, eyeing him curiously. He was clearly very upset. She picked up the gun and looked around. Where would he have no reason to look? She decided that her underwear drawer was as good a place as any. Once the Walther was completely hidden by lingerie, she walked back to Luke and touched his cheek. "I am sorry." He took a slow breath and relaxed his body. "Do you want to tell me what that was all about?"

"I hate guns," he said simply, then brought her

hand up to his lips for a kiss before getting back to unfolding the sofa bed as though nothing out of the ordinary had occurred.

She stood there, silently watching him with a straight face, as he went about fetching the bed pillows and putting a sheet on the mattress. Apparently, it was fine for her to divulge her most private, painful memories, but he didn't feel he could do the same.

Finally, he met her narrow-eyed gaze and threw his arms up in surrender. *"What?"*

"Is it that you don't trust me, or are you too much of a man to admit that you have emotions?"

He ran his hands through his hair with a frustrated sigh, then sat down on the edge of the bed. Patting the spot next to him, he invited her to join him. "It's not something I like to remember, but when I see a gun . . . it might as well be a poisonous snake. It scares the living hell out of me."

He shifted so they were facing each other. "I saw plenty of gunshot victims while I was working the crime beat. But one day, when I was trying to research a story about rival street gangs, I got to witness an actual shooting. A thirteen-year-old kid from one gang had found the gun his father had *forgotten* to put away. When a member of the other gang insulted him, he pulled out the gun and fired six times without stopping. One boy was lucky. He died instantly. Three others suffered for hours before they checked out, and two more were injured."

He had to take a slow breath before finishing. "I just stood there and watched it happen. It was over before I could even think to move. It's not like I have nightmares over it or anything, but I've never been able to stand having a gun around since then."

Kelly brushed a lock of hair off his forehead. "And the first thing I did when I saw you was pull a gun on you. I am so very sorry. But I've got to tell you, I couldn't tell that you were that frightened."

He smiled crookedly. "Writing the kinds of things I did, I had to learn to hide my reactions. The fact was, I could hardly hear you for how hard my heart was pounding."

She placed her hand on his chest. "It feels pretty normal now." She leaned toward him and brushed her lips over his. "Maybe, to be on the safe side, you should let me know whenever I do anything that makes your heart pound." As her mouth traveled to his ear, her hand moved over his nipple. "You just let me know, and I'll stop immediately." She felt his chest move with silent laughter.

"What if I don't want you to stop?" he whispered in her ear.

She eased him backward onto the bed, raised the hem of his shirt and kissed his stomach. "If you don't want me to stop, you should let me know that, too." She unbuckled his belt, undid the button on his jeans, and placed another kiss on his navel.

"Kelly?"

"Mmm-hmm?"

"Don't stop."

Acting out the promise she'd made that morning to thank him in an unforgettable way, she insisted he allow her total freedom to do whatever she pleased with his body, without his touching her.

She undressed him completely while he remained stretched out on the bed, then removed her own clothes. "Just to be sure you don't forget the no-touching rule," she said, placing both his hands at the top edge of the mattress, "I want you to hold on right there until I tell you it's okay to let go. Can you do that, or would you rather I get something to tie you in place?"

He bit his lip to keep from laughing. "I'll be good, mistress. I promise I won't let go until you order me to."

She gave him a regal nod of her head. "Very good. Now, no more talking."

He watched her kneel down on the bed beside him and guessed at what she was planning to do. He was wrong.

As light as a feather, she caressed his face with her fingertips. It was so gentle and relaxing, he closed his eyes to focus his entire attention on the sensation. The wispy touch moved to his neck, then his shoulders, arms, and hands, and back to his chest.

She was barely touching him, yet his skin tightened wherever she made contact and he began to anticipate the direction of her stimulation. Her fingers moved in circles and esses, grazing over his body hair, stroking every inch of him as though he was a gift she'd been given to explore. As her ticklish caress moved lower, he held his breath to prepare for the touch that would make him want to forget her orders, but his preparation was unnecessary. From his lower abdomen, she circumvented the obvious and moved on to his legs. He managed not to utter a complaint.

When she finally reached his toes, he exhaled heavily, thinking the slow foreplay was over. He was wrong again. A different sensation tickled his feet and his eyes opened to identify it. Once he saw that the implement of her new torture was her hair, he had to keep his eyes open to see what those beautiful tresses looked like draped all over his body.

The nerves beneath his skin were screaming for her to stop the torment, but he made himself hold still as she crawled upward between his spread legs. Rather than avoid the muscle that was standing at full attention for her, she wound a thick lock of hair around it from the base up. When he was completely wrapped, she placed a kiss on top of her creation, then very slowly raised her head so that her hair pulled tight then spiraled away from him. His heart was now pounding as hard as it had when he saw the gun, but he would die before asking her to stop.

She let him feel her hair brush back and forth across his chest, then began her third act. When she ran her tongue between his lips, he prayed that meant the tickling had come to an end, but it simply changed form. Without picking up her pace, her tongue covered the same ground her hands and hair had.

Again she made him wait for what he really wanted, but when her mouth finally closed over his erection, he decided her game had definitely been worth playing.

And play with him she did. Several times his hands lowered to touch her, to show her how much he was enjoying what she was doing to him, but each time he did so, she stopped pleasing him until he returned his hands to their holding place.

He tried to make it last, but it was too good. Again, she was the one in complete control. He was about to give in to her power, let her have him however she wanted him, when she abruptly released him. He couldn't stop the groan of near pain that came up from his chest.

She touched her finger to her lips and rose from the bed. Through the blurred haze of passion, he watched her walk across the room and come back to him with something in her hand.

"You didn't think I was going to forget about chapter five, did you?" she asked with a sexy smile as she crawled back up between his legs again.

With no further explanation, she squeezed the bottle of baby oil over the top of his penis, then across her big, beautiful breasts. He could barely keep from exploding as she smoothed the lubricant over him, then massaged herself. He knew what she was going to do, and yet, he still gasped as she enveloped his erection between her breasts and held them firmly around him.

Mere seconds later his entire body spasmed with the most intense pleasure he had ever experienced. Climactic waves continued to rock him long after he was spent, and she tenderly stroked him until every muscle in his body was completely relaxed again.

"You can let go now," she said, with an extremely satisfied smile.

He lowered his hands and pulled her on top of him for a kiss. "I hope you realize what you've done to me."

She arched one brow at him. "I have a pretty good idea."

"I don't think you do. I'll never be able to have sex with another woman again. You've ruined me."

She couldn't tell if he was serious or teasing. "Yeah, right. Knowing you, you'll be ready to go again in a half hour."

He smiled and kissed her nose. "That's not what I meant. You've surpassed all my fantasies, fulfilled every secret desire. I'd never be able to be with another woman again because all I'd be thinking about is you and this time we had together. It wouldn't be fair to her."

She made a face at him. "That's very flattering, but pretty hard to believe. I'm sure if you got zapped back to 1965 and saw Ginger again—"

He cut her off with a hard kiss, then said flatly, "I'm not going back. I'm staying here. With you. And I'm going to get you pregnant and be with you when you give birth, and still be around to get you pregnant again, if that's what you want. So stop talking about me going back!"

Chapter Seventeen

Kelly had no idea how to respond to Luke's declaration. He sounded perturbed, almost angry, with her, and yet, the actual words he had spoken suggested he was offering a commitment.

He sighed. "I'm sorry. That didn't come out right."

"Would you like to try again? I think I'd like to hear the revised version."

He rolled them both onto their sides so that they were facing each other more comfortably. "I can't explain it. Maybe there really is something to your reincarnation theory. All I know is I feel like I've known you for a lot longer than a week. And I want to spend a lot more time getting to know you even better. The thought of being ripped away from you just when I think I might have found someone . . ." He closed his eyes and pinched the bridge of his nose as he searched for the right words.

She wished for him to say what he had not been able to tell Ginger, even though she knew it was foolish of her to even let the thought enter her mind. When he looked at her again, his heart was in his eyes, but he didn't give her the words she'd hoped for.

". . . someone so . . . special. What if it's just a matter of you *wanting* me to stay?" He frowned a little. "You do want me to stay, don't you?"

She smoothed the wrinkle between his brows with her finger. "Yes, I would like you to stay . . . *if* that's what was meant to happen. I promise not to bring it up anymore, but until more time goes by, without your disappearing, I won't be convinced that I was wrong about you having some sort of mission to accomplish."

He accepted that much, but couldn't resist trying for more. He leaned forward until his lips were a breath away from hers. "What if the mission is to get you pregnant?"

She smiled softly and rubbed her nose against his. "If it is, I can assure you that I'm willing to work really, really hard at it."

His hand cupped her breast and gently kneaded the firm flesh. "There's no question that you worked really, really hard on your last effort, but I think I should tell you, it's pretty much impossible for you to get pregnant that way."

"Hmmph." She sat up and retrieved the bottle of baby oil. Nudging him onto his back, she poured a line down the center of his chest, and said, "If you think that, you must not have read *all* of chapter five."

"Ooh, that was a close one," Jezebel hissed snidely. "Tell me, Gabriel, how does it feel to have victory snatched away when you're so certain you can't lose?"

"There are still two weeks left," he said firmly.

"That's true, and I'll concede that he is more infatuated with her than he has ever been with another woman. *But*, our deal hinged on his actually telling her he loves her, then giving up his life to save hers. In case you weren't paying attention, Kelly has abandoned her plan to investigate Ginger's murder."

"As usual, Jezebel, the way your mind works eludes me."

She huffed and a gray cloud rose from her den. "By agreeing not to ask further questions around Charming, she has effectively eliminated the one chance she had of being in a life-threatening situation. Unless she steps in front of one of the few cars driving through that little village, there will be nothing dangerous for Luke to save her from."

"A lot can happen in two weeks," Gabriel replied confidently. "That is the beauty of the free-will system."

"You're fired."

Dillard was stunned. "Just because I didn't come back with the answer you wanted to hear—"

"You're fired because you are an idiot. I can't begin to imagine what you thought to gain with such a ridiculous story, but I'm not paying you for the time it took you to make it up."

"I didn't make up these reports."

"No? Then whoever did is just as big of an idiot as you are. There is no way in hell Duke McCoy and Luke Templeton are the same man."

Dillard had had enough. He gathered up his papers, but when he reached for the photos, his client slapped his hand down on top of them. "Those are mine, unless you want to pay me what you owe me."

"Sue me," the attorney said with a feral smile. "Or better yet, why don't you go to Reid O'Neill with your story. I'm sure he'd be willing to pay you some of his millions to have you point out the man who killed his wife thirty-two years ago."

As soon as the investigator left, Bruce Hackett squinted at the photographs one by one. He would have given up a fortune in legal fees to be the man administering the spanking to Kelly. But short of that, he would still have given a sizable amount to have been the man peeking through the kitchen window with a camera. As it was, he would have to settle for keeping the erotic pictures.

At least it was something in return for the advance retainer he'd paid that phony detective. Rather than use someone from the private investigative firm he usually employed through his legal practice, he had called an unknown, in hopes that his surveillance request would remain confidential and separate from his business. How could he have guessed that he'd chosen a complete incompetent?

When Evan Dillard had called and sounded so mysterious, he'd agreed to a personal meeting in his office that morning since no one else was due in. The visual proof that Kelly had indeed taken a lover was disappointing, but he figured he could put an end to that once he had some good dirt on Duke McCoy.

Instead of finding out that McCoy was a suspected drug dealer, a convicted child molester, or at least a married man, that idiot, Dillard, had come to him with an outrageous fairy tale about McCoy actually being a man who was executed for murder in 1965.

His parting shot echoed in his mind, and Bruce admitted that it wasn't the most professional thing he could have said. A man like Dillard actually might take the sarcastic suggestion seriously and use it to extort money from O'Neill. And it would be his fault for giving him the idea.

The wheels in his head turned this way and that until another idea occurred to him that would not only salvage the situation, but could get him a legal foot in the door of the prosperous O'Neill corporation. He mentally rehearsed what he could say to make it sound like he was doing O'Neill a favor by warning him of a possible problem before it happened, blaming the scheme entirely on Dillard, of course.

When he was sure he was ready, he called information and, though the discount store mogul's residence was unlisted, he got the number for the executive offices of O'Neill Enterprises. He tried calling it, on the off chance that someone was in on Saturday, but all he got was a recorded message instructing him to call on Monday.

It seemed that he was always having to wait for what he wanted, whether it was the business coup of a lifetime or the woman of his dreams.

Fortunately, he was a very patient man.

Kelly was well past the halfway point on her story outline by Sunday afternoon, and should have been rolling right along toward the finish, but she was having trouble concentrating on work today, and it was all Luke's fault.

Not that he was doing anything disturbing. He had been on the couch reading since he woke up Saturday morning. He didn't insist she pay attention to him, and, from personal experience, he knew better than to try to talk to her while she was creating. He even fixed most of their meals, so she wouldn't have to break her train of thought.

The problem was not what he was doing today, it was what he did last night, after they'd set the books aside.

He had made love to her. No fun and games. Not sex for the sake of sex, or sex for the sake of reproduction. *Love.* Beautiful, tender, sweet, magical love. Kelly wasn't sure if he realized it, but the difference had been very obvious to her, and what was left of the protective barriers around her heart had melted away.

She glanced his way, and he instinctively looked up from his book to wink at her.

She was completely, totally, head-over-heels in love with Luke, and she didn't know whether to sing or cry about it. Despite his determination to stay with her in this time period, she couldn't shed the feeling that he was only here temporarily and that something was about to happen that would cause him to be whisked away again.

Scenes from a time-travel movie she'd once watched kept popping into her head, as though there was an important clue or message in it that she needed to remember. Unable to move forward on her own story, she replayed the highlights of that movie in her mind, until she realized what it was that had been tiptoeing around the edges of her thoughts.

When someone goes back in time and changes an event, it can cause a chain reaction of changes into the future.

If Luke went back to 1965 and prevented Ginger's murder—and if she was in fact the reincarnation of Ginger—she, Kelly, would not have been born in 1966. She would simply not exist. That scenario did not bear thinking about.

On the other hand, if they were separate souls,

whether Ginger died or was rescued, she would have been born and continued on with her life exactly as it had proceeded originally. Except for one thing. She would not have been researching the case of Ginger's murder or Luke Templeton's execution.

And if he hadn't been electrocuted, he would not have been zapped forward to her.

In other words, if he changed those events in the past, she would not have met him in the future. Thus, it was probable that she would have no memory of him whatsoever, although he might remember everything.

Continuing along that line, she wondered what would happen if he found a way to return to 1997 after fixing the past in his favor. After last night, she was certain he was falling in love with her, even if he wasn't yet ready to say the words. Surely he would try to come back to her.

And she would think he was a crazed fan, or a lunatic. He would have a heck of a time convincing her that they had been lovers.

There had to be something she could do to smooth the way for him if such a situation came to pass. Gradually, an idea began to form, and she turned on her computer. Assuming that everything that occurred after Luke appeared in her life might change if he altered history, she needed to leave herself a message about him before he showed up. With that in mind, she changed the computer's internal clock to read January 1, 1997 and wrote herself a long, explanatory memo as part of her to-do list for the 24th of August.

That done, she readjusted the clock and got back to work on her story with renewed purpose.

As much as Luke was enjoying the book he was reading, he couldn't help but notice that Kelly had been doing more daydreaming than creating most of the day. Then suddenly, she got a burst of energy. Probably a new twist in her plot that would keep her occupied for a few more hours.

He really wanted to talk to her about his ideas, but he could make himself wait until she was ready to call it a day. So far, he had read two of her romantic suspense novels, the time-travel romance, and a straight mystery. He now understood what she meant about men thinking they were in love with her after reading her books. To his surprise, he liked reading the romantic stories, but he wasn't sure he could write one. The mystery felt more comfortable, and with his background, it would probably come together rather easily. He had even written down a few ideas about a crime-solving reporter.

He wanted to ask her opinion of those ideas, but was also anxious to discuss what he could do with them. If she was willing, he thought they could make it a joint effort. He would write it, with her guidance, and she could sell it under a pen name. That way, he could earn a living that wouldn't require him to have proper identification or credentials.

Of course, that also meant that they would be committing to a long-term relationship.

He let that awareness fully settle into his mind, examined it, and questioned how he felt about that. The words he said to her Friday night came back to him. Though they were said in the aftermath of incredibly great sex, he realized that he could comfortably repeat them this afternoon, sitting across the room from her. He actually *liked* the idea of having children with her and raising them together.

Unlike every other woman he'd known, the thought of spending an indefinite number of years with Kelly didn't make his stomach clench in panic. If anything, the sick feeling came when he thought of *not* being with her.

Did that mean he was in love with her?

At some point in his youth, he had come to the conclusion that in the search for the ultimate sexual experience, the truth could be stretched, with one major exception. He had decided that the one thing that went over the line was to tell a girl you loved her unless it was the absolute truth.

As the years went by, and he and his female partners matured, he began to believe that there was no such thing as true love. At least he'd never been certain enough of his feelings to make that special declaration.

So, did that mean he was in love with Kelly?

Maybe, but after all this time, he didn't want to jump to such a monumental conclusion too quickly. The reality was, he'd only known her a week. To be on the safe side, he decided to wait a month, and if his feelings for her hadn't lessened by then, he would tell her he loved her and wanted to spend the rest of his life with her.

Monday afternoon, Reid O'Neill cut his workday short to pay a visit to his oldest friend.

"That certainly is a mighty strange tale." Beau took another sip of his brandy. "You say this Bruce Hackett checks out as a legitimate attorney, and he gave you this information for free? He didn't want anything from you?"

Reid snorted. "Now I didn't say that. He clearly wanted some of my legal business, and if his tip turns out to be advantageous to us, he may just get some. If he'd called last week, before Junior found the newspaper clippings and those peculiar notations of Mizz Kirkwood's, I might have filed a complaint with the bar association. Today, though, I didn't think we could afford to ignore this additional peculiarity."

"I definitely concur with that. However, as I told Junior, I don't believe Mizz Kirkwood is the reincarnation of Ginger, no matter how much she resembles her. I also do not believe Duke McCoy and Luke Templeton could be one and the same. I was a witness at his electrocution, and I assure you, he did not escape from that room. He was incinerated to ashes."

Beau refilled his glass and took another swallow. "Aside from my disbelief that anything supernatural has occurred, however, something peculiar is very definitely going on with those two people. But there is still a vital piece missing to this curious puzzle. Let us put ourselves in a hypothetical situation and see what we come up with. If you were an author who wanted to find out about Reid O'Neill's past, particularly regarding his late wife, and the man himself had refused to give you the information you were seeking, who else would you go to?"

"His family, friends, and employees."

Beau held up a finger. "But you just made a promise in front of witnesses not to go around bothering those people with questions, and you're a well-known person with a reputation to uphold."

Reid rubbed his jaw as he considered the question, then stopped when a disturbing answer occurred to him. "I might try to find Ginger's best friend."

"Exactly what I would do. Let's see how right we are, shall we?" He looked up a number in his phone book and dialed.

"Jimmy Joe? Glad I caught you before you went home for the day. This here's Beauregard Ramey, Senior, up in Buford. How the hell are ya, boy?"

"Great," he replied with surprise in his voice. "It's been a very long time. Since my father's funeral, if I recall correctly. How is . . . everyone?"

"The little woman passed away two summers

ago. Her heart just gave out. Junior's still managing the O'Neill store up here. I hear tell the Jackson car dealerships are making more money than ever with you running the show. How's that pretty wife of yours doing?"

There was a pause before Jimmy Joe answered. "Mary Beth is . . . as well as can be expected. She keeps busy with her charity work."

"That nervous disorder still giving her problems, eh? Well, you're a good man for sticking by her. Speaking of Mary Beth, would you happen to know if she has had any calls or visits from a couple of strangers, a man and woman?"

"Not that I know of, and I discourage her from having company in the house when I'm gone. It seems to . . . aggravate her problems. Why do you ask?"

"Well, it seems this couple, one of whom is a famous author, has a real big interest in the past, particularly the time around when an old girlfriend of Mary Beth's passed on. This here is mighty important to me, Jimmy Joe. So I would sincerely appreciate it if you'd take a moment of your time to warn that pretty wife of yours not to talk to strangers if any should happen to come around when you're not home."

"I'll be happy to take care of that, Beau. Was there anything else I could do for you? Put you in a new Cadillac perhaps?"

Beau gave a hearty laugh. "As a matter of fact, I may be in to see you about that real soon. For now, just have a chat with Mary Beth and say hello to your mother for me when you see her."

Three hours later, Beau received a return call from Jimmy Joe reporting that the couple in question had visited his wife without his knowing about it. Unfortunately, Mary Beth didn't remember what they talked about. But she did recall that the lady was one of her favorite authors, and the man was the nephew of Luke Templeton.

"Another piece just fell into place," Beau told Reid over the phone as soon as he hung up from Jimmy Joe. "We now know that McCoy's motivation for resurrecting the past is to seek the truth or revenge, neither of which do we want to grant him. Her connection is most probably a personal relationship with him rather than Ginger, but nevertheless, she cannot be disregarded either."

"Where do you figure the attorney fits into the puzzle?" Reid asked. "Do you think he's working for McCoy?"

"Anything's possible, but that wouldn't make much sense since his call tipped you off to McCoy's identity."

"Perhaps that was the purpose—to put a scare into us and check our reaction."

"If it was, your reaction to his phone call was to drop everything and run straight here."

Reid was silent for a moment. "That doesn't prove anything. We visit each other all the time."

"It may not prove anything in a court of law, but if I were McCoy, it would be enough to make me believe that you have something to worry about and I'm involved in it."

Again Reid paused before speaking, and when he did, he couldn't hide the nervousness in his voice. "Even if he is suspicious about our . . . knowledge of what happened to his uncle, what could he do about it now?"

"I have been giving that a lot of thought. Considering all the pieces we now have, only one answer seems to come to mind. Mizz Kirkwood is about to write a new book, which will undoubtedly become another bestseller and maybe a movie. Her characters' names and the location will all be fictional, so she can't be sued for slander, but the story is based on a real crime. Imagine what will happen if she should mention that fact on a talk show interview. How long do you think it will be before the media puts it all together and starts hounding you for interviews?"

Reid inhaled sharply as a torrent of disastrous ramifications occurred to him.

"McCoy may not be able to do anything to any of us legally, but he wouldn't need to. I think they're setting us up for a public humiliation that could be mighty difficult to recover from, especially with your being in the retail business."

"Oh my. What should I do?"

"I think it's obvious that they have both become an inconvenience."

Reid took a slow breath. "Beau, you'd better think twice about the direction you're taking here.

Like I've said before, it's not like it was in the old days."

Beau snorted. "You were always the worrier, Reid, but you're just as wrong now as you were then. It's no different from what it was in the old days; only the dates on the calendar have changed. The power is still ours to use as we deem necessary. And I now deem it necessary."

Chapter Eighteen

"That's it!" Kelly announced after typing the words "THE END" at the end of her long synopsis. "I think it's good, but I'd appreciate it if you'd read it and give me your opinion. Unless you find some glaring hole, I can send it off to New York tomorrow, and we can move back to Atlanta permanently." She plugged the laptop into her laser printer and pressed the print key.

Luke set down the pad he was writing on. "Thank God. I've been trying not to complain, but I'm really getting tired of that poor excuse for a bathtub."

She straightened up the files and papers on the table while she waited for the printer to complete its job. "I'm sorry you had to suffer so much for little ol' me," she said with pretended sympathy. "But I promise to let you bathe in my magical bubbling pool tomorrow night to pay you back for putting up with my eccentricities."

He rose and walked toward her with a sexy grin. "In that case, I'm glad I managed not to complain out loud." He wrapped his arms around her. "I'm happy you finished. I can't wait to read it. And while I'm doing that, there's something I've been working on that I'd like you to—"

A knock on the cabin door surprised them both. Not only was it strange for them to have a visitor, it was nearly midnight. It was too dark outside to see who it was through the screen, and Luke motioned for her to let him go first.

A young black boy was standing there with an envelope in his hand. "You Mr. McCoy?" he asked.

"Yes," Luke said, opening the screen door to let the boy in.

Instead of entering, the boy held out the envelope.

Luke took it and noted that it was sealed and his name was printed across it in a childish scrawl. He thanked the boy and started to close the door, but the boy continued to stand there, staring up at him. "Was there something else?"

"I had to run a long way to get here, and now I has to run home. She said you'd gimme a big tip for bringin' this to you."

Luke glanced at Kelly and shrugged as she went for her wallet. "I'll give you a tip if you tell me who the 'she' was who gave this to you."

The boy fidgeted and looked down at his shoes. "I dunno. Just some lady."

"Young? Old? Dark? Light?"

He screwed up his face as he caught sight of the dollar bills in Kelly's hand. "Um, kind of in-between I think. I don't know her. You gonna gimme that tip, or not, 'cause I gotta go." Kelly passed him the money, and he took off down the road as though his life depended on it.

Luke watched him for a moment, then scanned the woods in front of the cabin.

"Open it," Kelly said impatiently.

Luke shut the screen door and carried the envelope over to a lamp with Kelly following closely. Inside was one sheet of plain folded paper with more of the childish scrawl:

I know who you are and why you are here. I could tell you what you want to know but I'm scared of being caught. Right now I'm hiding in the old Donley barn. I will stay there for one hour and if you don't come I'll go home. It's about a half mile down the road from where you are, in the opposite direction of town. Here is a hint of who I am— thirty-two years ago I made a phone call pretending to be someone who died that night. COME ALONE AND ON FOOT. If she shows up I ain't talking.

Luke and Kelly finished reading and looked at each other at the same time.

"Hannah?" Kelly asked.

"Highly probable. She's in between young and

old, and light and dark, and you said she seemed real tense when you tried to talk to her about her long history with O'Neill. Or it could be a Klan-style trap."

"I'd agree if we'd done anything even remotely suspicious since our lunch with them, but we've barely moved."

His mouth turned down on one side. "You think I should go?"

She skimmed over the letter again. "I wouldn't be able to resist if it were me. I'd be afraid, but I'd go. Of course, I'd also carry my gun."

"I won't carry the gun."

"Then don't go. If it is Hannah, you can try to catch her during the day sometime."

He ran his hands through his hair. "As a street reporter, I can tell you that stoolies rarely squeal in broad daylight. By tomorrow she'll have changed her mind about talking to me, and I'll have missed what could be my one opportunity to learn the whole truth."

"Maybe I could sneak down the road behind you and cover your back."

"Uh-uh. If it's legit, she could spot you and call it off. If it's a trap, they'll just pull you into it."

She touched his face. "Don't go if you think there's even the slightest chance that it's a trap. I couldn't stand it if anything happened to you now."

He smiled. "Weren't you the one who was so insistent that we had to find out the truth? What if this is it? The big chance to learn who did what to whom?"

It suddenly hit her how eerily close this was to the circumstances around the fictional climax that she'd just outlined, and she knew he had to go as part of his destiny. "If this is the big moment, and you discover the truth, it may mean you'll get sent back to the sixties. You'll be outside. Lightning could strike you and—"

"There's not a cloud in the sky."

"—and I won't even be with you when you disappear." She gazed deeply into his eyes, then took a calming breath. "It's your decision."

"I'm still a reporter at heart. I can't pass up a lead this good. Besides, my gut's telling me that I have to go, and it's always steered me right before. Just wait up for me, okay?"

She drew his head down for a long kiss and when she released him, her eyes were glazed with tears. "I'll wait for you, for as long as it takes. But promise me this, even if you get taken back there to stay, when it gets to be 1997, you come find me."

He tried to laugh. "I'll be almost seventy years old."

"I won't care." She kissed him one more time, then watched him walk out the door.

Luke couldn't figure out why he was doing this. It was in direct opposition to what he'd wanted to do since he'd landed here. He didn't care about the truth. He didn't feel the need for revenge. He didn't want to be hurled back into the Stone Age of technology. He wanted to stay here, now, with Kelly. So why did his feet keep propelling him toward a situation where the odds were stacked sky high against him?

He heard a sound behind him and jumped. There was enough starlight for him to see that there was nothing in the road he'd already traveled nor in front of him. It was probably a rabbit or a night owl that his footsteps had startled.

His fear rose another notch as he began to realize that there was something familiar about this walk he was taking, as though he'd done it before . . . *in the opposite direction* . . . like maybe after he'd been the special guest at a Klan party.

And yet, he couldn't make himself turn around. It was almost as if there were large hands at his back, pushing him farther and farther along that dirt road.

Kelly glanced at the clock. Only fifteen minutes had passed, barely enough time for Luke to reach the Donley barn. Why didn't she stop him from going? They could have at least tried to outrun fate. They could have packed up and returned to Atlanta tonight, even started a new life together in another state, far away from Charming and the dark shadows of the past.

She heard a twig snap outside and immediately thought that Luke had changed his mind and returned. Relief filled her mind as she prepared to welcome him back and tell him of her escape plan. She rushed to the screen door, but it opened before she got there.

It took her less than a heartbeat to realize that it wasn't Luke, but even that slight hesitation was too long.

A man in a ski mask, wielding a large serrated knife, grabbed a handful of her hair. She opened her mouth to scream, but his gloved hand clamped it shut again.

Adrenaline raced through her blood preparing her to fight back, but a wave of the deadly blade an inch from her eyes warned her against such action. Of all the things she and Luke had considered about the note, it had never occurred to them that it was just a ruse to get him away from the cabin so that she would be left unprotected.

As the man dragged her backward into the cabin, she forced herself to remember the basic lessons she'd learned in self-defense class. She had already lost the opportunity to scream or run. DON'T PANIC. DON'T STRUGGLE. TRY TO GET YOUR ATTACKER TO SEE YOU AS A REAL PERSON. GIVE HIM WHATEVER HE WANTS TO SAVE YOUR LIFE.

If this man was who she suspected, he was not prone to using the knife for anything more than control. If she delayed him long enough, Luke would realize the note was a hoax and come back. She forced her body to relax and made an attempt to speak in a calm voice against the man's hand. Slowly his grip loosened enough for her to say clearly, "Junior, is that you?"

His body tensed around her, and she knew she'd guessed correctly. "I've been expecting you," she continued, and he removed his hand from her mouth. "I wondered how long it would take for you to recognize me." She cautiously turned toward him and gazed up into the tiny eye holes in the mask. His disfigurement was almost, but not quite hidden and she wondered why none of those other women had noticed it. "If you want to tie me up to make love to me, that's okay, but it doesn't have to be that way. Wouldn't it be better if I could touch you, too?"

She could see by the rapid rise and fall of his chest that he was excited by her words. GIVE HIM WHATEVER HE WANTS TO SAVE YOUR LIFE. "I want to see your face when you enter my body, Junior. I want to hear you say, 'I love you, Ginger.'"

"You're *not* Ginger!" he shouted, taking a step back from her and swiping the air between them with his knife.

She told herself she could survive if she pretended she was acting in a movie. None of this was real. She just needed to give Luke time to return. She made herself smile softly. "Of course, I'm not really Ginger, but I look like her, and I can be her for you, in the way you always dreamed of her. Just say her name and look at me, and I will be her." Her heart was pounding so hard she could barely hear herself speak.

"Ginger," he whispered, and his knife hand lowered a few inches.

"You see? I am Ginger, but better than she ever was before. You don't have to tie me down or force me. I won't plead with you to leave me alone, or say mean things to you. I want you to make love to me. And I want to make love to you. *Willingly.*" She noted that he'd started breathing through his mouth. "Aren't you perspiring under that mask, Junior? It's awfully hot in here. Would you like me to take it off for you?"

"I'm . . . I'm too ugly," he murmured, turning his head to the side.

"Not to me, Junior," she said and very slowly raised one hand toward the mask and touched his cheek. "Don't you remember? All those years in school together. We even went to the movies that one time. None of the other girls would have ever done that. Only me. Because I loved you, secretly, just as you loved me. So, you see, I know the man inside, and he's handsome and gentle and kind."

"But . . . but you wouldn't go out with me a second time."

"I was young and foolish." She bowed her head in shame. "I let the other girls talk me out of it." Looking up at him again with big, sorrow-filled eyes, her voice caught in her throat. "I'm all grown up now. Can't you forgive me?"

He lowered the knife to his side, but kept a grip on it. "Could . . . could you call me . . . Beau?"

She gave him another smile. "I'll call you Beau, if you let me unmask you."

"All . . . all right."

She braced herself, then raised the ski mask as though she were unveiling a Michelangelo masterpiece.

Luke's gaze moved swiftly over the six men in white hoods who had rushed out of the woods just as the barn came into sight. One held a bull-whip, one had a shotgun pointed at him, one had an armload of rope, and the other three were lighting the torches in their hands. Considering his options, he went for a swift bullet-in-the-back finish and tried to run. On his third step the whip caught him around the throat and jerked him to the ground. Within seconds, the rope-bearer had him helplessly hog-tied.

"How impolite of you to try to leave your party before your guests have all been entertained."

Luke recognized the gravelly voice of Beauregard Ramey. He assumed three of the others were Junior, O'Neill, and Chapman. The two extra members were probably younger blood who would do the actual inducing of pain and suffering.

"I gather this means Hannah won't be meeting me," Luke said to the hood he guessed was Ramey.

"Excellent deduction, Mr. McCoy. We're curious as to what else you have deduced."

"You're all a bunch of assholes." That earned him a stinging slash of the whip across his back.

"It will go much easier if you don't try to be a comedian. Perhaps it will move things along if we tell you we already know that you're the nephew of Luke Templeton."

It took Luke a second to figure out the only way he could have come to that conclusion. "Mary Beth didn't tell me anything I didn't already know. We tricked her into talking to us."

Ramey let out a dry laugh. "Tricking a drunk doesn't take much talent. What I want to know is what she told you."

The last thing he'd wanted was for Mary Beth to suffer more than she already had. "I swear, she didn't say anything that made much sense. She, uh, she had just gotten invited to her high school reunion, and that was all she could think about. Her high school days." He knew he had to give them something to chew on. "She remembered how Junior had a big crush on Ginger and took her to the movies one time." He looked around the circle of men. "Do you remember that, Junior? How she tried to be nice to you?"

"I see that you're under the impression that Junior is with us tonight, but you're mistaken. He has a date with a pretty lady. I think you know her—long, strawberry blond hair, womanly figure—"

"No-o-o," Luke cried and tried to hurl himself at Ramey despite the binding ropes, but three rapid slashes across his back laid him flat.

"I bet you'd like to go see how she's doin' about now. And we'd be happy to oblige you, right after you make a full confession."

His back was on fire, and it was all he could do to hold down the bile in his throat. *Junior was playing his sick games with Kelly!* He had to get to her before he— He slammed the door on the image that flashed into his mind. "What do you want to know?"

"Everything. Who you are. What you think you know. What you and the author were planning to do."

Clenching his teeth against the pain, he gave the answers he thought they wanted to hear. "You're right. I am Luke Templeton's nephew. I grew up hearing the story about how my uncle was framed for murder, then was spontaneously combusted in the electric chair. I always wondered what really happened. When I met Kelly and told her about it, she thought it sounded like a good story.

"That's all there is to it. We were just trying to satisfy my curiosity and give her an unusual plot for her next book. We didn't mean to stir up any trouble. In fact, we were planning on moving back to Atlanta tomorrow. I swear you'll never see or hear from us again." *Hold on, Kelly, I'm doing the best I can.*

"What about the attorney's phone call? What was that all about?"

Luke turned toward the voice that sounded like Reid O'Neill. "What attorney?"

The whip almost came down on him again, but Ramey held up a hand and stopped its progress. "Bruce Hackett."

Luke squinted at him. "Kelly's attorney called you? About what?"

"Are you saying, you know who he is, but you didn't put him up to any phone calls?"

"I swear I didn't, but I'd really like to hear what he had to say."

"I think we can indulge you in that. He said there was a private investigator who had manufactured some proof that you and Luke Templeton were the same man. Apparently he thought he could blackmail us in some way and Hackett was giving us a warning."

"Hmmph. The impression I got from meeting Hackett was that he was more apt to do the blackmailing than the warning." He tried to make the connection between Hackett, a private investigator, and proof that he was Luke Templeton, but before he could work it all out, the loose circle of men around him began to shrink.

"Thank you for your opinion, Mr. McCoy. Unfortunately, we still feel it is in our best interests to eliminate you."

Luke was hoping he misunderstood, but as he watched the rope-bearer swing a long length up over a high tree limb and saw that the end of the rope was tied in a noose, his hope plummeted.

"Wait!" he cried as two of them dragged him over to the tree. "Why are you doing this?"

"Quite simply, we don't believe it is possible for you *not* to cause problems for us."

His feet were untied so that he could stand, then the noose was placed around his neck. "If you're going to kill me anyway, at least tell me what really happened to Ginger O'Neill and why."

Kelly glanced at the clock again. Another fifteen minutes had passed. She had to believe that Luke would be back soon, because she was no longer sure she could go through with this even if it did mean survival. She had managed to look right at Junior's face and smile adoringly. She had stroked his scars as though they were marks of beauty, and finally, she had made herself kiss him on the mouth. But when his hand closed over her breast, she almost lost it.

Taking a step back, she swallowed hard and made a decision. She couldn't just lie back and take it, no matter what the book said., "Beau, honey, would you like me to put on a sexy negligee for you? It will only take a minute."

"I'd rather see you in your bra and panties. Just take your clothes off." His tongue flicked out to wet his lips.

All she needed was a few seconds in her lingerie drawer. "Okay. I can do that. But I'm not wearing anything very pretty. I have some very sexy things right here . . ." She took a step closer to the drawer. "What color do you like? Black, white, red?" That got a definite reaction. "Would you like to see me in the red? It's very sheer, with just a little black piping. I could even put on a pair of red high heels—"

"Yes. I . . . I imagined you in the red."

She opened the drawer, but he barked at her.

"No! Not like that. Take your clothes off first, like you don't know I'm watching you. Then get out the other things and put them on. Slowly."

It took all her willpower not to go for the gun immediately, but the risk would be much less if she went along with his game. She lowered her eyes and kept telling herself she would have control of the situation in a moment. She forced herself to pretend she was doing this for Luke, and from the sound of Junior's erratic breathing, she was succeeding in throwing him off balance.

She tried to drag the striptease out, praying that Luke was only seconds away, but eventually, she had nothing more to take off. It was time to switch from passive to aggressive behavior.

She turned her back on him, supposedly to get out the red lingerie. As her fingers closed around the grip of the gun and her thumb released the safety, she hummed a little tune and wiggled her bare hips back and forth to hold his gaze.

Another rule suddenly popped into her head: IF YOU'RE GOING TO PULL A GUN ON YOUR

ATTACKER, YOU'D BETTER BE READY TO PULL THE TRIGGER. She took a deep breath in preparation. This cretin had trespassed into her home, had threatened her with a deadly weapon, and clearly intended to assault her. She was justified.

She whirled around, bracing the gun with both hands, and aimed for his kneecap, but as she fired, he lunged at her.

"You bitch!" His weight slammed her against the dresser, then onto the floor. "You wanted to play Ginger, now you can die like her!"

She knew her chance was gone. She now had to shoot to kill before he cut her with the knife, or got the gun away and used it on her, but her weapon was pinned between their bodies. She kicked and pushed and struggled, but he seemed to have a hundred arms and legs.

The battle lasted several seconds before the second shot was fired.

Luke heard the shot and, for a split second, thought they'd decided to forego the hanging and just give him a bullet in the back after all.

"Where the hell did that come from?" Ramey shouted as the man holding the shotgun aimed it toward the woods.

It took Luke a moment to understand that he might have an ally hiding amidst the trees. Good God! Kelly had come to rescue him. A minute later and it would have been too late. The noose had already been tightened around his neck and three men were pulling on the opposite end as a fourth anchored it around the base of the tree.

He was already on his tiptoes with his neck stretched as far as it would go. He figured the next hard yank would break his neck, or at least close off his windpipe.

"Let him down!" a man yelled from the woods.

Instantly the gun bearer fired one of his two bullets toward the voice. A heartbeat later, the stranger fired again, striking the gun bearer between the eye holes of his hood.

"I can pick you all off one at a time, or you can clear out of here now!"

The men released the rope and Luke slumped to the ground. As he gasped for air and rubbed his throat, the five remaining men took off down the road. Soon there was the roar of an engine and a pickup truck went flying by in a huge cloud of dust.

By the time the dust began to settle, Luke saw his savior coming out of the woods and moved toward him. In a raspy voice he asked, "Where's Kelly?" Then he recognized the man. "Cowboy?"

The man held out his hand. "Evan Dillard, private investigator. I assume Kelly is still at the cabin. I followed you here."

"Dear God! Come on. She might be in trouble!" He began running as fast as he could and Dillard quickly caught up with him.

"You're welcome."

Luke frowned at him. "I'll thank you when you explain why you waited so long to save me if you followed me here."

"I wanted to make sure they were serious before risking my own neck."

"You killed that man back there."

"He shot at me first. You figuring to turn me in?"

"I didn't see a thing."

"Why do you think . . . Kelly's . . . in trouble?" He didn't have the breath to run and talk.

"If they were telling the truth, the sickest one of the bunch went to pay her a visit while they were occupied with me."

"Shit! I camped in the woods . . . for three days . . . waiting for y'all to make a move . . . and nothing happened. I figured . . . following you . . . was going to lead me to . . . the main action."

"I don't get it. Why were you watching us at all?"

"Hackett hired me to . . . get the goods on you . . . so that . . . he could look like a hero . . . to the lady. But he fired me . . . when I told him . . . what I found out."

"Which was?"

"That you are . . . Luke Templeton. I sure hope . . . my saving your ass . . . has earned me . . . an explanation of how . . . that's possible."

"Sure, right after you explain why you were

still watching us if Hackett fired you . . . not that I'm ungrateful.''

"I don't like losing a case . . . especially if it's not my fault. I was . . . determined to learn . . . the truth about you. Besides . . . curiosity . . . was killing me.

"The truth might be easier to accept if you hear it from someone else." The light from the cabin was in sight. *"Kelly!"*

A surge of adrenaline helped Luke pick up his speed the last hundred yards while Dillard slowed to a stagger behind him.

"Kelly!" he shouted again as he tore open the screen door and bolted inside . . . then came to an abrupt halt.

He blinked and rubbed his eyes, unwilling to believe what he was seeing.

His beautiful Kelly was lying naked on the floor like some broken doll. He wanted to deny the blatant evidence before him, but her chest was covered with blood and her lifeless eyes were staring up at him.

Chapter Nineteen

It was a thousand times worse than when he'd found Ginger.

"Aw shit," Dillard cursed behind him. He placed a hand on Luke's shoulder. "I'm sorry, man. Look, it isn't good to remember her this way. Why don't you go outside, and I'll call the cops—"

"There's no phone," Luke told him in a flat voice. He couldn't pull his eyes away from her. "And the local cops might cover it up anyway. You've got to get the county or state guys in here."

"Don't touch anything," Dillard said. "Especially not the gun."

Luke glanced at the Walther on the floor. "The gun's hers."

"Did you ever touch it?"

He shook his head. *Why did she insist on having the damn thing at all?*

"It looks like she injured him."

Slowly, Luke turned his head and saw the bloodstains leading out the door. He nodded, but it didn't take any of the pain away. "You can take her car if you need to."

"Thanks, but mine's not far from here. You gonna be okay if I leave you here alone?"

Luke nodded again. *Maybe, if I'm lucky, the boys in hoods will come back and finish me off.* Somewhere at the edge of his consciousness, he heard Dillard leave the cabin. He knew the crime scene had to be preserved, but he couldn't just leave her exposed like this, not with all the men who would soon be traipsing in and out. He got a sheet and neatly covered her body, then kneeling down beside her, he closed her eyelids.

He could stand it now. Despite the dark smear that automatically appeared through the sheet, he could pretend that Kelly was only sleeping. He found her hand and covered it with his own. It was still warm.

Gradually, numbness reduced the pain, and his heart and lungs began working on automatic pilot. This wasn't the way it was supposed to be. *He* was the one who was supposed to die, not her.

"*Why?*" he cried to heaven. "How could you let this happen to her?" Suddenly a rush of tears flowed from his eyes. "Why would you spare me and take her?"

For a few moments, he gave in to his grief, then tried again to get through to God. "I know I haven't always been . . . what You might have wanted, but she was so good. You performed some kind of miracle before to bring me to her. I'm asking You to perform another one now. Let me switch places with her. Let me be the one lying here with a bullet in my chest. Let me die in her place!"

He waited for the miracle, but nothing happened at all. "What am I supposed to do without you, Kelly? You were so sure that I had to go back and fix things. How do I fix this?"

By going back.

His head jerked from side to side. He would have sworn he'd heard Kelly's voice. It wasn't just a memory of words she'd spoken before. She was trying to tell him something!

"What?" When he heard no response, he tried to gather his mental faculties to figure out the answer on his own.

If he could get back to 1965, to before Ginger's murder, he could alter history. He could change things so that Kelly would never have been investigating that case because it wouldn't have happened. And then there would be no reason for anyone to want her dead.

It seemed simple, but how was he supposed to get back there? Kelly only said they'd know when the time came. He rose and walked away from her to try to clear his brain a bit more. Pacing back and forth, he forced himself to be analytical.

He got here by electrocution. It must be the answer for a return trip as well. There was no lightning streaking down from the sky. No high-tension wires in the neighborhood. He didn't see an electric chair sitting around. They were lucky they had a generator in this primitive—

He abruptly stopped pacing in front of the bathroom. The answer was right in front of him. It had to work. Urgency filled every cell in his body. He had to be gone before Dillard returned.

As quickly as possible he turned the water on in the metal bathtub and tore off his clothes. He remembered laughing at Kelly's ugly electric lamp with the fifty-foot extension cord that allowed her to move it from one end of the cabin to the other, but he wasn't laughing now.

He removed the lamp shade and switched the light on and off to be certain it was working, then he unscrewed the lightbulb. Carrying it into the bathroom, he allowed himself ten seconds to reconsider what he was about to do.

He had no doubts. If there was even the slightest possibility that this could ultimately save Kelly's life, it was worth the risk. He lowered himself into the tub and turned off the water.

Bracing himself against the metal sides, he took a deep breath and plunged the top of the lamp into the water.

"Good morning, Atlanta! It's seven a.m., and we're going to start our rush hour this beautiful Friday morning with the number-one hit that's rockin' the nation, '(I Can't Get No) Satisfaction,' by the Rolling Stones!"

As Mick Jagger wailed out his complaint, Luke rolled over and turned off his new clock radio. As much as he liked the music when he was wide awake, he wasn't sure it was that much better than a jangling alarm first thing in the morning.

He started to stretch, and was surprised to find that his entire body was aching as though he'd been doing heavy labor all night.

A whip coming down on his back. Running. A woman covered with blood. A metal tub. Electrocution!

Luke bolted upright and looked around his bedroom. He'd made it! He was back. What had the radio announcer said? It was Friday morning and the Rolling Stones were at the top of the chart.

Quickly, he got out of bed and put on the boxer shorts he'd dropped on the floor last night. Seconds later, he retrieved the morning's newspaper from in front of his apartment door. Beneath the *Atlanta Journal* banner was a confirmation of the date: Friday, July 9, 1965.

Now that he was sure he'd arrived in time to make a difference, he set the paper down on the sofa and went to the bathroom.

There, he received his second surprise. The image reflected back at him in the mirror had his old haircut. He dipped his head down, then examined the top of his scalp with his fingers. It was perfectly healthy. A glance down at his calf told him the same thing. He no longer bore any sign of having been electrocuted.

But, of course he wouldn't, he reminded himself. It hadn't happened yet.

He thought about his boxer shorts being exactly where he'd left them and how everything in the apartment looked exactly the way it did . . . *before he went to sleep last night.*

Could he have dreamed that he was electrocuted? The longer he was awake, the less real it all seemed. He sat down and tried to run through the sequence of events as he remembered them, but the images in his mind were no longer as clear as they were when he first woke up. *Just like in a dream.*

He had a call from Ginger. Found her murdered. Was arrested. Sent to the electric chair. Traveled forward in time.

What?

He saw the technology of the future. And learned that cheeseburgers could kill you, and that Ronald Reagan had been elected president.

What?

Kelly. Beautiful Kelly. She looked like Ginger only she was all the things Ginger wasn't. She was truly the girl of his dreams.

Exactly.

Luke scratched his head. He had never had a dream that seemed so real, or was so complete in every detail, or that went on for so long. Nearly two months of time passed between Ginger's mur-

der and his execution, then there was the whole
week with Kelly . .

If it had all been real, including his traveling
through time, then he had to prevent a murder
tonight, or at least see to it that the real guilty
parties were arrested. On the other hand, if it had
only been a weird dream, he couldn't afford to do
anything about it.

He could see how it would go now. He notifies
the police about some Klan members planning to
rape and murder one of their wives. They act on
his tip, but nothing like that happens. Everyone
thinks he's just trying to get revenge against the
Klan for what they did to him a few months ago.
He gets fired, or burned on a cross. Either way,
he's screwed.

There had to be some way that he could know
for sure whether it was real or a nightmare. Then
again, perhaps it was a little of both—a premonition of danger. He tried to remember what he had
done during the day on July 9th in his dream. If
there was some event that he could accurately pre-
dict before it happened, that would be enough to
convince him that he had to risk warning the au-
thorities. Unfortunately, his recollection was that
he stayed in his apartment working on an article
all day until he'd received the call that sent him
racing up to Charming.

His gaze fell on the newspaper. Could he pre-
dict something printed inside before reading it?

Probably, but since it was the *Journal*, he might have seen it or heard about it in advance.

He needed an outsider to supply unquestionable proof, but he couldn't very well walk up to Reid O'Neill or Junior Ramey and ask if they were planning on committing any crimes that night.

He stopped and repeated the thought he just had. How did he know about Junior Ramey? Oh yes, that article he did about some of the younger members of the Klan. Who else?

Suddenly the perfect answer came to him. Hannah. He had no way of knowing who she was or her connection to the O'Neills prior to his strange dream. Hadn't he told that to Kelly when she first asked him about the housekeeper?

More than likely, she lived somewhere near Charming and the number of Negroes—blacks— Again he stopped and questioned why he'd thought that, but it wasn't proof of anything. Anyway, the number of her people was limited in that area. It couldn't be that hard to find a mulatto named Hannah, even if he didn't know her last name. As insurance, however, he decided he'd better take the entire stash of cash he kept on hand for "greasing his way to the truth."

Minutes later, he was dressed and thinking he could grab some sausage biscuits and coffee on the way to Charming, when he realized that wasn't possible in 1965. He slowed down long enough to make a breakfast to go, then headed out.

Now that he was in a hurry, he missed the superhighways that Kelly had introduced him to, but at least he was getting an early start.

Logic took him to Buford first and polite questions led him to the areas where he might find a woman with light brown skin. Luck led him to a grocer who knew Hannah.

"Y'all got laundry fo' her t'do?" the grocer asked, obviously looking for an explanation as to why this white man was in his store.

"Yes," Luke replied, quickly improvising. "I've never brought it to her myself, but the housekeeper was sick today, and now I'm afraid I've gotten lost."

The man was satisfied with the story and gave Luke directions to Hannah's house.

It wasn't much more than a shack, but it had clean curtains on clean windows. When no one answered his knock, Luke went around back where he could see about a mile of clothesline stretched back and forth between poles and enough laundry twisting in the warm breeze to clothe a small army.

A young woman was forcing a wooden clothespin over a wet sock.

"Hannah?"

She turned around and Luke could see she was a young teen, definitely not old enough to be Hannah. He could also see by her skin color and features that she had even more white blood in her than Hannah did.

"Mama," she called over her shoulder. "There's a man here to see you."

Mama came out from behind a sheet, wiping her hands on her apron. She looked very much like a young version of the Hannah he'd seen in his dream. The way she looked him up and down before speaking was also very familiar. "Yes?"

"What's your name?"

She eyed him suspiciously, but gave him an answer. "Hannah. If y'all have laundry that needs doin', I'm all filled up for today. People usually brings their baskets by six."

"That's okay," he assured her with a wave of his hand and a friendly smile. "I don't need you to do any laundry for me. I just need to talk to you for a few minutes."

"Talkin' don't get my work done. 'Scuse me."

She went back behind the sheet, and he followed her. After she bent over to get another wet item out of a basket on the ground and took two clothespins out of her apron pocket, he leaned over and picked up two more pieces.

She was clearly horrified. "You crazy, mister? What you think you's doin'?"

"I thought if I helped, we could talk."

She snatched the things away from him and dropped them back in the basket. Her gaze darted from side to side as though she was afraid someone had witnessed the crazy white man in her yard and would blame her for the indiscretion.

"Sorry. How about if I paid you?" He pulled

out his wallet and extracted a twenty-dollar bill. "You don't even have to stop working while we talk. Okay?"

She decided this offer was much more reasonable and stopped hanging laundry long enough to tuck the money into her apron pocket.

"I know this is going to sound a little nuts, but I had a dream last night, actually it was more of a nightmare, and you were in it." The only way he could tell she was listening was because her frown deepened. Hopefully she was superstitious enough to believe in dreams. "Anyway, I think it was a premonition of something bad that might happen tonight and I have to stop it. Unfortunately, I'm not sure if I can trust the dream unless I can prove that some of the other things that were in it are true."

"Mister, you sho' talk a lot without sayin' nothin'."

"What I have to ask you is very personal, and it's really none of my business, but someone's life may depend on your answer." He recalled the tidbits Ramey had fed him to satisfy his curiosity while he had a noose around his neck and hoped he had drawn the right conclusions. "Do you still have a, uh, *personal* relationship with Beauregard Ramey?"

Her eyes widened in shock, and she called to her daughter, "Sugar, you go on in and wring out that load that's been soakin' for Mama." She waited a few seconds, then spoke to Luke in a hushed voice. "She don't know who her daddy is, and I don't want her to till she's old enough to understand how things are for us."

"Did you used to . . . clean his house?" he asked carefully.

She looked away. "I wasn't much older than her when he started payin' my mama to send me up there. We was dirt poor, and I was the oldest of six. At first I just cleaned, then he . . . offered me some pin money."

She hung another piece of laundry before continuing. "When the baby started showin' he sent me away so's his wife wouldn't know. But he wasn't a bad man. He bought this house for us and kept sendin' money. Still does. And he sent me lots of customers to make sure I didn't ever have to sell myself or my daughter the way my mama had to." She took a slow breath and returned to her chore. "Did you get your money's worth or do you need somethin' mo'?"

He'd gotten much more than his money's worth. She'd given him proof that he hadn't simply had a bad dream last night. "I'm sorry, but I do need something else." He took his wallet back out and handed her another twenty-dollar bill. "Sometime tonight, Ramey, or one of his friends, might come to you and order you to make a phone call to a man named Luke in Atlanta. He'll tell you to cry and say that your husband has beaten you and beg Luke to come rescue you immediately. He'll use your daughter's future to force you to do it."

Luke could see by the look in Hannah's eyes that she knew Ramey was capable of doing that, and that she was incapable of refusing him. "It's me that he wants you to call. You have to do as he says, but when you hear the phone ringing on my end, I need you to pretend that I've picked up the phone, even though I'm not going to be home."

Although it didn't seem possible, her face tensed even more. "Can you do that? For your daughter's sake, can you convince him that you're talking to me? Because I can assure you that you won't be happy with what's in store for you and your daughter if you can't."

She repeated what he'd asked her to do and decided it wasn't too great a task for an extra twenty dollars.

"Remember," he said, walking away. "Your daughter's life may depend on your being a good actress."

He knew that was a white lie, but he needed to be positive that she would follow through. From what Ramey had revealed, she was rewarded for her cooperation with the permanent live-in position in O'Neill's house. Her silence was guaranteed by the knowledge of what would happen to them if she ever told anyone what she knew about that night.

As he drove away from Hannah's house he

could finally think about what meeting her really meant. For whatever reason, he had been given a glimpse of the immediate and distant future. If he ignored the premonition, disaster awaited him. As Kelly had told him to begin with, he had a mission to accomplish.

He considered calling Ginger and warning her, but he couldn't take the chance of altering anything about tonight. He knew the general timing and order of how events would proceed this evening. If he called her, she might say something to her husband about it, or she might go visit her mother so that she wouldn't be home alone. Either way, the original plan to kill her and frame him would not necessarily be canceled, only changed or moved to another night. A warning to her could result in everything occurring differently.

Then he would be right back where he started— not having any idea of what was coming or when. No, he knew the only chance he had of making things right was to let as much of it proceed as it had in his dream, then throw a monkey wrench in at a crucial moment.

He drove part of the way back to Atlanta to avoid being seen anywhere near Charming before the sun went down. It was imperative that Ramey believe he had nearly two hours between Hannah's call and his coming to Ginger's rescue.

The next thing he needed to do was arrange for the cavalry to arrive in the nick of time. He saw a phone booth outside a truck stop and pulled in for lunch, a fill-up, and the call that could save both his and Ginger's lives.

He had spoken to Special Agent Carl Hastings once before, after the Klan had punished him for his annoying behavior. Carl was part of a secret task force assigned to disrupt Ku Klux Klan activities in Georgia and had asked Luke to notify him if he picked up any solid information on his travels. Luke figured this was solid enough for J. Edgar Hoover himself to show up.

It took all the dimes he had to reach someone at the newspaper who could take the time to go searching through his desk and find Agent Hastings's business card. He then had to buy gas before the attendant was willing to part with a dollar's worth of change. After that, he was put on hold for five minutes while someone went to find Hastings to take the call. Eventually, however, the red tape had been cleared away.

Once Hastings remembered who Luke was, he was all ears.

"This isn't just a Klan meeting, Carl. It's a sacrificial mass, and the Imperial Wizard himself, Beauregard Ramey, will be conducting the services."

"I don't suppose you'd like to tell me how you got this information."

"I'm sorry. You know I can't reveal my source. But I will tell you that I found out about it because of one of the stories I've been working on. Have you heard of the Lake Sidney Lanier rapist?"

"Sure. Odd profile."

"Wait till you meet the man himself." Luke could almost see Carl straightening up in his chair.

"You know who it is?"

"Not only do I know the crackpot's name, I'm going to let you have the honor of catching him with his pants down."

"Ooh. Sounds like fun, but it's not my jurisdiction."

"Normally that would be true. But you see, his little routine is the opening act for tonight's main event. Festivities are expected to begin about eight o'clock, but the gang might not all be in attendance immediately, so I'd suggest you keep your approach as quiet as possible so as not to tip off any latecomers."

"You're sure this has all been planned in advance?" Carl asked incredulously.

"Yep. But that's not as strange as it sounds. You see, the rapist is none other than Junior Ramey, son of the Imperial Wizard."

"No shit! After months of sitting around with our thumbs up our asses, this is almost too good to be true. Every man in the agency is going to want to be in on it."

"The more the merrier," Luke assured him. "There's no telling how many white hoods will be present."

Luke gave Carl directions to O'Neill's house and explained that extenuating circumstances pre-

vented the Klan from holding this particular mass
outdoors. He assured him he would see him there,
then hung up.

Luke acknowledged that he'd just told another
white lie, but if he hadn't, the FBI's involvement
would not be justified. And they were the only
law enforcement agency that he could trust not to
sweep everything under the carpet.

The truth was, a meeting *would* be held tonight,
but at the lodge, as everyone would later testify
in court. What no one would ever say, though,
was that three of their members had stepped out
for a while.

Based on what Beau Ramey had admitted to
him, he had been honest about Junior's part. His
father's warped sense of humor had allowed him
to make sure Ginger was "firmly secured" before
he and Reid entered the picture to render her punishment. She had been found guilty of adultery
and consorting with the enemy, and had been sentenced to death.

However, no one but Reid and Beau knew
which one of them actually put their hands
around Ginger's throat and choked the life out
of her, and that was the one fact Beau had been
unwilling to reveal . . . probably because of the
others who were present at his hanging. Apparently, everyone in the upper level of the group
knew the rest of the story and had assisted in
framing Luke. He, too, had been found guilty of

crimes punishable by death. His sentence just took longer to carry out than Ginger's.

He had only been able to estimate the times based on the facts he had, but he was fairly sure he was close enough for everything to work out as planned. By eight o'clock, he was hiding in the overgrown bushes that surrounded O'Neill's property. Not knowing for certain where everyone would be coming from, he just kept scanning the area.

He was thinking that it was just as well that the cavalry was late, when he caught sight of Junior sneaking up to the side of the house. As he watched him pull the ski mask down over his head, Luke was overwhelmed with images of Kelly lying in a pool of her blood.

In that instant, he knew he hadn't dreamed the whole thing. He had really lowered her eyelids to conceal the vacant stare. He had *really* placed his hand over hers and felt the ebbing remnants of her body heat. This demented animal, who was now climbing through a window not a hundred feet away from him, had killed Kelly. Or rather, *would* kill her, in the future.

He had never before known the urge to murder another human being, but he did now. Although he started to rise in response to that urge, logic returned and held him in place. He had thought this all out. He could not act on impulse. He had to wait for the FBI, and they had to wait until O'Neill and Ramey entered the house and were about to kill Ginger. They all had to be caught together so that no one would pose a threat to Kelly in the future.

Junior would rape Ginger. He knew that and tried not to think about it. Hopefully, he would stick to his usual routine. The important thing was that she would survive.

He heard her cry out once, then it was quiet again. It was nearly nine o'clock. Hannah would have made her call by now, and he would have been driving like a madman to get here.

Where the hell were Hastings and his men?

His panic increased when another half hour passed without the FBI making an appearance, and he saw O'Neill and Reid approaching the house on foot. They barely glanced around before casually entering the front door. They were obviously confident that their plan was foolproof.

Would Junior still be with Ginger, or would he be waiting for them downstairs? How long would they talk to one another before getting on with their business? Would they take advantage of Ginger's spread-eagled position as Junior had? Beau hadn't mentioned it, but now Luke was hoping that he and Reid had given in to their lower instincts when faced with such an opportunity. Anything to prolong the inevitable until the agents got here.

But several more minutes passed, and there was still no sign of them. He didn't know what difference he could make against the three of them, but he had to make an effort to stop them. Trying not to think about the size of the knife Junior was carrying, he grabbed a broken limb off the ground and headed toward the front door.

"Psst. Templeton!"

Luke whirled around and saw Carl and a small army of men running toward him. "Where the hell have you been?" he whispered urgently. "They're upstairs and they're going to kill her!"

The front door had been left unlocked, as Luke knew it would be, but instead of his walking through it into a trap, he had used his knowledge to set one.

"Wait outside," Carl ordered and another agent remained behind with him.

Suddenly there was a lot of shouting and some thumping, and Luke let out the breath he'd been holding. It was done. Ginger had been saved from death, and the guilty parties would be arrested.

And Kelly would be alive and well when he went to look her up in 1997.

Minutes later, Reid, Beau, and Junior were all led outside with their hands cuffed behind them.

"Is Ginger okay?" Luke asked Carl as soon as he came out.

The agent grimaced and shook his head. Poking his thumb toward Reid and Beau, he said, "The two of them were strangling her when we burst in on them. Pretty-boy Floyd over there was so busy playing with Mr. Happy he didn't even hear us come up behind him."

Luke struggled to take in all the information at once, but one point took precedence. Ginger didn't survive. She died anyway, just as she had the first time. The only difference was who was arrested for it. "Wait," he said catching up to Carl. "Did you say they were *both* strangling her?"

"Yeah, they—"

"He *made* me do it!" O'Neill whined loudly. "I didn't want to do it, but he took my hands and held them—"

"Shut up, you whimpering little snot!" Beau shouted at him.

"Both of you shut up!" Carl ordered. As several dark sedans pulled up in front of the house and the agents loaded up their prizes, Carl turned to Luke. "Look, we don't need you tonight, but it would help if you'd stop by headquarters tomorrow morning and give me a statement. I'm going to have a hell of a time explaining how a dozen federal agents ended up handling a local homicide."

"Sure thing," Luke promised. After all, it was his fault. The least he could do was try to help with the paperwork. He waited for the ambulance to arrive to take Ginger's body away. He figured it was the right thing for him to do. But when they carried her out on the stretcher, he turned and walked away. He didn't need to look beneath the sheet. He'd already seen her death face.

His legs felt like they weighed a ton as he walked toward where he parked his car. A rumble of thunder sounded in the distance, and he shook his head. That's just what he needed now—to have to drive all the way back to Atlanta in a thunderstorm. Better yet, maybe the cloudburst would open up over his head and soak him to the skin even before he got to his car.

That thought didn't make him move any faster, however.

Why hadn't the agents gotten there in time? Why couldn't he have saved both Kelly and Ginger?

A streak of lightning lit up the sidewalk in front of him, and he stopped in his tracks. Of course! Why hadn't he realized it? Kelly had been right about that also. He couldn't save them both because they were the same person . . . sort of. Ginger had to die in order to be reborn as Kelly. *His* Kelly. His ideal woman.

Only one problem existed with that analysis. He was here, in 1965, and she was there, in 1997. Regardless of what she had said about waiting for him for as long as it takes and not caring if he was an old man the next time she saw him, he couldn't believe he had been put through all this, only to have to wait thirty-two years to be with her again.

Another streak of lightning cut through the sky and hit a tree in the yard across the street. That one was close, he thought, and found the energy to walk a bit faster. But as he hurried along, he recalled Kelly saying something about lightning and being out in the open . . .

At the same instant as he realized what it meant, the third bolt struck him dead on.

"Foul!" Jezebel cried. "That was interference."

"Nonsense," Gabriel replied. "I didn't do a thing. After two electrocutions, he's a walking lightning rod. It was bound to happen."

She grumbled unintelligibly for a moment, then reminded him, "You haven't won yet. He may have risked death to save her, but he failed to tell her he loves her."

"I'm well aware of that, but as I've said before, there's still plenty of time."

"In case you've missed count, ten of his twenty-one days are now gone. I would hardly call eleven days *plenty* of time."

Gabriel laughed off her needless reminder, but he was secretly very worried. Knowing what he did about Luke and Kelly, eleven days' time was not nearly enough. It was going to take a miracle to pull this one out of the fire, and his noninterference promise was really starting to chafe.

Chapter Twenty

Luke had been positive he'd been struck by lightning, but he was still standing in the same spot, on the same street, in the same clothes. The other two times he'd been electrocuted, he not only traveled in time, but place as well. Yet, he had felt the searing pain hit his chest and shoot through his limbs. He had seen the glowing aura appear around him.

He glanced up at the sky and noticed one thing that was different. There wasn't a cloud in the sky, where seconds ago, he couldn't see a single star. Not knowing what else to do, he kept walking toward his car.

His confusion mounted when he reached the vacant lot on the corner where he had parked earlier and saw a house and a fenced-in yard. Thinking he might have made a wrong turn in his dazed state, he backtracked all the way to the O'Neill house.

Only it wasn't there either. In its place was a two-story apartment building. He was definitely in the same neighborhood he'd been in minutes before, but it had changed.

By the few lights on in the houses, he guessed his watch was showing the right time—ten-fifteen. It was the date that had him baffled. Please, God, he prayed, let me be in 1997 again.

He rejected the idea of knocking on a stranger's door at such a late hour to ask a stupid question. Instead, he decided to walk to the cabin and simply hope Kelly was there. It hadn't seemed like it was that far when they'd driven the distance, but his body was beyond exhausted when he finally reached the dirt driveway.

He tried not to worry when he saw no lights in the cabin. She could have gone to sleep early, he told himself, but then he realized that her car wasn't there. Since there was no nightlife in Charming, he doubted that she was out for the evening. Of course, there was a chance she was at her house in Atlanta. He decided to let himself in and take a look around before trying to figure out what to do next.

Climbing in the back window and finding and lighting a kerosene lamp was easy enough. It was also easy to see by the dust and cobwebs that no one had been in residence here for a while.

He was too tired to think. If he could just sleep for a few hours, he was certain he would come up with a plan of action. Thankfully, the bathroom was in working order and the owner had left some clean linens in a drawer of the chest. Within minutes of opening the windows and doors to let in some fresh air, he stretched out on the couch and fell into a deep sleep.

The sun was high in the sky when he awoke the next day. As he helped himself to a can of corned beef hash that had been left in a cupboard, he came up with a reasonable explanation for Kelly not being here.

The first time he traveled in time, he arrived on the same day as it had been thirty-two years earlier. If that was the case again, today was the tenth of July, several weeks before Kelly moved into the cabin. That meant he had no choice but to get himself to Atlanta.

That also meant that it was prior to the time they'd actually met. Now that he was rested and not too hungry, his brain began functioning again, and he quickly deduced that his biggest challenge might not be hitching a ride to Atlanta. After he got there, it was possible that Kelly would not know who he was.

If he walked up to her door, and she didn't recognize him, what could he do? Knowing that she was leery of male fans who developed crushes on her, he would undoubtedly have a difficult time convincing her that she should let him in.

When the answer didn't come to him immediately, he decided that improvisation was sometimes the best plan of all.

He felt it was a good omen when a trucker picked him up minutes after he stepped onto the main road to Charming and drove him to within ten miles of Kelly's town house. He considered taking a taxi the rest of the way, but he had less than three hundred dollars left of his stash, and remembering the price of a cheeseburger convinced him to use the bus system.

By the time he was standing at Kelly's front door, he had made a decision. In case she didn't know him, telling her the truth was bound to intrigue her enough to get her to listen to him, as it had the first time. He was praying for instant recognition, though.

As soon as she opened the door, he had his answer. She had no idea who he was. But God, he was glad to see her. He desperately wanted to take her into his arms and never let her go again, but he couldn't afford to frighten her.

"Hi," he said instead. "My name is Luke Templeton, and I have a very strange story to tell you."

Kelly forced a polite smile. "I'm sorry. I make it a policy never to listen to anyone else's plot ideas. I don't co-author or ghostwrite, and I don't want to risk the chance of someone accusing me of stealing their story. I don't wish to be rude, but I am working and—"

He stopped her from closing the door on him. "No, please. You don't understand. I'm not talking about a story for you to write. This is something that actually happened, and you were involved in it."

She was losing patience with him. "Nor do I write nonfiction. I'm sorry. I'm really not interested—"

"Your attorney's name is Bruce Hackett," he said quickly. "And since he helped you get divorced from Will, he has suddenly decided he's in love with you."

She looked at him sideways. "Do you know Bruce?"

He hesitated. "Not really. But I can tell you some other things that might interest you." He sorted through his memories to choose something that wouldn't make her think he was a nutcase. "You've been having a hard time coming up with a new story and someone has offered you the use of their cabin up by Lake Sidney Lanier as a sort of retreat."

She shook her head. "It's not a bad idea, but no one's made that offer."

"They will. Okay, how about this? You have a Walther PPK because you like James Bond movies."

"You could have read that somewhere," she said, frowning. "I have to go now."

She tried to close the door again, but he pressed his hand against it. "You accidentally got pregnant in the sixth year of your marriage to Will Kirkwood, you miscarried, and afterward, he never touched you again."

Kelly gasped. "How do you know that? Did he tell you?"

Luke made a face at her. "That cocky son of a bitch? You know he'd never admit that, especially not to another man. And by the way, he's been trying like hell to get you to reconcile with him."

She stared at him for several seconds, then took a deep breath and stepped outside onto the porch with him. "Okay, you've got my attention. How do you know these things?"

"Could we sit down? It may take a while." She shrugged and sat down on the top step. Before he joined her, he took his wallet out of his back pocket and handed it to her. "Please look through it, and note the birthdate on my driver's license."

"There's something familiar about your name, but there's no picture on this," she said before checking the birthdate.

"Licenses didn't have photos on them when that one was issued."

She squinted at the small print. Her voice was heavy with sarcasm after she read it. "You want me to believe that this is *your* license, and that you were born in 1930?"

"Yes. Keep looking."

She checked his various pieces of identification, thumbed through the thick wad of twenty-dollar bills, then glanced at the photos.

Luke held his breath as he waited for her to see it, and when she did, her wide-eyed stare let him know it did the trick.

"Who is this?" she asked pointing at a photo of him and Ginger at the beach. The bathing suit she was wearing gave a hint to the time period.

He pulled the photo out of its plastic case and showed her the date on the back—June 3, 1965.

"Am I related to her?"

"Not directly," he said, avoiding a lie. "Her name is Ginger O'Neill."

Her mouth dropped open. "You're kidding! I was just— Now I know why your name sounded familiar. Wait here!" She jumped up, went inside, and came back out with a folder full of papers. It took her another few seconds to find what she was looking for. "I guess I couldn't see the likeness because of the bad copy." She showed him an article that contained a photo of Ginger O'Neill.

It was coverage of the murder and the arrest of her husband and the two Rameys. Luke skimmed the article until he came to his name. "That's not true," he said. "This suggests that the Klan had something to do with my disappearance."

"*Your* disappearance?"

"Yes, mine. I'm *that* Luke Templeton." He could see she didn't believe him, but then, she hadn't believed him immediately the first time either. He began by telling her a little more about how she came to be at the cabin and went forward from there. By the time he got to the point where they had lunch at O'Neill's, an hour had passed, and she invited him in for a cup of coffee.

Because she started asking questions about details, it took him another hour to bring his tale up to date. The only part he left out was how their personal relationship had developed. His instincts told him that would scare her off before he ever got back on base.

"Wow," Kelly said after he told her about the lightning bolt striking him. "That's some story. In fact, I wish I'd made it up so that I could use it for my next suspense."

"But it *is* your next suspense," Luke insisted. "And while I was spelling it all out, I thought of a way that I can prove it to you. Remember the private investigator I mentioned, Evan Dillard? You could take my fingerprints to him and ask him to verify who they belong to."

"I hate to be so skeptical, but you could have paid him in advance to say whatever you want. Besides, if you were never arrested, would you even have prints on file anywhere?"

Luke's shoulders slumped. "No. I hadn't thought of that."

"Look, as much as I've enjoyed being entertained, it's getting late, and you never actually got around to telling me why you're here."

"I . . . I had nowhere else to go. I was hoping . . . you could give me some advice. Whether or not you believe what I've told you, I have a real problem. All I have is the clothes I'm wearing and the money in my wallet. It's going to be tough finding work without believable identification or references, but I'm sure I'll figure something out.

Meanwhile, maybe you could tell me if there's a YMCA or really cheap motel where I can stay until I get reoriented."

"Sure," she replied with a smile. "In fact, I'll give you a ride."

"In your new black Camaro."

She nodded, and was about to say something about his knowing that, too, when the phone rang. She went to the kitchen to answer it. A few seconds after the conversation began, she gave Luke a peculiar look and turned her back so that he couldn't hear what she was saying. When she returned to the living room, her expression was one of bewilderment.

"That was a friend of mine," she said. "She called to tell me about someone she works with who has a cabin by Lake Sidney Lanier that I could rent if I wanted to get away from the city for a while."

Luke sent up a silent prayer of thanks for the timely intervention. "I hope you turned it down."

She slowly lowered herself back down onto the couch. "Is there anything else coming up that I should know about?"

He had to fight the urge to tell her. "I'll let you know if I remember anything else."

"You know, your story gave me an idea. I've been thinking of hiring some help. How do you feel about being a research assistant slash bodyguard slash jack-of-all-trades? The job would include room and board."

"It's a deal," he said, with a broad grin. "Plus I get to use your whirlpool at least once a week."

Her eyebrows raised. "How do you know—" She changed her mind about that question. "One other thing. I want your written permission to write that story."

"Done."

As Kelly settled into bed that night, she wondered if she had completely lost her mind. Will and Bruce would surely think so. Jack, of course, would send her a congratulatory bouquet.

Even if she did have the feeling that Luke's story was on the level, she shouldn't have invited him to stay in her guest bedroom. Prudence had caused her to lock her bedroom door, but it would hardly keep him out if he was intent on getting in.

Her intuition told her she was safe with him, but her intuition had also told her to trust Will and Bruce.

Before she fell asleep, she promised herself that if Luke made one wrong move, even *one* ungentlemanly advance, she'd throw him out.

Ten days later, she was wondering how she could get him to be less of a gentleman.

Their relationship had started out a bit on the tense side, but as the days passed, and he did nothing to justify her nervousness, she began to relax. To her surprise, he made an excellent research assistant, and in practically no time, she had her new synopsis written and had begun on the actual book.

He also proved to be a valuable addition to her household with regard to general maintenance. He even seemed to enjoy cooking for her.

And he was a charming, entertaining companion when they weren't working. Whether they went sightseeing, shopping, or stayed home, ordered pizza, and watched movies, they had a good time together. She had dates without actually having to *date*.

Best of all, his presence discouraged Will and Bruce from dropping by whenever they felt like it.

Luke was a busy author's dream-come-true.

Except when she slipped into bed at night. None of the dreams she had there came true.

Wasn't that a laugh? The famous romance author was having fantasies about her live-in help and didn't have the nerve to act on them. It didn't matter that her heroines had no trouble seducing reluctant heroes. She couldn't do any of those things herself. It would be different if Luke made the first move. . . .

But she didn't see any possibility of that happening. He was too much of a gentleman. Or maybe he was afraid of how she would respond. After all, he was still fairly dependent on her. He couldn't afford to be fired for sexual harassment.

Yet, every so often, she caught him looking at her in a way that was so adoring it would make her chest ache, but then he would always turn away. At those moments, she felt nearly certain that he was just waiting for a sign from her . . . a sign that she couldn't bring herself to give without a guarantee that she wouldn't be rejected.

Luke was ready to tear his hair out. This was the eleventh day of being with Kelly without being *with* her. Ten nights of sleeping twenty feet away from her. Eleven days of waiting for her to show some sign of attraction to him.

He had wanted to convince her that she was perfectly safe with him in the house. He had wanted her to feel comfortable with him. Unfortunately, he had succeeded so well, he was now afraid of doing anything that would upset that comfortable relationship. He didn't dare do anything that would jeopardize what little he had with her.

He couldn't stand much more, though. If she didn't make a change in their relationship soon, he was going to have to risk making a pass at her. He decided to give her one more week, and that was it. After that, he'd go back to doing things his usual way.

He glanced up from the book he was reading. Her eyes were focused on the screen of her laptop computer, as they were most of the time now that she was working on her new book. He could only hope that as she started to write the more romantic scenes, she'd start thinking about spicing up her own life.

Kelly could not believe what she was reading, yet she had to. Luke had no way of knowing the password to put an entry into her calendar, and even if he had somehow figured it out, she had given herself a cryptic message within this unbelievable message to convince herself of its validity.

No one knew the name of her favorite doll's make-believe boyfriend when she was a little girl. She did not have a single doubt that she had personally written this letter to herself. She didn't know when or how, but she was certain she had done it.

Before she shut down for the day, she had decided to check on how the last two weeks of August looked. If they were still clear, she was going to schedule in a research/vacation trip with Luke to some romantic hideaway, in hopes he would get the hint.

To her great surprise, she found a very long letter to herself when she brought up August 24th. It told her the same story Luke had when he first arrived, along with her own expectation of possibly forgetting everything about their time together once he changed history.

It also informed her in very explicit terms what their relationship had been like.

Suddenly, everything made sense. Her feelings about him, the way he looked at her, why he would be willing to wait for as long as it took for her to fall in love with him all over again.

With her confidence level spilling over the top, she walked over to him, and sat down on his lap. As he tried to recover from the shock, she said, "It seems that there was a little something that you neglected to tell me about us, but I had the foresight to leave myself a note. Apparently, we managed to generate a lot of heat when we put some effort into it. One thing I didn't understand, though. The note told me to ask you if you'd like me to give you another haircut. Do you know what that means?"

His mouth curved into a sexy grin. "Yep. But it's one of those things that requires showing rather than telling."

The way his hand slid down her back and over her bottom made her shiver. "I can hardly wait," she whispered and tilted her head for the kiss she'd been waiting a lifetime for.

After he was assured that the memory wasn't nearly as good as the real thing, he eased her away so that he could see her eyes. "There's something else I neglected to tell you."

She narrowed her eyes suspiciously. "Am I going to like it?"

"I hope so."

"Okay then. You can tell me."

He gave himself a chance to reconsider, but he'd postponed this moment too long already. Putting all his thoughts and feelings into three little words, he said, "I love you."

And in the echo of his declaration, a double rainbow arched across the heavens over Atlanta.

Former business executive Marilyn Campbell turned in her briefcase a few years ago to follow her dream of becoming an author. The dream has since become a reality with the publication of two contemporary category romances, three psychological suspense novels, seven futuristic/time-travel romances, two novellas, and a screenplay. Marilyn resides in Florida with her two children.

WE NEED YOUR HELP
To continue to bring you quality romance
that meets your personal expectations,
we at TOPAZ books want to hear from you.
Help us by filling out this questionnaire, and in exchange
we will give you a **free gift** as a token of our gratitude.

- Is this the first TOPAZ book you've purchased? (circle one)

    YES   NO

    The title and author of this book is: _____

- If this was not the first TOPAZ book you've purchased, how many have
you bought in the past year?

    a: 0 - 5   b 6 - 10   c: more than 10   d: more than 20

- How many romances in total did you buy in the past year?

    a: 0 - 5   b: 6 - 10   c: more than 10   d: more than 20 ____

- How would you rate your overall satisfaction with this book?

    a: Excellent   b: Good   c: Fair   d: Poor

- What was the main reason you bought this book?

    a: It is a TOPAZ novel, and I know that TOPAZ stands
       for quality romance fiction
    b: I liked the cover
    c: The story-line intrigued me
    d: I love this author
    e: I really liked the setting
    f: I love the cover models
    g: Other: _____

- Where did you buy this TOPAZ novel?

    a: Bookstore   b: Airport   c: Warehouse Club
    d: Department Store   e: Supermarket   f: Drugstore
    g: Other: _____

- Did you pay the full cover price for this TOPAZ novel? (circle one)

    YES   NO

    If you did not, what price did you pay? _____

- Who are your favorite TOPAZ authors? (Please list)

- How did you first hear about TOPAZ books?

    a: I saw the books in a bookstore
    b: I saw the TOPAZ Man on TV or at a signing
    c: A friend told me about TOPAZ
    d: I saw an advertisement in_____magazine
    e: Other: _____

- What type of romance do you generally prefer?

    a: Historical   b: Contemporary
    c: Romantic Suspense   d: Paranormal (time travel,
       futuristic, vampires, ghosts, warlocks, etc.)
    d: Regency   e: Other: _____

- What historical settings do you prefer?

    a: England   b: Regency England   c: Scotland
    e: Ireland   f: America   g: Western Americana
    h: American Indian   i: Other: _____

- What type of story do you prefer?

    a: Very sexy   b: Sweet, less explicit
    c: Light and humorous   d: More emotionally intense
    e: Dealing with darker issues   f: Other

- What kind of covers do you prefer?

    a: Illustrating both hero and heroine   b: Hero alone
    c: No people (art only)   d: Other_____

- What other genres do you like to read (circle all that apply)

    Mystery   Medical Thrillers   Science Fiction
    Suspense   Fantasy   Self-help
    Classics   General Fiction   Legal Thrillers
    Historical Fiction

- Who is your favorite author, and why?_____
  _____

- What magazines do you like to read? (circle all that apply)

    a: *People*   b: *Time/Newsweek*
    c: *Entertainment Weekly*   d: *Romantic Times*
    e: *Star*   f: *National Enquirer*
    g: *Cosmopolitan*   h: *Woman's Day*
    i: *Ladies' Home Journal*   j: *Redbook*
    k: Other:_____

- In which region of the United States do you reside?

    a: Northeast   b: Midatlantic   c: South
    d: Midwest   e: Mountain   f: Southwest
    g: Pacific Coast

- What is your age group/sex?   a: Female   b: Male

    a: under 18   b: 19-25   c: 26-30   d: 31-35   e: 36-40
    f: 41-45   g: 46-50   h: 51-55   i: 56-60   j: Over 60

- What is your marital status?

    a: Married   b: Single   c: No longer married

- What is your current level of education?

    a: High school   b: College Degree
    c: Graduate Degree   d: Other: _____

- Do you receive the TOPAZ *Romantic Liaisons* newsletter, a quarterly newsletter with the latest information on Topaz books and authors?

    YES   NO

    If not, would you like to?   YES   NO

    Fill in the address where you would like your free gift to be sent:

    Name:_____
    Address:_____
    City:_____Zip Code:_____

    You should receive your free gift in 6 to 8 weeks.
    Please send the completed survey to:

    Penguin USA•Mass Market
    Dept. TS
    375 Hudson St.
    New York, NY 10014